PENGUIN BOOKS AND BLUE SALT
GHALIB DANGER

Neeraj Pandey is a National Award–winning film-maker whose work includes *A Wednesday* and, most recently, *Special 26*. This is his first novel.

Blue Salt is an imprint dedicated to noir and crime, established by the bestselling writer S. Hussain Zaidi and co-published by Penguin.

GHALIB DANGER

NEERAJ PANDEY

BLUE
SALT

PENGUIN BOOKS

An imprint of Penguin Random House

PENGUIN BOOKS

USA | Canada | UK | Ireland | Australia
New Zealand | India | South Africa | China | Singapore

Penguin Books is part of the Penguin Random House group of companies
whose addresses can be found at global.penguinrandomhouse.com

Published by Penguin Random House India Pvt. Ltd
4th Floor, Capital Tower 1, MG Road,
Gurugram 122 002, Haryana, India

Penguin
Random House
India

First published by Penguin Books India and Blue Salt 2013

10 9 8 7 6 5 4 3 2

ISBN 9780143421016

Typeset in Adobe Garamond by SÜRYA, New Delhi
Printed at Repro India Limited

www.penguin.co.in

MIX
Paper from
responsible sources
FSC® C047271

For *Shakkar*

ACKNOWLEDGEMENTS

Arrah zilla gharba
Toh ka cheez ke darr ba?

This loosely translates as:

If Arrah is where you are from
Then what is there to fear?

I was born and brought up in Calcutta but my roots are in Arrah, Bihar, and this is the saying that I was brought up on. It has dictated my choices in life and I believe that it has served me well.

In short it means: NO FEAR.

Thanks and gratitude are due.

To Dad, for making me understand very early on that success is both boring and overrated. The more solid learning in life lies in our failures.

To Mom, for letting go.

To Bhai and Bhabhi, for their unconditional love.

To S.N. Sharma sir, for being the best teacher that I have ever had.

To Sid and Harsh—don't be like me.

To Vasu and Yashu, for being the magic in my life.

To N.K. Choubey, for introducing me to Ghalib at an age when I should have been playing soccer or doing . . .

To Maami, for supporting him.

To Shital and Namrata, for just happening. You both are my rock.

To Hussain, for extorting this book.

To Chiki, Tanvi and the entire team at Penguin, for their faith and the hard work that they have put in.

To Anupamji, for taking the word 'impossible' out of my vocabulary.

To Naseer bhai, for taking out the thinnest script in the pile.

To Mubina and Sameer, my caring blackmailers.

To Binay, Nitish, Munish, Vineet, Amit, Ina, Sanjay, Puneet, Anju, Shila, Aubin, Shree, Rajesh, Gautamji, K.P., Qamar, Ishrat, Vikram, Karan and Jimmy, for all those nudges and pushes.

To the Internet, Google and Wikipedia, for happening in my lifetime.

A big thanks to my staff, my foot soldiers, for putting up with my erratic schedule with a smile.

Love,
Neeraj

PROLOGUE

2007—La Chapelle, Paris, France

Kamran Khan was staring at the Nokia phone on the table. He was in the kitchen of a three-bedroom apartment on the top floor of a four-storeyed apartment on Rue de Cail in La Chapelle, Paris. Also known as 'Little Jaffna', this was a small, colourful neighbourhood right on the edge of the 10th arrondissement. The quarter was slowly waking up but Kamran was already dressed for work and staring at the phone.

Actually, he had been staring at it for the last ten minutes or so as if waiting for it to throw up the details of the last received call which had come some eight hours ago. Kamran had been curious and patient in equal measure all his life but today was different. That phone was not his. It was Sonia's and Sonia was sleeping in the bedroom upstairs; still, Kamran could only sip his coffee and stare. He had been awake all night but was unable to summon the will to pick up that phone.

A moment later, he let out a sigh, smiled and mumbled:

> *Kahoon kis se main ki kya hai*
> *Shab-e-gham buri bala hai*
> *Mujhe kya bura tha marna*
> *Agar ek baar hota!*

He was not sure if he understood it completely but it just seemed apt for the occasion. His intuition and memory endorsed it. He looked around.

1

It was a nice apartment and had been home to them for the last four years. Everything, every little thing around him, had a backstory. There were nice, sweet memories that . . .

Fuck it. Let me have a look.

Kamran took a couple of steps towards the table and froze.

No. This is not right.

He walked back and reclined against the gas counter. He heard steps as he took another sip. Sonia entered the kitchen and looked at him. He looked at her. She was standing in her black nightdress. The one amazing thing about their relationship was that every morning, on first seeing her, Kamran always remembered the first time he had seen her.

The feeling back then was a cocktail of desire, some more desire and then some more.

And back then it was not a great time and surely it was not a happy place. The only constant was that she was as stunning, if not more.

She hugged him tightly. Kamran's forty-year-old body responded. Chemicals started debating and arguing.

That was Sonia for you.

'Hi. You are up early?'

'Good morning.'

'Good morning. Coffee?'

Kamran raised his cup. Sonia smiled and headed towards the coffee machine. Kamran scanned her, looking for a telltale sign. He was very good at this. His whole empire had been built on this talent. That it had got reduced to ashes is another story.

He watched her as she went about the business of making a cup of coffee, but noticed nothing out of the ordinary.

No tell. That's the tell. This is bad. Really bad. I am fucked.

'I will see you in the evening.'

'Can you drop these off before you leave for the office?'

Sonia peeled a sticky note from the fridge and walked towards him. Kamran took the note and looked at it.

'You will get these at Pierre's.'

Kamran looked at her. She caught his look and worked on it like a wringer. He blinked. She came closer.

'You okay?'

'Yes.'

'Sure?'

'Is it going to rain today, Sonia?'

'Do you want it to rain?'

'No.'

'So it won't.'

Kamran smiled at her and then kissed her. It lasted a touch longer from his end than the regular, everyday goodbye kiss.

Still no tell. This is going to be really, really bad.

When he went downstairs, Sonia was at the window waving at him. He waved back and continued walking. Paul, the florist, called out to him.

'Bonjour!'

'Bonjour!'

'Is it going to rain today, Kamran?'

'Of course, Paul. You can place your bet and give me my twenty.'

'But you never take it even when I give it to you.'

'If I take your money then you will stop winning. That's how it works. You keep my share for now.'

Paul was an honest man and so he never quite understood what Kamran meant.

Pierre's was just around the corner. Kamran entered the store. He knew the layout inside out. There were five rows of branded consumerables lined up neatly one after another. And then, of course, there were the dairy and meat products kept in freezers lined in the inverted U. Kamran picked a basket and started on the list.

He was on the fourth item on the list when he realized that

the pregnant woman in front of him in the second row was not just another customer. This was the third time Kamran had caught her looking at him.

He scanned the store. There were faces there that he had never seen. It had never happened in his three years in La Chapelle. The cashier, Julia, was a little too engrossed in her magazine today. There was a man looking at a cookie pack diligently. Actually, a little too diligently. The couple in the next aisle glanced at him in sync.

Kamran didn't waste another moment. He walked towards the pregnant woman with a smile.

It's in her handbag.

'Bonjour!'

The woman was surprised.

'Bonjour!'

'Puis-je vous aider?'

'Merci.'

Kamran signalled at her bump and asked, 'Quand vous êtes dus?'

As the woman fumbled for an answer Kamran caught her by her neck and drew the gun out of her handbag. The woman screamed. The other 'customers' in the store could barely react before Kamran had his hostage fully secured. Everyone sprang into action.

It was Kamran's SP 2022 trained at the woman's temple against nine other SP 2022s trained straight at him. Amid all the screaming and threatening, Kamran started to slowly inch towards the exit using the woman as his shield. He had barely reached it when he heard the sirens closing in on him.

Eleven National Police cars of various makes converged at the scene as Kamran froze at the glass door. The cops alighted and took position. A flash blinded Kamran. He retreated for a moment and then glanced at the terrace of the building across the street. A couple of snipers had already taken their positions. He looked around and spotted a few more. He looked ahead and saw the cops training their guns at the exit. He looked behind him. The cops in the store had also taken their positions.

He looked at his hostage. She was crying and pleading.

Kamran tightened his grip around her and kicked at the door. A hinge came undone and the door spilled on to the street. The cops took a step back. He walked with his hostage right on to the middle of the street and looked around. A helicopter flew right over his head.

His hostage was still crying and pleading. Kamran smiled.

You should have had the stomach for it.

Kamran reached for the stuffing under her jacket.

She didn't have any. Kamran lost a step. She was actually pregnant.

His grip loosened. The woman was surprised. She looked at Kamran. The gun dropped from Kamran's hand. The woman took a step and then another and then started running towards the cops lined on the other side of the street.

Kamran could only register a cacophony of overlapped screams. Cops on the street as well as cops from inside the store were all training their guns at him and were asking him to kneel on the ground.

And through that pandemonium he filtered out someone shouting his name. He didn't respond. It came through again. He turned. Sonia was standing behind a police cordon and screaming his name.

Wow!

Sonia was crying and screaming for him and standing next to her was SI Avinash Sharma of the Mumbai Police.

Really!?! Am I fucked or what?

He didn't know exactly when he was floored and pinned down but, while they were handcuffing him, Kamran Khan started counting, out of a very old habit.

CBI
Interpol
Maharashtra Police, India
National Police, France
Eleven police cars
About thirty-five cops
Six snipers

He then saw a couple of police choppers arrive at the scene and assume position overhead. Kamran smiled.

Not bad! Not bad at all.

1

2013—Taloja Jail, Maharashtra, India

The Maharashtra state government analytically distributes its bad apples in three baskets: the Arthur Road Jail in Byculla, the Taloja Jail and the Thane prison. These three house the undertrials. Inter-gang rivalry had initially led to this judicious move of distributing them with discretion but then, as politics bedded crime, the choice of jail by criminals themselves also came into play.

That is to say that the law had not chosen the Taloja Jail for Kamran Ali Khan. Kamran Ali Khan had chosen Taloja for himself.

Situated about fifty kilometres from Mumbai, it was the resort prison. The jail takes its name from a village nearby. It accommodates 2427 prisoners. Kamran had company in the form of Somali pirates, Bangladeshi migrants, members of the Indian Mujahideen and the Students Islamic Movement of India (SIMI), some accused in the 2007 Malegaon blasts. The other inmates included Mukhtar Sheikh and Pratap Khatri, the two notorious underworld rivals.

Taloja was tucked away nicely from civilization and hardly attracted any attention.

But today was different. The first OB van arrived at around 4 a.m. Soon others started trickling in one after another. By daybreak, the land outside the jail started resembling a picnic spot. And by eight that morning, the jail authorities had to step in to restore some order as the media was almost threatening to go inside and get their sound bites.

Damodar, an inmate, was worried that he was getting late. He had been servicing Kamran for the last three years but today was different. He quickly brushed the black leather shoe one last time and held it against its counterpart. They shone exactly the same. He picked up the shoes and then a hanger, which had a blazing-white cotton shirt and a pair of royal-blue denims, and a rolled bunch of newspapers.

He rushed out to the barracks, towards Kamran's cell. The other inmates saw him and were reminded of the occasion. There were murmurs and whispers all along. Damodar actually enjoyed these occasional moments of attention. He was facing trial for multiple marriages. He had been getting married for the fifth time when he got arrested. How he manoeuvred this extraordinary arrangement for more than fifteen years won Kamran's admiration and he was promptly chosen to be part of his service.

Kamran didn't like hangers-on. But, in this world, you do need service.

Damodar reached Kamran's cell. It was a surreal sight that made him marvel every time he entered the den. The small cell resembled a scaled-down deluxe five-star hotel room. It had a small bed in a corner with a couple of pillows that actually looked soft. A twenty-one-inch LCD TV was wall-mounted. There was a Blu-ray player on a small shelf below it. A couple of latest releases were piled on top of it. The floor was actually tiled. There was a stand with an iPod and a small wireless speaker. Once every month the iPod would travel to the outside world, get loaded with new Hindi film songs and travel back to Kamran's cell. There were a few books kept on one corner stand along with some scented candles. Farther down was a shower curtain and Damodar could hear the water running. He could make out Kamran's figure in the bath.

Damodar kept the shoes on the floor. The clothes were then neatly laid out on the bed. The newspapers were unrolled. Damodar then took out a couple of cell phones and laid them next to the newspapers.

He was confused whether he should leave or wait.

When in doubt—go!

Damodar remembered Kamran's words and left.

Kamran sensed Damodar leaving. He knew exactly when Damodar had entered, what he had carried and when he went. As the water sprayed on his face, Kamran stood still and took a moment to acknowledge the significance of the day.

It had been six long years since La Chapelle. Four years since he had been extradited to his homeland.

Kamran shut off the shower and stepped out in a white towel. Time had been kind to Kamran. He looked younger and fitter than his forty-six years. The fact that he had never felt short of anything during his entire stay had something to do with it. He was in jail all right, but he lived the life that he best could under the existing circumstances. Be it food, clothing, hygiene or exercise, Kamran had managed to get his way because of Pramukh Joshi, the home minister.

Pramukh Joshi was more than happy to help because of a small pen drive that Kamran had in his custody. But then, that's another story.

Kamran looked at the bunch of newspapers. He picked one up and saw his photograph.

The headline read 'JUDGEMENT DAY?'. The strapline read 'End of the road for dreaded Gangster Kamran Khan aka Ghalib Danger?'.

Assholes. Why do they use this photo again and again?

He glanced through the other newspapers. Minor aberrations

apart, the gist was the same. A watch beeped. Kamran picked up a phone and called the only number stored on it. The display showed 'Calling Babu'.

Babu was sweating like a pig and running along JP Road in Andheri West when his phone rang. He couldn't decide whether to take the call or ignore it. Finally he took the phone out of his pocket without breaking a step or cutting his pace. The display read 'Unknown number calling' but Babu knew exactly who it was.

'Salaam alaikum, bhai.'

'Wa'alaikum salaam. Is Lala gone?'

'Just about to shoot him, bhai.'

Some way ahead of Babu was Lala, running breathlessly and splattered all over with blood, mud and grime. He must have fallen a few times and had badly bruised himself.

'Keep the phone on.'

'Yes, bhai.'

The chase continued for another two minutes before Lala slipped and fell again. Babu caught up with him.

Kamran kept listening. He had been waiting for this moment. Lala had evaded him for a very long time. But Lala's time had run out today and this was great timing for Kamran. This was close. Really close. Kamran could hear some heavy breathing and Lala pleading. Kamran stood still.

Lala was catching hold of Babu's feet and screaming into the phone that Babu held out to him.

'I am so sorry, Danger bhai. This was a huge blunder . . . A huge one . . . I swear on my mother . . . I am never going to cross—'

Babu was counting. The moment Lala had had ten seconds of audience, Babu pulled the trigger, the nozzle touching Lala's head. Lala's head sprayed. His body fell, struggled and then gave up.

Kamran disconnected. He threw the phone on the bed, switched on the iPod and shuffled for some time. He then selected Play and Gulzar's lyrical voice started with *Ibteda* from the album *Ghalib*.

Kamran Ali Khan started getting ready. This was going to be a long day and it had started well.

Morning shows the day.

As he was putting on his favourite black Russell and Bromley the words that poured from the wireless speaker were:

> *Hain aur bhi duniya mein*
> *Sukhanwar bahut acche*
>
> *Kehte hain ki Ghalib ka hai*
> *Andaaz-e-bayan aur*

2

'Tum mere paas hote ho goya
Jab koi doosra nahi hota'
—Momin

Legend has it that the great poet Mirza Ghalib was ready to trade his entire diwan, his whole repertoire, for these eleven words written by another poet, Momin.

Kamran loved this story. Eleven simple words crafted and strewn together in the right order against the weight of two hundred and thirty-five ghazals. One line against an entire life's work.

He remembered that one word that he could trade everything in his life for.

Salma.

Fragile as glass. Beautiful as a prayer. Touch of a healer. Voice that could replace music. Eyes that could create magic.

Salma was all of the above and also his doom. Kamran remembered the time Salma had bitten him on the shoulder and asked, 'Why do we lose appetite when we are in love?'

'What? Are you sure? My intake *toh* has doubled.'

Kamran remembered his answer and shook his head. This was from around twenty years ago. He used to be a taxi driver and she had lived in the same mohalla as him, near Byculla, called Jangpura. It's another story that Kamran had once come quite close to killing her.

On the subject of killing, Kamran's judgement day had made three people seriously anxious.

Farookh Khitkhit, Yakub Mental and Sonia.

Kamran was where he was because of them. And they understood that if Kamran were to be acquitted there would be a bloodbath in the offing.

Farookh Khitkhit's real name was Farookh Ali. Though Farookh was very talkative and a cribber, he never used a cuss word. He hated people who did. In his presence people made sure they used the right vocabulary or shut up. He had once cut a man's tongue for saying *bahenchod*. He had inherited his share of the underworld from his father. But there was a problem. His father had married twice and he had two stepbrothers who also had a share in the inheritance. Farookh didn't approve of this and so he called for both the brothers and started to negotiate with them. The two stepbrothers were a bit crass. Farookh tried to ignore them but the meeting became very heated after fifteen minutes and Farookh shot and killed both the brothers and then went to their house and killed their mother and the elder one's wife. The younger one's wife was spared because Farookh had always liked her.

He liked her to the extent that he called her Mohabbat. But Farookh never forced himself on her. He just kept sending her gifts, money. Once in a while he used to go to her place. No one had the guts to stop him. He used to sit in the drawing room. She used to stand behind the curtains.

'Some tea, please. And kindly make it yourself and serve it yourself, please.'

The following routine ensued every time. Mohabbat made tea and served it herself. Farookh watched Mohabbat walk from the kitchen up to the table, bend a bit, place the tray on the table, do a salaam and go back to where she came from. Initially, Mohabbat scorned him but Farookh's tenacity got to her eventually. Mohabbat was a study in curves. A glimpse of skin here and there and Farookh used to look like a robbed bank. There was no physical contact at all during these meetings but if you were in the room your completely drained phone could charge in a second.

When Farookh got up to go after placing an envelope full of currency notes on the table, Mohabbat would ask, 'Was the tea okay, Farookh saab?'

'I feel intoxicated.'

'You are generous. Salaam.'

But after eight years and more than a few thousand cups of tea, fate smiled on Farookh. While serving tea that evening Mohabbat asked him to wait for dinner. A regret crossed Farookh's mind as to why he had made love to his wife that afternoon. But then he was reassured when he remembered that he had taken all his pills that morning.

As Farookh was having dinner, Mohabbat fanned him.

'Please join me.'

'In the bedroom, Farookh saab.'

Farookh became sure that there was a khuda.

Their first kiss lasted an eternity. In the bedroom, as Mohabbat undressed, Farookh became sure of another thing. Miracles happen to those who believe in them. When the bra came off, Farookh had smoke coming out of his ears. He got up and rushed towards Mohabbat and kissed her again. They then proceeded towards the bed and Farookh was fast losing control of himself—till he ripped off the salwar and felt that something was not right. He looked down at Mohabbat's body and found the strangest-looking truth staring at him.

Mohabbat was not a woman-woman. Farookh gasped and cursed in his mind for the first time in his life.

My fucking stepbrother was not fucking straight.

He shivered and pushed Mohabbat away. Mohabbat smiled slowly.

'Farookh saab! You got fucked without getting fucked *na*?'

'You . . . You . . . You bitch.'

'Your measly allowance doesn't work for me any more. I loved your stepbrother and he loved me, God rest his soul. I have waited eight years for this day. Your entire reputation will go down the drain if word gets out that your taste is such. Here is what you will do . . .'

Mohabbat rattled off a list of demands. Farookh was stupefied.

'I am going to kill you.'

'You can, but you won't unless you are in a tearing hurry to tell the world what a big *chutiya* you are.'

Farookh started to get dressed when Mohabbat politely threatened, 'You will have to keep coming here from time to time and have tea with me, Farookh saab.'

'You can shove the tea up your . . .'

'No! Seriously. It soothes me when I see your fuckface. You *will* keep coming personally.'

From that day onwards Farookh would visit Mohabbat once every fortnight, and in case he missed it one brief telephone call would expedite his visit.

He also started using a few cuss words every now and then. He also completely lost interest in women.

How Farookh Ali became Farookh Khitkhit is, however, not that dramatic a story, even though it was one of Farookh's favourites.

Fifteen years ago, it was the annual dons' conference in Dubai. The chosen twelve were invited to the Boss's place for a three-day seminar on how to take their illegal businesses to the next level. It was Farookh's first time with the big fish. On the last day of the seminar, a party was organized which was attended by Hindi film stars, builders and businessmen.

Farookh was a couple of drinks down when he and a builder started arguing about the quality of Dubai's duty-free. A little later the topic changed to the Mumbai Police and then it shifted to Indian politics and from there to the film industry. The arguments grew in decibel till they started pissing off a man who was dressed formally and was wearing shades indoors. He turned and—

'*Aye khitkhit!* Keep it down.'

Farookh swivelled around and was about to abuse him, when he realized who the man was and froze. His mouth uttered an apology automatically.

'Sorry, bhai.'

Yes. Dawood had that effect on people.

Though the name Khitkhit stuck, Farookh was proud.

It was like the Pope had baptized him in person.

But today Farookh was a very worried man. Though he was sitting on his terrace swing in his mansion in Heera chawl, watching TV, surrounded by all his people . . . by his own people . . . he was still gripped with fear. Farookh knew that the chances of Kamran getting out of jail were slim.

But what he also knew was that Kamran had lived all his life on slim.

Once again the reporter started her commentary on Kamran. Farookh took the remote and switched off the TV. He was in his late fifties but he looked older. Farookh got up from the swing. The people around him became uneasy. He walked up to the wall and picked up the twenty-one-inch LCD TV and started walking towards the edge of the terrace. The plug came flying out of the socket. Farookh walked to the edge and dropped the TV over the wall.

It missed a few people by inches as it came crashing on to the street. When they looked up and saw Farookh Khitkhit, they promptly resumed whatever they were doing, without saying a word. Farookh took out his cell and redialled the last number.

'It's me Farookh Khitkhit, again. Please transfer the call to the doctor.'

Pause.

'Yes Doctor, Khitkhit again. The burning sensation in my chest is not going. Anxiety is still there, Doctor. Hmmmm . . . No. No. No tension, Doctor. Yes, I took the tablet. Take one more? Okay. *Khuda Hafiz.*'

Farookh disconnected and saw Babloo, his most trusted hand, rushing in.

'Khitkhit bhai . . .'

'What happened?'

'Lala is gone.'

'What?'

'Lala got shot about half an hour ago.'

'Hey! Where is my pill?'

A man rushed in with a box of pills and a glass of water. Farookh took a pill and washed it down, hurriedly gulping down the water.

'And?'

'Bhai, bets are getting placed over Kamran's judgement and . . . and . . .'

'And?'

'And also over who Kamran is going to go after first. You or Yakub Mental. And . . . and . . . ?'

'And?'

'And the odds are not looking good for you, Khitkhit bhai.'

Farookh quietly took another pill and washed it down.

'Where is Mental?'

'Dubai.'

'Call in everyone. And everyone means everyone. No one goes anywhere till I say so.'

'Okay, bhai.'

Babloo rushed off. Farookh stood there. He could feel a flutter in his heart. He needed to sit down. As he rushed towards the swing he remembered the time Kamran, Yakub and Farookh himself were sitting in a police van after being arrested. Kamran was the youngest of the three and this was his first arrest. While Farookh and Mental were tense and worried, Kamran was cool as ice. Kamran also had the audacity to look them in the eye and ask, 'Between the two of you who is Mental and who is Khitkhit? Also, who the fuck gave you guys names like that?'

Khitkhit, then, was tempted to say, 'Mine was given by Dawood.'

But he refrained because he was travelling in a police van and was surrounded by cops.

As he recollected this incident, Khitkhit felt he should have one more pill.

3

Yakub Mental was not worried. Not only because he was in Dubai but because he was a *Mental*, slang for insane. His real name was Yakub Anwar. Unlike Farookh, Yakub was very crass. He couldn't construct one sentence without using a few cuss words.

Yakub was born in Dongri, the breeding ground for many infamous criminals. He committed his first murder when he was nine years old. It was a contract killing. A *supari*.

Shankar Anna, who had had a meteoric rise in the underworld, had antagonized both the local police and the reigning dons. Shankar didn't live by any code. He was ruthless and had no regard for anyone. Battle lines are constantly drawn and redrawn in the underworld but Shankar had been doing something different. It was the eighties and while the old guns were being marginalized by the young Turks, Shankar had come out of nowhere.

Shankar Anna was a Tamilian who organized and mobilized his community. Unemployed youths were drafted and hordes came to join him from back home.

In one single day his men had carried out two murders. Sub-inspector (SI) P.K. Kamte was shot in broad daylight while he was on his way to duty. Later, the notorious criminal Hemant Chowksi was stabbed and shot right outside his nightclub. These two murders had rocked the city.

The message was loud and clear. Shankar instilled fear in those who thought of themselves as fearsome. He started extorting extortionists and opened a parallel judiciary system, which meted out instant justice.

In a first of sorts the police and the underworld came together to eliminate this common threat. Information regarding Shankar Anna was exchanged diligently. But still no one was willing to take up the job of eliminating him. This was because the two failed attempts on Shankar's life had seen the contract killers punished in a way that had shocked the world.

The two killers had been blinded and their arms chopped off. But they had been spared to tell the story.

Shankar Anna had fiercely loyal people around him who would put their lives in line for their *brother* without a blink. Everyone gunning for him was lost for answers, till the wife of an ageing don Fali came up with an answer.

It has to be a kid. An eight- or nine-year-old. And it has to be done at the upcoming Ganeshutsava that Shankar has organized himself.

That day, the underworld and the police were convinced that Fali's empire was actually created by Najma Begum, his wife.

The hunt for the kid resulted in Yakub getting shortlisted. His biggest accomplishment till then was that he had nearly killed a twenty-six-year-old for pushing him at a cinema ticket counter.

The interview went something like this.

'Can you kill someone?'

'How much money will you give?'

'This is someone very strong, powerful. Do you understand powerful?'

'How much money will you give?'

'You may go to jail?'

'How much money will you give?'

'You might get killed if caught.'

'How much money will you give?'

'You do not know us. We do not know you. You will be on your own.'

'How much money will you give?'

'If you squeal we know where your family lives.'

'*Ae gandu!* Do not threaten me. How much money will you give?'

The interviewer forgot his next question.

'Two thousand.'

'Add twenty before that. Half advance. Half after work.'

Pause.

Najma Begum, sitting in the other room, nodded.

As Yakub was coming out of the room, counting his advance, he heard the interviewer telling someone, 'The bugger is a *Mental.*'

Yakub had liked the sound of it. It was then and there that he decided on his new name.

Yakub Mental. Fucking good ring to it.

Shankar Anna's assassination was the most sensational murder in the history of the Mumbai underworld. Yakub had breached security with a puja thali in his hands. He had entered the pandal and then looked at all the exits. Planning was never his strength. Guts were. He had waited for the *aarti* to get over. Shankar had stood up after the puja and Yakub had walked towards him. No one bothered to stop the pleasant-looking kid carrying the thali. Yakub removed the gun from under the garland, shot Shankar four times and fled. A huge commotion facilitated his exit.

Yakub was on the run for six days before the police caught him. But the underworld would not wash their hands off their most promising star. In a smooth sequence of events, the trial resulted in Yakub going to the Bhiwandi Remand and

Correctional facility. The threat from Shankar's men dissipated with time. Yakub had numerous fights inside—and no prizes for guessing who won them.

Yakub Mental never looked back after the day he stepped out. His growth was subsequently charted over extortion, drugs and women trafficking. He had a couple of wives, several kids and you could throw in a few mistresses as well.

Yakub had shifted base to Dubai two years ago, and today, instead of being massively worried, he was finding the whole situation very funny.

He was sitting in his office in Kings Hotel with Sultan, his right-hand man. The glass panel had a view of Burj Khalifa and Yakub couldn't control his laughter.

'Bahenchod. This can only fucking happen in India. They catch the asshole in Paris. Get him back home. Feed him the best fucking meals for five years. Take fucking good care of him and now they are all fucking set to release him. This is only fucking possible in India.'

'True, Mental bhai.'

'How is that chutiya Khitkhit?'

'Shitting bricks.'

'And what is the fucking betting scene?'

'First Khitkhit, then you.'

'Do we have a fucking shooter ready in Mumbai?'

'Fuck it *na*, Mental bhai.'

'No. Someone should remind the motherfucker who his dad is. Of all the fucking people in this fucking world it's me and Khitkhit that he wants to kill. What about the whore Sonia? She fucked him and then fucked him over and got him to bite the fucking dust. He doesn't have any fucking problem with her?'

'Bhai. News is that she is going to have it the worst.'

'And me? He is going to fucking kill me over the phone or what?'

Sultan started laughing. Yakub shook his head. Sultan's phone beeped.

'Mental bhai, this Nigerian party wants to meet up tomorrow.'

But Yakub was not listening.

'Bastard. You know what happened once? This is the first fucking time I met this asshole. We were travelling in the same fucking police van. Kamran, Khitkhit and me. Now, Khitkhit is fucking tense. Me a little bit. But this bastard is humming a song while we are sitting there tight. He then cracks a joke and then looks us in the fucking eye and asks, "Between the two of you who is Mental and who is Khitkhit? Also, who the fuck gave you guys names like that?" I was fucking tempted to strangulate him then and there and tell him that I gave myself the name, asshole.'

'Forget it, Mental bhai. Like you said, is he going to kill you over the phone or what?'

They started laughing again. But deep inside Yakub knew he had distorted the story a little bit. Back then he hadn't thought of strangulating Kamran. Then he had just marvelled at the rookie's guts. Farookh Khitkhit and he were both pros and yet scared. This was a first-timer who was enjoying danger.

Fucker has the best fucking name in our business. Ghalib Danger.

Yakub acknowledged that in his head. He knew that Kamran never issued empty threats. He tried anticipating Kamran's next few moves.

The only problem was that Yakub Mental didn't have the brains for it.

4

'It's time.'

The jail superintendent called for Kamran. The lock was opened. Kamran stepped out. A small posse of cops surrounded him. One took his hand. The inmates froze. Some in respect and some in fear. Some smiled and greeted him. Kamran smiled back. Damodar stepped forward with a box of sweets.

'Who got married, Damodar?'

'No ... no. Advance congratulations for the judgement today. You are going to be a free man.'

Kamran smiled and took a kaju katli. He looked around.

Five years ... five godforsaken years.

In the five years of his confinement, Kamran had worked a lot on himself. He had internalized all his anger and pain. No one could see the angst behind the cool smile and the easy demeanour. He was coiled and believed that releases should happen at the right time. Whether they are physical or emotional.

A Ghalib couplet that he loved was:

> *Qaid-e-hayat-o-band-e-gham asl mein dono ek hain*
> *Maut se pahle aadmi gam se nijat paye kyun*

Kamran was never sure if he completely understood Ghalib but then he just happened to love Ghalib's poetry after he was named Ghalib Danger. How Kamran Khan became Ghalib Danger is another story and it will come in good time, of course.

Kamran sat in the van parked inside the jail compound. There were two escort vehicles each at the front and the rear of his van. A group of seven cops sat with him inside.

Kamran counted.

Not bad.

The gates opened and the convoy started to proceed. A sea of reporters swarmed around. Kamran saw them through the netted window. There were some who had covered him for the last five years. They came right in the path of the convoy and the cops on standby had to intervene. It took twenty minutes for the convoy to cover a distance of not more than fifty metres and get on the main road.

Kamran saw a helicopter overhead.

Not bad at all.

The escort vans accelerated. The media was also in tow. A few eager reporters were on bikes riding pillion and shooting the scene with their PD cameras. One of the cops screamed at them to back off. The bikes held back. Kamran looked around. Everyone looked glum and serious. SI Kanitkar was known for seldom smiling, but even the remaining six officers were just staring at him blankly.

Kamran started his ritual.

'So Kanitkar saheb. All well at home?'

SI Kanitkar, who had accompanied Kamran on four earlier occasions and who knew exactly what was coming, shook his head.

'Once there was this seemingly happy couple. One day the wife reminds the husband that she loves him very much. The husband says that he loves her very much too. More than her own life, she says. The husband says, ditto. After a moment the wife asks him what he would do if something happened to her . . . if she died. The husband promptly replied that he would go mad . . . go crazy. The wife then asks him if he would remarry. To which the husband says, you can't trust a crazy guy. He can do anything.'

The cops in the van stared at him. Kamran waited. A giggle started somewhere followed by another and then another and suddenly there was laughter all around.

SI Kanitkar couldn't help it either and burst out laughing too. The van now resembled a group going for a picnic.

'That's better. We are not going for a fucking funeral, are we?'

Kamran threw his head back. He knew that it would take them around fifty minutes to reach the sessions court in Sewri. He loved these drives. It was like a teaser, a trailer of his freedom. His heartbeat quickened and Kamran's mind wandered back to where it all started. Kamran shuffled his memory deck and out came a card saying . . .

. . . Qasimgarh!

Qasimgarh is one of the eastern-most districts of Uttar Pradesh. Kamran Khan was born here in the year 1967. Quite a few important people were born that year, as it happens with virtually every year, but 1967 was even more special. Destiny had brought about a number of births that year in different parts of the country, its design both intricate and brilliant.

Immensely popular personalities from the Hindi film industry like Akshay Kumar, Ajay Devgn, Madhuri Dixit and Juhi Chawla were all born in 1967. Little did they know that their professional worlds would be rocked by a man who was born in a remote, insignificant village called Jiria in Qasimgarh.

How? Well that's another story.

Kamran was born prematurely, in a village which did not even have basic amenities like clean water and power. Forget hospital; there was no doctor. Kamran's mother, Fatima, had lost four of her earlier ones during pregnancy. Kamran's father had expired a few months back in a rail accident. His mother had then wanted to kill herself but had lived for her child. Fatima prayed five times a day asking Khuda to take her but spare this one.

The midwife who delivered Kamran gave him fifteen minutes to live.

But little Kamran decided to hang around. It was as if the infant knew and understood the value of life. And the value of his survival to his mother. As if the infant understood that he had to fulfil not only his destiny but also shape the destiny of several others.

As if . . .

Fatima named him Kamran, which meant successful. He meant the world to his mother. She could have remarried but she didn't. Kamran went to the local school as his mother toiled for a better life for her son. But he was not into studies at all. He was a true-blue *haraami* in his school. He made life miserable for his teachers. His mother quickly reconciled herself to the fact that he was not going to be a babu, a big man.

What she didn't know was that Kamran could not bear the thought of his mother working as a part-time servant in four houses, just so he could go to school. He had seen the way people looked at her. In his head he was clear that he needed to work, earn money and not learn the fucking history of the British Empire.

Kamran started working in a garage. There were only tractors around that area and a few jeeps but there was enough work to be done, especially in the harvest season when there were more breakdowns. It made up for the lack of work during the remaining year. Kamran started making money until Fatima could finally stay at home.

For Kamran, dignity was the key to a man's character. He worked hard, slept less, just to keep Fatima from toiling at a job he considered beneath her.

As he grew, Qasimgarh started seeming too small for him. He wanted to leave but couldn't afford to take his mother with him or leave her behind. He started dealing in small businesses but soon got tired and bored. There was only so much that one can do in a place like Jiria. He built his reputation brick by brick. If he took a loan, he paid it back on time. If he had promised anything to anyone, he was sure to keep his word. He was there at marriages. He was there at funerals. He was resourceful and enterprising. He rallied his people around him. He was always eager to listen, to help. Sometimes it doesn't matter if one can actually solve the problem. Just an honest hearing is enough.

Fatima sensed that Kamran had to be let go. Jiria was not his world. In her heart she knew that he was meant for bigger things. So late one night when Kamran was having a smoke on the terrace, Fatima joined him.

'I thought you were asleep, Ammi.'

'You are keeping me awake these days.'

'Really?'

Fatima smiled.

'I am tying you down, Kamran.'

'No. You are not.'

'Shut up and listen. I can't bear to live without you around. I can't bear not to see your face every morning, night or at my will. But more than that I cannot bear the fact my Kamran is wasting his life here.'

'But . . .'

'Ssshhhh. I want you to be a very big man, Kamran.'

'That I will surely become. You tell me how big?'

'But for that you need to go.'

'I will. At the right time.'

'You are waiting for me to die?'

'Don't you say that.'

Kamran hugged Fatima tightly.

'Never ever say that.'

'Kamran, I want to see you make something out of your life in my lifetime.'

'I will.'

'You should say "Inshallah!", beta.'

'I was just making a promise to myself before saying that.'

'I will miss you.'

'I will get you there the instant I can.'

'*There* where?'

'Bombay.'

'You want to go to Bombay?'

'I spoke to Khalid mamu the last time he was here. He told me that he could get me in the taxi line.'

'Don't stop there, Kamran.'

'I won't.'

'You should say "Inshallah!", beta.'

'I was making a promise to myself before saying that.'

That night both Fatima and Kamran cried and laughed a thousand times. This is the strange thing about love. It hurts and heals at the same time. There were *sher*s of Ghalib that Kamran had attributed to the emotional signposts of his life. That evening was a signpost and the couplets that he had assigned to it were:

> *Dil hi to hai na sang-o-Khisht dard se bhar na aaye kyun*
> *Roenge ham hazaar baar koi hamen sataaye kyun?*

> *Ghalib-e-Khastaa ke ba Gair kaun se kaam band hain*
> *Roiie zaar-zaar kya, kiijiye haaye-haaye kyun?*

5

It took Kamran a few weeks to plan his trip. He called his uncle Hamid who was very happy to hear that he was coming. Then Kamran started ensuring that Fatima's stay in the village would be comfortable. He looked ahead and tried to fix and arrange things for his mother in advance, even getting the roof of his house fixed, though the monsoon was months away.

Finally, the day came. Word had spread that Kamran was going to Bombay and the entire village turned up at his house that morning. It was a big deal. The last guy that had left Jiria had been Hamid. He had run off to Bombay about fifteen years back. Took him three months to reach the city. When he got there, he had just enough money for one meal. Hamid was very hungry but he had heard of the Haji Ali Dargah and went there to offer his prayers. He also bought some food with the money that he had and fed it to the beggars lined up outside.

Hamid got married a few years later and though he had had his share of ups and downs, his family never went to sleep on an empty stomach. Now, Hamid was a driver in a public listed company. How many people could achieve that? Hamid was the role model for the entire village.

A tractor was decorated especially for this day. Everyone stood patiently outside the door. Inside, Fatima recited the outward journey *dua* and tied a *taveez* on his wrist. Once the rituals were complete, Kamran looked at Fatima and smiled.

'I will see you soon.'

Fatima couldn't hold back her tears. She hugged him tightly. He was her only reason for existence. She still felt worried about her twenty-four-year-old. For a moment she wanted to be selfish again. But, it was just for a brief greedy moment. She summoned all her strength and sported a smile.

'Inshallah.'

They stepped out of the house and the crowd surrounded him. Everyone started talking at the same time.

'Bhaiyya, we have to rush or we will miss the train.'

'He won't. I have already sent Babloo. He will keep the train standing till Kamran boards. Kamran you don't have to rush.'

Someone shoved an envelope in his face.

'Beta, just give this to Hamid and ask him to pass it on to Jumman and tell him that it is for his sister-in-law's uncle's daughter's husband.'

'Keep this. You will get hungry. Don't take anything to eat from strangers. They mix something in the food that puts you to sleep and then run away with your stuff.'

'Take care. Be well in the big city and stay away from women.'

'Khuda hafiz, beta.'

This went on till Kamran boarded the tractor. As it started moving, the crowd moved too and followed it till the road. Kamran caught one last glimpse of his mother and his heart ached. He consoled himself saying that this was all for the better.

The tractor cut through the fields and headed towards the station. Four of his friends were with him on the tractor. Bunty, Mohsin, Sameer and Chote were all very excited. They knew that a part of them was leaving for Bombay with Kamran.

The train had indeed been waiting for him. The stationmaster was on the platform, looking anxious. Babloo was waiting next to him.

'See. Here it comes.'

'Thank god.'

Kamran and his friends were getting off the tractor. Chote couldn't contain himself.

'Master saab, Kamran bhaiyya is going to Bombay.'

'It's now known to all the four neighbouring villages, beta.'

'Master saab, the train is still . . . ?'

'It's been waiting for the last half hour. Passengers for the next few stations decided to walk and must have reached home and also had dinner by now.'

The group boarded the train and then proceeded to install Kamran in his seat. Other passengers were politely asked to adjust and cooperate. His luggage was placed nicely. Kamran had an aisle reservation but his friends politely got a window seat vacated for him.

'Uncle, bhaiyya likes to smoke please.'

As Kamran settled in his seat, Chote started bawling.

'What happened, Chote?'

'Bhaiyya, you are going. Why are you going?'

'*Bhonsdi ke!* For you. Unless I go and make a man out of myself, how the fuck will I be able to call you guys there? Stop crying and wipe your face.'

Chote wiped his face. Kamran issued the last set of instructions.

'You guys have to take care of my mom. Be responsible. I will call you guys to Bombay, one after another. Work hard. Keep people around you happy. Stop chasing girls now.'

They all nodded in sync.

'We can do that once I come back for my holidays.'

Kamran smiled. They all hugged him for the last time and were refusing to let go when the stationmaster intervened again.

'Beta, just wanted you to know that there are three other trains waiting behind us now.'

The train finally left for Jiria.

The young Kamran spent the night awake looking at the world he was leaving behind and thinking of the world that lay ahead. He was a bit of everything—sad, happy, anxious. He remembered things he had heard about Bombay.

It was a city that never sleeps, they said.

How is that possible?

Kamran landed at the Kurla Terminus on 2 August 1991. The first thing he did once he set foot in Bombay was to recite a prayer his mother had taught him.

*Allahumma innee as-aluka khairaha wa a'oodhu bika min
sharriha
Allahumma habbibna ilaa ahliha wa habbib saalihi ahliha
ilayna*

O Allah! I beseech from you this city's goodness and seek
refuge in you from its wickedness
O Allah! Let its inhabitants love us and let us love its
virtuous inhabitants

While he was muttering this with his eyes closed, a porter noticed him. When Kamran opened his eyes he found himself facing the porter.

'Are you a bhaiyya?'

'Yes! Kamran bhaiyya.'

'Need help?'

'No.'

'Looks heavy.'

'It isn't.'

Kamran started walking. The porter started walking alongside.

'Just ten rupees.'

'No.'

'Eight.'

'No.'

'Okay, five.'

The porter snatched Kamran's luggage despite his protests.

'You need a taxi?'

'No.'

'Where do you have to go?'

'Beykalla.'

'Byculla?'

'Byeculla.'

'No bus to Byculla.'

'But mamujaan said that . . .'

'They stopped the service yesterday only. Everybody was taking taxis so the government stopped the bus service.'

'Ohhh! Now?'

'Either you walk or you take a taxi.'

'How much for the taxi?'

'They charge anything here, but my friend will take you and he will charge you only by the meter. You are a good man, I can tell.'

Kamran smiled. They emerged from the station. The porter led Kamran to the taxi stand and whistled. A cabbie promptly came on the scene. The porter started helping Kamran with the luggage.

'Raju, this is Kamran bhaiyya. He has to go to Byculla.'

'This address.'

Kamran handed him a chit of paper.

The porter continued, 'Take him nicely and charge him only by the meter. No extra. Do you understand?'

'Yes.'

'Thank you.'

Kamran handed him a tenner with his thanks. The porter looked at the note.

'I don't have five in change.'

'No problem. I will give your friend five short. You guys can sort it out later.'

The porter went blank. Kamran got into the cab and it moved out of the station. The porter smiled and made a prediction in his head—*This one will make it.*

In the cab, Kamran passed the same fountain for the third time.

'Bhai, I am seeing this fountain for the third time.'

'You will see it one more time. They've planted four of these on the way to Byculla.'

'Oh! Nice.'

So Kamran saw the fountain one more time before he reached Karampura, Byculla. The cabbie stopped his taxi right at the entrance of the mohalla.

'Ask in any of those shops. It should be very close.'

'How much?'

'One forty-five.'

'I am not asking the time, my friend. What is the fare?'

'That, my friend, is the fare.'

Kamran looked at him.

'How far is the nearest hospital?'

'Very close. About three kilometres. Why?'

'And the police station?'

'Two kilometres. Why?'

'I was wondering how much time each one of us is going to take to reach our destinations after I thrash the living shit out of you. Four fountains is fine but why did the people open the same set of shops at all the four places?'

The cabbie went mute.

'I will ask one more time. What is the fare, my friend?'

'Forty-five.'

'So here is forty. You can collect the remaining five from your friend at the station. Now can you help me with my luggage?'

The driver not only did so but also helped Kamran till he located the address.

That evening when the taxi driver narrated the entire incident to his group over drinks, the porter laughed out loud.

This one is definitely going to make it.

6

Karampura near Byculla was a quiet mohalla, nicely tucked away from the main city. It housed mainly migrants from the northern part of the country. People who had migrated here in the fifties and the sixties had built it both by design and default. That generation ensured that the tradition and culture of their native places survived in this metro at all costs. It was a melting pot of lower-middle-class people dabbling mainly in leather goods. There were others who were mechanics and drivers. Some were employed privately while others operated taxis. People here knew each other well compared to those who lived in high-rises where one didn't even know the next-door neighbour.

The Karampura of 1991 was a great place to live in. It would give you a pat on the back at night after you had faced a long day of getting slapped around in the city.

Hamid rushed out to welcome Kamran. He had always been very fond of Kamran. They hugged each other and smiled.

'Mashallah! You have become big.'

'You are seeing me after a long time.'

'How is baaji?'

'Very well. She sent you some gujiyas.'

'No problem finding the house?'

'Not at all. People here are more helpful than I had thought.'

Kamran suddenly remembered the cabbie who was still holding his luggage.

'Thanks, bhai. You can keep it down there.'

The cabbie put the luggage down and scampered away. Hamid called out for his son.

'Arif! This is your Kamran bhaijaan. He is going to stay with us. Take his bags to the loft.'

Arif took the bags. Kamran spotted a woman and two very cute children, about three or four years old, looking at him from the window.

'That's Nusrat on the right and that's Zeenat. And that's your mami.'

'Salaam, mami.'

In response, the mami shouted: 'Arre Arif, once you have kept the bags go and fetch some flour. We have a guest. I will have to cook more rotis.'

She went inside with her daughters. Hamid was embarrassed but Kamran smiled and put him at ease.

'So, I have a spicy mami.'

'She has a quite a tongue but she has a nice big heart.'

'That you would know better.'

'Don't try to be a smartass.'

They smiled as he led Kamran inside the *kholi*. It was just one room with the kitchen in one corner. There was a ladder and a rope hanging. It led to the loft. Hamid led Kamran to the loft. You couldn't stand in there. Just crouch.

'This is all that I could achieve, Kamran.'

'It's huge. Back home they are all very proud of you.'

'I am getting late. We will catch up in the evening. You can take some rest.'

'I need to freshen up.'

Hamid smiled.

'You should have taken the Gorakhpur Express. It gets you in time for freshening up. Now you will have to wait till the evening, beta. The municipality is going to be nice to you only in the evening now.'

Hamid left Kamran wondering.

But they said that this city never slept.

This was Kamran's first learning in this city.

'The time of your dump shall be decided not by your constitution but by the Bombay Municipal Corporation.'

The next day itself Kamran joined Chohan motor training school. He used to drive a tractor but didn't have a driving licence. Hamid would take Kamran around the city and teach him various routes whenever he had the time.

'They say there are always two options before you—the long route and the short route. But my experience says that there is a right route and then there is a wrong route.'

'How do I know which is right and which wrong?'

'Usually the right one is a little longer and the wrong one shorter.'

Hamid smiled like a professor. Kamran was not convinced at all.

A day in Kamran's life would start at four-thirty in the morning. He would take his plastic Dalda container and stand in queue for the latrines. He would count the number of people ahead of him. Usually he was number eight or nine. The turnout at that hour was impressive. Kamran often wondered if these guys slept at home. Within a very short time, BMC had adjusted his bowel settings and Kamran would be up and running by 6 a.m.

Mami served him breakfast and dinner with an occasional jibe. Kamran would give a happy retort or ignore her, depending on the intensity of the jibe and the level of his exhaustion.

After his morning classes he would head straight for Pinto's garage. Hamid had helped him get a job there. These were not tractors like back home but high-end cars and Kamran was hired as an apprentice. Kamran didn't like the downgrade but he knew it was just a matter of days. Or cars.

He got his licence on the same day he received his first pay in Bombay. He went straight to the post office and sent half to his mother by money order. Then he went to the Haji Ali Dargah and spent half of the remaining amount feeding people. From there he proceeded to the Heera Panna shopping arcade and spent the rest of the money buying gifts for Hamid, his wife and the kids.

For himself, he kept a one-rupee coin from his first earning. The rest was all well spent, he felt.

When mami saw the suit piece that Kamran had got for her, she had tears in her eyes. The kids were extremely happy with the goodies. Hamid was wise enough to be proud rather than happy. Kamran became sure of something.

Money can buy happiness. It can buy smiles. Can make one forget pain. Those who say it can't can go fuck themselves. Money is not a bad thing in itself.

He knew there was something twisted about that thought. It was a signpost moment and the couplet assigned later to it was:

Hamko ma'aloom hai jannat ki haqeeqat lekin
Dil ki khush rakhne ko, 'Ghalib' yeh khayaal achcha hai

His mami warmed up to him and Kamran realized that there was actually a very soft heart behind that threatening exterior. Kamran became a favourite with the kids and the youngest, Zeenat, became his favourite. It was Kamran's duty to drop Zeenat to school in the morning. He used to buy her something or the other every day. When Arif and Nusrat accused him of being biased, he didn't stop; he just made sure they didn't catch him. They became so close that Zeenat wouldn't go to bed unless Kamran told her a story. He was horrible at it but the three-year-old Zeenat didn't judge him. She simply loved him unconditionally.

Hamid soon arranged for a cab for Kamran to drive. Roshan

bhai had a fleet of taxis and Kamran became one of his operators.
Kamran would get to drive the graveyard shift, which was from
nine in the night to six in the morning. He could still work at
the garage during the day for a few hours. Pinto was so impressed
by this hard-working boy that a financial arrangement was
worked out.

Kamran would spend a couple of hours in the garage every
evening and then do the night shift.

Eight months went by. Everything was going really well till
destiny decided on an upgrade.

Kamran was sleeping in the loft after a night's work when
Hamid woke him up.

'Kamran! Kamran! Get up! Arre get up.'

'Wh . . . What happened?'

'You have to go to Kurla station.'

'No, I don't have to.'

'Arre! Open your eyes. You have to go to Kurla for a pickup.'

'Who's coming?'

'Mohsin's uncle Abbas bhai and his family.'

'Why is Mohsin not going?'

'He is a tailor. He can't get them to sit in a sewing machine
and bring them here. You are the driver. Take Jumman's cab.
They are due to arrive in an hour.'

'But how will I identify this Abbas bhai?'

'Just look out for the meanest-looking haraami at the station.
And hurry.'

'But . . .'

Hamid was gone before Kamran could say anything. After
ten minutes he was on his way to the Kurla station, muttering
abuses under his breath. He reached the station just in time.
The train had just arrived and people were still getting off. It
was a huge crowd that Kamran found himself staring at from
the connecting bridge.

'Meanest-looking haraami . . . Now which one is that going to be?'

He started looking around. A couple of moments later his eye caught a middle-aged guy fighting with a porter in an extremely agitated manner. The guy then caught the porter's collar, causing him to trip and fall.

'That's my haraami.'

Kamran rushed towards the guy.

And it was then that he noticed her . . .

. . . right behind the haraami.

As he walked towards her, his legs started giving way. His heart ran out of oxygen. She was the most beautiful thing he had ever seen in his entire existence. She was embarrassed because of how Haraami was conducting himself and that made her seem even more beautiful. Her hair fell across her face. Her eyes blinked in anxiety. The rosy-red lips were desperately trying to calm Haraami.

Kamran's all-time favourite woman was the Hindi-film heroine Madhubala. She was the most beautiful woman in his opinion. And not many people would disagree with him. In fact, on his list, the one to five slots in this category were all given to Madhubala.

But that afternoon at Kurla station, platform number three, near A.H. Wheeler registration number 4156, right outside bogie number 7724, Madhubala was demoted to the second place.

Destiny's upgrade for Kamran Khan was an angel born to a haraami.

Unke dekhe se jo aa jaati hai muh pe raunak . . .
Wo samajhte hain ki beemaar ka haal achha hai . . .

Dekhiye paate hain ussaak buttoon ee kyaa Faiz . . .
Ek Brahman ne kaha hai ki ye saal achha hai . . .

7

Kamran walked up to the guy, pulling the porter away and mockingly reprimanding him.

'Scram. Scram right away. Salaam alaikum, Abbas saab.'

'Wa'alaikum salaam. Who are you?'

'Kamran. Mohsin sent me for you, Abbas saab. There is a taxi waiting for you outside.'

'He didn't come?'

'No.'

'Why?'

How the fuck do I know?

'He is a tailor and he doesn't know how to drive.'

'So he sent you. He could have at least come with you.'

Yes, but for the first time Mohsin has done the right thing in his entire life. What's her name, Haraami?

'Salma, take those bags.'

'*Ji*, abbu.'

Salma, your soft, fair, delicate hands are not meant for this. You don't have to take those bags.

'No. I will take those.'

'Take these too.'

Kamran noticed the mother for the first time.

'Sure.'

So Kamran didn't allow Salma to carry any bags and carried the entire family's luggage to the taxi stand himself. He was so preoccupied that his brain did not even register its weight. He

threw the bags into the boot and opened the door for Salma.
The mother and the daughter sat in the rear seat. Kamran and
Abbas sat in the front. Kamran adjusted the rear-view mirror.

Dear Salma—First of all, let me tell you that you have a
beautiful name. That it rhymes with kalma *is not a mere*
coincidence. I have always wondered what the purpose of rear-view
mirrors was in life. I have no reason to look back whatsoever. But
today the great purpose has been revealed to me. By adjusting this
mirror to see you I am also adjusting my destiny. You can look
whenever you want and you will find me waiting for your look.
Ignore what is to my left and what is to your right. You don't have
to worry. This is a half-hour journey but I will take about an hour
and a half. And if you smile, I will stretch it by another half an
hour. I also want to tell you that . . .

'What are you thinking? Let's go.'

'Ji, Abbas saab. You first trip to Bombay?'

'Yes. Why?'

'Nothing. It's a beautiful city.'

The Bombay darshan started. Kamran from his experience
knew exactly how to stretch the half-hour journey. From Kurla
he headed straight for Bandra. Kamran wanted to see her face
again and again. Abbas caught him checking her out.

'You should keep your eyes on the road.'

'Ji.'

'Where are you from?'

'Ji, Qasimgarh. I am staying here with Hamid Ali.'

'That driver.'

'Ji. He is my mamu.'

'You are Fatima's son.'

'Ji.'

'When did you come?'

Kamran looked at Salma and started rattling.

'It's been eight months now. I started learning how to drive the day I arrived. Also started working in a garage. Did not take a single rupee from anyone. Started paying for my stay also. Every month I manage to send something for my mother and at the same time save some for myself. You see, one has to plan something for the future or else how can you survive? There are things to do. Tomorrow one has to start a family and then there will be more responsibilities with kids and all.'

Salma smiled.

And now Haraami is going to enjoy an extra half an hour in this cab.

'You should keep your eyes on the road.'

'Ji.'

'So you drive a taxi?'

'Ji. For now. But I have plans.'

'Of course you have. Keep your eyes on the road.'

Dear Salma, as you can see, it seems very unlikely that your father and I will get along well. Kindly note that I am trying very hard. Also note that the colour blue suits you very well though I doubt if there is a colour that doesn't. Please remove the careless strand that's falling on your face again. Actually, on second thoughts, leave it like that. I will remove it for you some day. And please don't bite your lips. They will get hurt. You have to take good care of them. For me.'

'Watch out. Eyes on the road.'

'Ji.'

Dear Haraami, what fucking 'eyes on the road', 'eyes on the road' again and again? Have you even fucking seen your daughter properly, you idiot? You should have kept her back home. Actually NO! It's good that you brought her to Bombay. But my advice to you is to mind your own fucking business and not worry about Salma any more. I will take care of everything. Just be nice to her. Okay?

'Are you saying something to me?'

'What, Abbas saab?'

'You mumbled something?'

'It was a prayer.'

The taxi finally reached Karampura. Mohsin and the other relatives had been waiting for the last one and a half hours.

'Why did it take you guys so long?'

'Ask him.'

'I brought them via Bandra.'

'Why? Why not through Tilak Nagar? It was half the distance.'

'Because, Mohsin, today there is a rally at the Chota Maidan. We might have got stuck there for hours.'

'Oh.'

Everyone had alighted and the world was taking Salma away from Kamran. Kamran got all the stuff out and sat in the taxi. Salma was hugging an aunt at a distance.

Lucky aunt.

Kamran started buying time by starting and shutting off the ignition.

Dear Salma, just give me one look. My world, which stands pillaged, ruined and empty the moment you got out of my taxi, will get another lease of life if you look at me. And please hurry or that Haraami will intervene.

'What happened, Kamran?'

'It's not starting.'

I told you. Are you sure he is your father?

'I think the carburettor is choked.'

'Do I get someone to push it?'

Relax, motherfucker. All I am asking for is a look.

'I think I can manage.'

'Mohsin! This chap needs help. Just get four of your guys to push this taxi out.'

Salma, please turn and look at me before Haraami gets run over by this cab.

Salma felt something and turned. It was Cupid poking her with his arrow. She turned and looked at Kamran. Kamran's hand went out of control and the ignition worked up the car.

Thank you, Salma. We will meet soon. Take good care of yourself because from now on, you are not yours or Haraami's. You are mine.

He looked at Abbas and smiled.

'See . . . It started. Khuda hafiz, uncle.'

'Khuda hafiz.'

The cab screamed out on to the main road.

Hamid was in the company parking lot at Nariman Point, chatting with the other drivers when he saw Kamran screeching Jumman's cab to a halt. He rushed towards Kamran.

'What the hell are you doing here?'

'I need to have a quick word with you.'

'Arre, Jumman would be waiting for his taxi.'

'Mamu! Easy. I just want to know how long Abbas Haraami is going to stay here.'

'Have you gone crazy?'

'Please tell me what you know. He is here for good, right?'

'No.'

'He is not settling here?'

'No. He is just here for his daughter's marriage.'

'Which one?'

'The only one. Salma.'

'With whom?'

'Final talks are on. The man is a widower but he is loaded and has a seven-year-old kid.'

'Don't break my heart.'

'That's true.'

'I want to tell you something.'

'Don't. I can figure. And let me tell *you* something. Forget about her. You don't know Abbas bhai. We don't call him Haraami out of affection.'

'Mamu, you don't understand. Salma looked back for me. That's a sign.'

'I look at Madhuri Dixit's posters and find that happening all the time. She is always looking back at me. But it hasn't got me anywhere, has it?'

'You don't check the mirror when you shave or what?'

'Scoundrel. Go and return the cab to Jumman immediately.'

'Okay. Don't worry too much if you see less of me in the coming days.'

'Try not to get thrashed.'

Kamran returned the cab to Jumman but before he did that he opened the rear door and sat in the same place where Salma had sat on the way back from the station. He closed his eyes. He was not sure what he was trying to feel or what he was trying to do but he was just following his heart.

Jumman who was watching him was sure that Kamran had started drinking or doping or both.

That night Kamran couldn't sleep.

Kamran was not aware but sixty metres away Salma was also having trouble sleeping. A face flashed before her eyes, every time she closed them. There was something nice about the taxi driver.

Kamran's biggest emotional signpost . . .

The couplets:

> *Dil-e-naadaan tujhe huaa kya hai?*
> *Aakhir is dard kee dawa kya hai*
>
> *Ham hain mushtaaq aur woh bezaar*
> *Ya ilaahee! Yeh maajra kya hai?*
>
> *Main bhee munh mein zabaan rakhta hoon*
> *Kaash! poocho ki 'muddaa kya hai?'*
>
> *Jab ki tujh bin naheen koee maujood*
> *Fir ye hangaama, 'ei khuda, kya hai*

8

The business of love gets even more complicated when you are running against time. Kamran knew that the odds were against him but he was not deterred. He needed an ally.

A really strong ally.

Zeenat wondered why Kamran uncle was being extra nice to her that morning when they were on their way to school. The chocolates tasted really nice, however.

'I will give you another packet in the evening. Okay?'

'Okay.'

'Zeenat . . .'

'Hmmm . . .'

'Do you like me, Zeenat?'

'Yes.'

'How much?'

'Very much.'

'Good. Do you want a new aunt?'

'No.'

'But an aunt will love you too. She will give you toys, sweets and anything that you want.'

'Okay.'

'So you want an aunt?'

'Okay.'

'Good. Now what kind of aunt do you want?'

'A nice one.'

'Do you know Salma aapa?

'Who?'

'Your friend Aafreen's aapa who has come to stay with her.'

'Yes. Salma aapa. I know. Why?'

'Now pay attention. This is an important question. Who would you like to have as your new aunt? Someone strict like your mom or someone loving and sweet like Salma aapa.'

'Someone like Salma aapa!'

'Okay. Now the thing is that in order to get a new loving and sweet aunt like Salma you will have to do a few things. Are you ready?'

'Yes.'

'The first thing is that you will have to promise that this will stay only between us. Promise?'

'Promise.'

'The second is that we can't afford to get caught.'

'If we get caught then will be out.'

'Exactly. You are so smart, Zeenat.'

'I am sad.'

'What happened?'

'I suddenly remembered the doll we saw last week which you didn't buy for me. She was so cute na, chachu?'

Kamran realized that he was dealing with a born negotiator.

'That doll, Zeenat dear, will be coming home tonight.'

'Really?'

'Really.'

'Let's talk about Salma aapa now.'

'Great. I want you to go and meet Aafreen and then I want you to pass this letter to Salma aapa when no one is looking.'

'Okay.'

'Remember, no one should notice.'

'I am sad.'

'Yes, I remember. The blue dress . . . right?'

'Right.'

'It's on its way too.'

'You are the best.'

'I know. And please don't be so sad so often.'

'Okay. Salma chachi is very beautiful, chachu.'

'Please take this before I faint, Zeenat.'

'Okay.'

They had reached the lane adjacent to Mohsin's house. Zeenat took the letter and ran towards the house. Who would suspect and stop a three-year-old angel. She ran inside the house and took some time locating Salma. She spent some time with Aafreen. Once she located Salma, Zeenat went and straightaway hugged her. Salma was surprised. Zeenat kissed her on the cheek. Salma kissed her back. Zeenat smiled, pressed something into her hand and ran off.

Salma was wondering what this was all about when she noticed the folded envelope in her palm. Her mother happened to enter the room at the same moment and Salma instinctively hid the letter in her dupatta.

Zeenat found Kamran waiting outside nervously. She strolled up to him and kept on walking. Kamran caught up with her.

'What happened?'

'It's delivered.'

'Safely.'

'Looks like it. I even hugged her and kissed her. She kissed me back too.'

You are worth the doll and the dress and much more, Zeenat.

After her mother was gone, Salma went into the bathroom and opened the envelope. There was a handwritten letter inside.

Dear Salma,

The moment I looked at you I realized what love is. I am very bad with words but I am still writing this letter in the hope that you will understand even what I won't be able to explain. My mother used to talk about *hoor*s. I understood the meaning of that word when I saw you at the station the other day. You almost killed me with the way you looked at me.

I need to see you again. I may not survive otherwise. I beg you to consider because I truly believe the following.

Why have you come in this world?

For me.

Why have you come to Bombay?

For me.

Is there anyone in this entire universe who can love you more than me?

No.

Is there anyone who can make you more happy than me?

No.

Salma, this for me is love. I can do anything for you and when I say that, I mean ANYTHING.

Just meet me once. Then I will respect whatever decision you take. Just give me an hour. It is my promise that your wish will rule.

Zeenat will come by again tomorrow. Your answer is the key to my life now.

Yours or Not?
Kamran.

Salma's face turned red. Her hands started shivering. Her pulse was racing. This was the first time someone had written a love letter to her. This was also the first time someone had acknowledged her as the custodian of his life.

Love, life, death ... these were very heavy words to an eighteen-year-old. She stepped out of the bathroom drenched in her own sweat. Through the entire day her mind kept asking and answering questions. When night came, sleep abandoned her. Kamran's face, his words on paper were all that she could think of.

Her heart was beating and stopping in turn. And the rhythm of every beat would echo a name:

Kamran.

She started to cry. This was such a wonderful feeling but why was it happening when her destiny was to follow her father's wishes and marry someone else? She wanted to be loved. She wanted to make her own choices but what about her family then?

People from the prospective groom's family were coming to see her in a few days. What if word got out that she was seeing someone? This was not possible. It would mean humiliation. She would not let this happen to her or her family.

Salma got up and shredded the letter into such small pieces that it was impossible to tear them any further.

She cried through the night but her mind and heart were made up.

No love for me.

Still, the moment she saw Zeenat the next day, her heart betrayed her resolve. Zeenat came and hugged her and then kissed her, looking at her in anticipation. Salma just hugged her. When Zeenat let go, she saw tears in Salma's eyes.

This was Salma's answer.

Zeenat went back empty-handed.

'Did she give anything?'

'No.'

'Then?'

'She was crying.'

'What?'

'She was sad. She was crying.'

Kamran stopped walking. He had received the message.

That evening Zeenat was back at Aafreen's house. At an opportune moment, she handed Salma the second letter from Kamran. She rushed again to the bathroom and started reading.

Dear Salma,

Zeenat tells me that you were crying when she met you. If it is because of me, then this is something that I will never forgive myself for.

But if it is because of the fact that you are unable to follow your heart then trust me I am your answer.

Salma, we are born once, but if we make the wrong choices we die every day, every moment.

If your heart is whispering, talking, then listen to it. I am just asking for an hour from you and again I promise you that your wish will rule.

I am going to be there at the Haji Ali Dargah from nine in the morning tomorrow. Please be there whenever you have the time and intent.

Whatever time you choose to come, I promise, you will find me there.

When you cried, Salma, I wanted to burn down this entire world because I felt it was the world that had made you cry.

Is there something wrong with me having that
feeling for you?

Yours surely . . .
Kamran.

Salma kissed the letter and started crying again. Once she
exhausted all her tears, she made a fresh resolve.

This nuisance must end. And this man can go to hell.

Kamran Khan was at the dargah for three consecutive days.
He had been spending every moment there for the last three
days waiting for the *deedar*, the *jhalak*. Salma was in his prayers,
his memory and his imagination. He was totally besotted with
her. This feeling was both tearing him apart and holding him
together.

A nine-year-old kid who used to live in the dargah premises
had been watching him very closely.

Towards the evening on the second day he came up to
Kamran and offered him some tea. Kamran took a glass. The
kid sat next to him.

'What is your name?'

'Kamran.'

'Woman trouble?'

Kamran was taken aback.

'It's written on my face?'

'Yes. See that man.'

The kid drew his attention to a helper near the gate. The
helper, who would be in his seventies, was guiding people
around the dargah.

'Yes.'

'His name is Junaid. He is also waiting.'

'Oh . . .'

'For the last forty years.'

Kamran looked at the kid.

'What's your name, kid?'

'They call me Chintu.'

'You want to say something?'

'Good luck.'

Salma tried shutting out all thoughts of Kamran but they kept seeping in. She didn't want to think about him but he always forced his way into her dreams. In her dream Salma saw Kamran waiting for her at the dargah and smiling. A little later she saw herself walking towards him down the causeway.

Kamran, on the other hand, knew that it was a test. Not once did he lose either faith or hope.

It was on the fourth day that he saw what he had been waiting for.

Salma was walking towards him and she was wearing blue.

> *Ishq mujhko nahin, vehshat hi sahi*
> *Meri vehshat teri shohrat hi sahi*
>
> *Qata keeje na taalluk hamse*
> *Kuch nahin hai to adavat hi sahi*
>
> *Hum koyee tarqe-vafa karte hain*
> *Na sahi ishq museebat hi sahi*
>
> *Kuch to de ae falke-na-insaaf*
> *Aaho fariyad ki rukhsat hi sahi*
>
> *Mere hone mein hai kya rusvaai*
> *Ye vo majalis nahin khalvat hi sahi*
>
> *Ham bhi dushman to nahin hain apane*
> *Ghair ko tujh se mohabbat hi sahi*

9

Salma knew that the world, her family would think that she was wrong. But she couldn't stop herself now. Something told her she should meet him once . . . just once . . . hear him out and then never ever meet him again. This would be their first and last meeting.

What if he was not at the dargah any more? It had been three days and that was a long time. It would be nice if he were not there. All the tall claims of love would be proven false and that would put an end to this stupid story automatically. It would be best if Kamran was not there.

Salma asked her mother if she could go to Haji Ali that morning. Mother appreciated religious leanings and consented. Abbas was a bit surprised but then how can you say no to a trip to the dargah?

Abbas asked Razzaq's sister Reshma to accompany Salma. He wanted to go himself but he had an appointment with his dentist. The mother couldn't go because her knees had been aching badly since last week. Salma had chosen her moment wisely.

Abbas gave Salma a set of instructions but she was busy readying herself for the big moment. The moment she would meet Kamran she would terminate this nonsense. You can't just fall in love with someone so quickly and, even if you do, you cannot expect her to love you back.

She would ask him to forget her completely. After all, her wish would rule.

Salma filled in Reshma on the way. Reshma was a city girl who was always looking for a bit of thrill and romance. Her own life was a nice mix of both. Reshma was flirting with one Asif and romancing with one Rajesh. Abbas, unknowingly, had provided Salma with the perfect ally.

Kamran was sitting on the steps and leaning against the pillar when he saw Salma accompanied by Reshma walking on the causeway towards him.

Hazaaron khwahishen aisi ke har khwahish pe dam nikle
Bahut nikle mere armaan, lekin phir bhi kam nikle

Nikalna khuld se aadam ka sunte aaye hain lekin
Bahut be-aabru hokar tere kuuche se hum nikle

Mohabbat mein nahin hai farq jeenay aur marnay ka
Usi ko dekh kar jeetay hain, jis kaafir pe dam nikle

Magar likhvaaye koi usko khat, to hum se likhvaaye
Hui subaha, aur ghar se kaan par rakh kar kalam nikle

He got up slowly. Salma and Reshma reached him but didn't stop walking. They went inside the dargah and offered their prayers. After that they went to a secluded corner. Kamran followed them there. Reshma looked at her watch.

'One hour you wanted and one hour you have got. Salma, don't you run away with this *chikna*.'

Reshma went away, leaving them alone. Salma's heart raced. She couldn't dare to look at Kamran and kept staring at the ground. Kamran couldn't bear to take his eyes off her. They stood there in silence.

'Thanks for coming.'

'I just came to say that this is all wrong and . . .'

'You look beautiful.'

'. . . I can't do this.'

'I just knew that you would come.'

'My family's reputation is at stake.'

'You have no idea of what you are doing to me.'

'I am going to get married in a few months.'

'I can just keep looking at you all my life, Salma.'

'Kamran, are you even listening to me?'

'I am and I am ignoring it because you are saying all the wrong things.'

'Kamran, please don't do this to me.'

'What?'

'Don't fall in love with me, Kamran. Please.'

Salma started crying. Kamran wanted to hold her but resisted the urge.

'I have already fallen in love, Salma.'

Salma looked up finally. She saw him. Kamran had a smile on his face but his eyes were swelling with tears.

'Why are you doing this to me?'

'This is our destiny, Salma. Accept it and embrace it. I will make sure that everything turns out right.'

'But how?'

'Do you like me, Salma?'

Salma kept looking at him. Kamran's eyes drilled a hole in her heart. Ages passed.

'Do I matter, Salma?'

'I don't know. I hardly know you.'

'But you still came today.'

'I came to say that that I cannot do this, Kamran.'

'But you wore my colour, Salma.'

Salma didn't know how to answer that.

'What did you ask for at the dargah, Salma?'

'One is not supposed to share it.'

'If it was not me in your wishes, then you can walk away right now, Salma. I swear on my mother that you will never see my face again.'

Salma didn't move. Kamran got his answer. Time seemed to stand still.

'What do I do, Kamran?'

'Give yourself a chance.'

'How?'

'By giving me another chance. I want you to meet me tomorrow. Let me figure out something. There has to be a way out, Salma.'

'My father will kill me if he comes to know about this.'

'Can you trust me, Salma?'

Salma knew that she was getting into a mess but her heart egged her on, saying that this was a good mess. Kamran repeated the question.

'Can you trust me, Salma?'

'I trust you.'

'I will live with it for the moment, Salma. I will take that for the moment.'

The lovers stood there in the corner till the hour passed. They kept looking at each other, punctuating the tension with innocuous questions about each other. Chintu came in with two glasses of tea. He winked at Kamran before leaving.

Kamran wanted to hug her a million times in that hour. Salma was worried a million times that Kamran would actually do so. Kamran wanted to kiss her a million times in that hour. Salma was worried a million times that Kamran would actually do so.

Reshma came as the sun was setting.

'Salma, you okay?'

'Hmmm . . .'

'Hey chikne! You didn't try anything naughty, right?'

'I wanted to but chose to wait.'

'Wait for what?'

'Wait for Salma to first say that she loves me.'

'Wow, chikne! She is soon getting married by the way.'

'I know. To me.'

'You are crazy.'

'Of course. She made me.'

Reshma smiled. In a flash she regretfully realized that both Asif and Rajesh were nothing like this Kamran.

'I like you.'

'Me too and that's the reason I want you to do something for me, Reshma.'

'What?'

'I want you to come to Liberty Cinema tomorrow at noon.'

'You want us to see *Phool aur Kaante* with you?'

'No, that's running houseful and is at the Super Cinema. We are going to see *Lamhe.*'

'But that is a flop.'

'Precisely. I need a quieter place.'

'Chikne, you are either an idiot or a genius.'

'Depends on which you like more.'

Salma and Reshma broke into laughter. Kamran stood there fixed to the ground as they started walking away from him. Salma kept turning and looking at him all through the walk down the causeway.

Khuda ke vaaste parda na kaabe se uthaa zaalim
Kaheen aisa na ho yaan bhi wahi kaafir sanam nikle

Kahaan maikhaane ka darwaaza Ghalib aur kahaan vaaiz
Par itna jaantay hain kal voh jaata thaa ke ham nikle

The next day Kamran and two burqa-clad women entered the balcony section of Liberty Cinema to watch *Lamhe*. They took the corner seats in the house. The seats were divided though. Reshma was seated alone in a row. Kamran and Salma were seated in the row right behind her.

'Did you sleep well, Salma?'

'No. I Just kept thinking about you. You?'

'I just kept dreaming about you.'

'What have you thought about us?'

'I am still thinking.'

As Anil Kapoor's character in the movie *Lamhe* got more and more baffled about his feelings for the younger Sridevi, Salma became more and more sure about her feelings for Kamran.

Some time in the second half of the film Kamran asked Salma, 'Do you like me, Salma?'

Salma put her head on his shoulder.

'You know what the problem with this film is?'

'What?'

'They are so bloody confused about their feelings.'

'I am also confused about us, Kamran.'

'That, my love, is the problem.'

'How do we solve it?'

'You can begin by admitting what your heart says.'

Another song started and ended.

'I think I love you, Kamran.'

'You think?'

'Yes. I think.'

'I will live with it for the moment.'

When the prospective groom's family was to visit Mohsin's house, Kamran asked Salma to just take it easy. He needed more time and anything rash at this point of time would jeopardize everything that they wanted.

The widower's family came and of course liked what they saw. Salma was looking striking. What the groom's family didn't know was that she was glowing because she was in love and was flushed with it. What they also didn't know was that Kamran was the first to have seen her that evening. An arrangement had been made with Ruslaan, the owner of the neighbouring house, to ignore Kamran's presence for an hour that evening.

Kamran had scaled the walls and had entered the bedroom where Salma was sitting decked and ready. The moment she saw him, she broke down. Kamran hugged her tightly.

'I am scared.'

'Don't.'

'Can you kiss me?'

'Why?'

'Because I love you.'

Salma had hugged Kamran tightly. Her nails dug into his back.

'I will live with it for the moment, Salma.'

So while Abbas Haraami was extolling the virtues of his beautiful, honourable daughter to the guests, Salma, upstairs, was sharing her first kiss with Kamran. It was so passionate that they were both intoxicated once it ended. Kamran wanted to go beyond the kiss. Salma was aware of what was happening downstairs.

As Kamran had held Salma's delicate body, he knew that she would be the bane of his life.

Now, standing behind the walls while the details and the negotiations of her marriage were being worked out, Salma smiled and bit her lip.

She knew she was Kamran's.

Salma had both faith and hope now.

Hazaaron khwahishen aisi ke har khwahish pe dam nikle
Bahut nikle mere armaan, lekin phir bhi kam nikle . . .

10

Salma and Reshma arrived at Nariman Point in a taxi. They were in burqas again. Kamran had sent a note through Zeenat asking Salma to be there that evening at five. This time Reshma had made the excuse of taking Salma to her place.

Kamran kept looking at Salma while answering Reshma.

'Hey chikne! You are playing with fire.'

'Thank you.'

'Only half an hour today.'

'Go get some peanuts.'

Reshma shook her head in irritation and left them alone.

They went and sat on the edge of the stretch.

'What happened?'

'They liked me.'

'Of course.'

'They are meeting again day after to finalize the date for the nikaah.'

'Pointless.'

'You are smiling.'

'Roshan bhai is handing me my very own taxi tomorrow morning. A brand-new beauty. I am going to come to your place and ask for your hand tomorrow itself. So my dear, the meeting day after tomorrow is pointless.'

'And what makes you sure that my father will agree.'

'If he doesn't, we will elope. We should give him a chance. If he rejects us, then we will do what we want.'

'He will not agree, Kamran.'

'Why? How am I lacking?'

'You mean besides being illiterate and a taxi driver?'

'Well, at least I am better than that forty-three-year-old widower with a seven-year-old.'

'I am afraid abbu wouldn't think so. You will still just be an illiterate taxi driver in his eyes.'

'Do you have any idea what people call your dad behind his back?'

'No. What?'

'Never mind. I will come tomorrow evening and we will see what happens.'

'Okay.'

'And open your mouth and tell him that you are in love with me.'

'He will kill me. But I will.'

'If he raises his hand on you then I will . . .'

'Shut up.'

They sat in silence for some time wishing for all the clocks and watches in the world to stop.

Salma bit Kamran on his arm. Kamran didn't flinch.

'Kamran?'

'Hmmm.'

'Why do we lose appetite when we are in love?'

'What? Are you sure? My intake *toh* has doubled.'

'Abbu won't agree, Kamran.'

'We should still give it a go.'

'We are going to be together forever, Kamran?'

'I was four and a famous pir landed at Qasimgarh. Ammi took me to him and the pir told her that the world would be at my feet some day. The pir said I would get anything that my heart truly desired. So, to answer your question, Salma, we are going to be together even if all the haraamis of this world come together and oppose us.'

'Don't curse!'

'Who cursed?'

Salma bit him again.

'I love you.'

'I love you.'

'I want to live my whole life for you.'

'Hmmm.'

'And this may sound funny but I am not scared at all, Kamran.'

'That's good.'

'What do they call abbu behind his back?'

'Never mind.'

They spent the evening seeing the sun go down. This was an evening they would remember for the rest of their lives.

'Hey chikne. Timeout. You okay, Salma?'

'No. Salma tell her that you are pregnant.'

Salma turned pink.

'Some day I am going to kill you, chikne!'

'Please wait till I get married and have a dozen children.'

'Her father is going to chop off your thing if you even think about that.'

'Ouch.'

Salma turned a shade darker. Reshma took her hand and they dashed towards the taxi stand.

Kamran decided to hang around for some time. Since morning, he had a nagging feeling that something wasn't right but was unable to put a finger on it. Now that he was alone, it came back to haunt him. He reanalysed the situation in his head.

CASE ONE: He goes to Haraami and asks for Salma's hand in marriage. Haraami says YES! Matter over.

CASE TWO: He goes to Haraami and asks for Salma's hand in marriage. Haraami says NO! They elope within a week. Matter over.

Where else could this go?

Kamran searched for an answer through the night and then deduced that maybe it was just his anxiety reacting to the situation. Love took over uneasiness and Kamran closed his eyes wishing all would go well the next day.

Roshan bhai, the owner of a fleet of taxis, was very proud of Kamran because he found him both hard-working and honest. When Kamran shared his current situation with Roshan, he figured the chap needed some help and support. He immediately suggested that Kamran get his own exclusive taxi and also not work nights any more. He made an arrangement whereby Kamran could own the taxi after a few years once he had paid a certain amount of money every month. Roshan even offered to lend him money but Kamran declined. He was doing fine for the time being.

The next day, Roshan bhai handed over the keys of the new taxi to Kamran. Kamran acknowledged the debt and thanked him. He then drove straight to the dargah. He had prayed for this day and his dua had been granted. He was dressed in his Friday best, a white shirt with white trousers, as he planned to head straight to meet Salma's family after this.

Kamran closed his eyes and thanked Sayyed Pir Haji Ali Shah Bukhari at the *mazaar*. As he stepped out he bumped into Chintu.

'You are shining, Kamran bhai.'

'Pray for me, Chintu. It's a big day.'

'Nothing wrong can ever happen to you, Kamran bhai.'

Kamran ruffled his hair and gave him a fiver. He then sprinted down the causeway towards his parked taxi. He quickly started the taxi. As he put it into gear, he saw an elderly man waving ahead. Kamran leaned to tell him that he was not running fares but the man spoke first.

'Beta, can you take me to Mohammed Ali Road?'

Kamran couldn't say no. He looked at his watch and did a quick calculation.

What timing? First to Mohammed Ali Road ... drop this gentleman ... then head to Salma's. Should still make it on time. My first fare? Can't say no.

'Please sit.'

The gentleman sat in the rear seat. Kamran noticed that he had a nice air about him. He was dressed in a white Pathani and was in his mid-fifties. Kamran entered Mohammed Ali Road to see a sea of vehicles ahead of him. He asked himself to relax.

But his patience started waning as he moved only an inch every couple of minutes. It didn't help that the driver ahead of him was even slower. He screamed, 'Do you even have gears in there?'

The gentleman in the rear seat smiled.

'Relax, beta. It will clear out in a few minutes.'

'With this guy in front of me, I really doubt it.'

'Do you have to be somewhere?'

'Yes. I am going to be late and I cannot afford to get late today.'

'You want me to get down here? I mean I can walk ...'

'No ... no. It's okay.'

Suddenly, Kamran spotted Ruslaan stopping his bike on the other side of the road. Ruslaan was Mohsin's neighbour who had helped Kamran for his secret rendezvous with Salma a couple of evenings before. Ruslaan got down from the bike while the pillion rider took charge and kept the accelerator going.

Kamran saw Ruslaan walking towards his cab determinedly. He saw Ruslaan taking out a gun from under his shirt and as soon as he reached the taxi Ruslaan shot the elderly man in his chest.

Four shots in four seconds ... all into the chest of the elderly man.

As Ruslaan turned he caught a glimpse of the driver. He froze. Kamran looked at him in shock. Their eyes locked. After a frozen moment, Ruslaan started running towards the other side of the road. He reached the bike and sat on the rear seat. The guy accelerated the bike and they were off in a matter of seconds.

The public, which was witness to the shoot-out, rushed to have a glimpse of the man inside the taxi. Kamran turned to find large circles of blood on the man's chest. The man was wincing in pain, gasping and bleeding profusely.

Kamran knew that he couldn't lose time. He quickly got out of the taxi and then started screaming at people to make way for him. A couple of pedestrians and other drivers also joined in. In a matter of minutes, the crowd had cleared out a path for him. Kamran rushed back to his taxi and started it. He kept screaming and tore through the road. He had never seen a shoot-out and had never imagined that he would be a witness to something like this.

Kamran speeded towards the K.L. Hospital, the nearest in the vicinity.

The pir who had prophesied that Kamran would get whatever he wanted in his life was absolutely right.

He would.

Whether he would be able to keep it, however, was something that the pir hadn't commented on.

11

Kamran reached the emergency room at K.L. Hospital in little time. A couple of wards boys were chatting outside. Kamran shouted for help. They took a stretcher and rushed towards the taxi. Kamran opened the door and the ward boys were horrified at the sight of the man in the rear drenched in blood and gasping for breath.

Kamran pulled the man out of the taxi and laid him on the stretcher. The ward boys were confused over whether they wanted to help him or not. Kamran wheeled the man into the emergency. A nurse appeared before him.

'What happened?'

'He . . . This . . . Somebody shot him.'

'Who is he?'

'Sorry?'

'Who is he?'

'I don't know.'

'Who are you?'

'Why don't you call a doctor first?'

'How are you related to the patient?'

'I am not. He was in my taxi.'

'Stop shouting. You drive a taxi?'

Kamran calmed himself.

'I drive a taxi. He was my fare. We were in traffic. Someone shot him while we were stuck in traffic.'

'It's a police case. Stand there.'

'Aren't you going to call a doctor? This man will die.'

'But . . .'

'What's happening here? What's with this shouting, sister?'

Kamran turned to see a doctor standing behind him.

'Doctor, this man was shot at while he was travelling in this chap's taxi. Multiple gunshot wounds. Police case.'

'Roll him in immediately.'

'But Doctor . . .'

'Are you deaf?'

'Sorry, Doctor.'

The nurse rushed out shouting for help. The doctor held Kamran back.

'When did this happen?'

'About . . . twenty . . . odd minutes back.'

'Where?'

'Mohammed Ali Road.'

The nurse came back.

'Doctor! There is a call for you.'

'I will take it later.'

'Doctor, you would want to take this.'

There was a tone shift in the way the nurse spoke to the doctor. The doctor walked towards the reception. The receiver was off the hook, waiting in anticipation. The doctor picked it up.

'Hello . . . !'

'Doctor, I am the guy who pumped four bullets inside the man that you are so eager to help. If you do help him, I will have something as nasty as this in store for you and your family.'

The line went dead.

The doctor's hands started shaking. He kept the phone down. He saw the ward boys preparing to take the stretcher into the operation theatre.

'Hang on. Did anyone call the police, sister?'

'No, Doctor.'

'No one will touch him until the police arrives.'

Kamran was surprised at his sudden change of stance.

'But he will die by then, Doctor.'

'We can't attend to him till the police arrives.'

'But Doctor . . .'

Kamran found the doctor walking away. The nurse followed the doctor and soon the ward boys were also gone. Kamran started feeling lost but realized that this was the time to act. He rushed over to the injured man and started searching through his pockets. He came up with a wallet. A driving licence stated that the man was called Mirza Azmat Ali Khan. There was a small blue telephone diary with chronological alphabetical flips. Three alphabets on each flip and the last two flips had four alphabets each.

The small diary was full of telephone numbers.

Kamran shut the diary and closed his eyes and reopened the diary again. It opened at M and the first handwritten entry on that page was Munna. Kamran rushed toward the PCO and dialled the listed number. It kept ringing for some time and just when Kamran felt that it would disconnect, the call went through.

'Hello.'

Kamran dropped a one-rupee coin.

'Hello. Do you know someone called Mirza Azmat Ali Khan?'

'Who is calling?'

'Do you know someone by the name Mirza Azmat . . .'

'Yes. Who is this?'

'He has been shot.'

'What?'

'Yes, he was travelling in my taxi and someone shot him. I brought him here to K.L. Hospital but these guys here won't admit him till the time the police comes and I fear that it will be all too late by then.'

'Is the doctor around?'

'He got a telephone call or something and he just went away.'

'Is Mirza saab okay?'

'No.'

'Is he . . . he . . .'

'He is alive. Yes.'

'Do you know J.K. Hospital?'

'Yes.'

'Can you get him there?'

'Yes. I can.'

'Okay get there as fast as you can. I will be waiting there.'

'Okay.'

Kamran ran back to the stretcher. Mirza was still gasping. Single-handedly, Kamran wheeled the stretcher out of the lobby and took it to his taxi. He took Mirza in his arms and put him in the rear seat. The seat was soaked in blood. Kamran himself had bloodstains all over him.

Kamran knew that generally it took about fifteen minutes to get to J.K. from K.L. Hospital. He also knew that Mirza didn't have fifteen minutes. He had stopped gasping and was unconscious now.

Kamran reached there inside of ten minutes. He saw a group of four people waiting in the emergency. Behind them there were doctors, nurses and ward boys. As soon as Kamran's cab stopped, they all rushed towards him. They took control of the situation in a moment. Mirza was wheeled into the operation theatre of the J.K. Hospital in a matter of minutes.

While Mirza was getting operated on, Kamran sat outside the operation theatre hoping he would survive. Someone came and gave him a glass of water. Kamran thanked him. The crowd kept getting bigger and Munna had to instruct his boys that barring a few everyone was to wait outside. A few were crying but the general feeling was that of anger. Kamran noticed that some of the people had guns tucked away.

Who is this fucking man?

His mind struggled with the image of Ruslaan's face staring at him after the shoot-out. Random questions popped up in his mind.

Why would Ruslaan do this?

Who was Mirza?

Was this the infamous underworld dealing a hand?

Kamran then remembered that he was supposed to be at Salma's place. He looked at himself, all soiled in Mirza's blood.

What the fuck!

The reason that Kamran had that blood on him was a man called Murli Highway. Murli Shetty became Murli Highway the day he bought his twenty-fifth truck. He ruled the Bombay–Goa NH-17 and controlled all the smuggling on this route. Murli's wife had died in childbirth and he lived with his twelve-year-old daughter, Laxmi.

Of late, Murli had been accepting the most impossible of suparis or contract killings. But that was not the only thing. The icing on the cake was that Murli protected his clients with utmost secrecy. If Murli made a deal, no one besides him would ever get to know about who got whom killed.

Murli, of course, charged a premium. But it was worth it because even if it was a botched attempt, Murli would never give away any information.

Someone hired Murli and Murli hired Ruslaan.

Ruslaan knew that this was actually worse than it looked. He reached his hiding place in Mahim and the first thing he did was call Murli Highway. Murli was sitting in his sea-facing flat in Bandra when he received the call.

'Hello.'

'Is it done?'

'I have shot him four times. They have wheeled him into J.K. Hospital.'

'How is it looking?'

'Bad.'

'Good. Because if he survives then it will be bad for us.'

'Murli seth . . . there is a problem.'

'What?'

'The cabbie saw me doing Mirza.'

'What the fuck are you saying?'

'It's bizarre. The fucking driver happens to live in my mohalla. His name is Kamran. He saw me clearly.'

'Then why did you leave him?'

'I don't . . . know. Didn't strike me.'

'Then you are fucked.'

Sub-inspector Promod Gupte reached the hospital and had to tear through the crowd to get inside. It was late at night but the crowd had only swelled. Munna spotted him and joined him in a corner.

'How is Mirza saab now?'

'Don't know, Promod saheb. These doctors are still inside.'

'But how the hell was he alone?'

'Karim had fever and you know Mirza saab. He got adamant and insisted that he wouldn't break his routine. I called him up saying that I would be there in twenty minutes but he didn't wait.'

'Any idea who did this?'

'No. You will have to give me a name on this one, Promod saheb.'

'I am trying. Where is the cabbie?'

Munna pointed to Kamran. Promod walked over to Kamran. Kamran saw a uniformed officer and instinctively got up. Promod motioned for him to sit and then sat beside him.

'What's your name?'

'Kamran Khan.'

'Tell me exactly what happened. Try not to miss anything even if you think that it's insignificant.'

Kamran was tired. He had already done this a few times but he had no choice. He narrated everything all over again in the exact same manner, leaving out one bit of information like every other time.

'Did you see the shooter?'

'No.'

'Anything?'

'No.'

'The shirt colour or something?'

'Some shade of blue.'

'Nothing else?'

'No.'

'Do you know anything about Mirza saab?'

'Not really. He seemed nice . . . That's all.'

'No one in this city does this, Kamran. You are different. People are not known to help anyone in such situations.'

'I felt I . . . I had to.'

'We will have to take your taxi.'

'It's outside. The keys are in there.'

'I will need you at the Crime Branch tomorrow at eleven.'

'Crime Bran . . . ?'

'Don't worry. I will need you for not more than ten minutes.'

'Okay, sir.'

The operation theatre doors opened and the doctors came out. One of the doctors announced:

'He is under observation for the next 48 hours. He has lost a lot of blood and we could take out only three bullets. The fourth one is still there inside but it's not a problem and we are not going to do anything about it at the moment. We can only comment on his condition after six hours.'

The crowd wanted to ask questions but the doctors were gone before they could react. Promod patted Kamran on the back and left. On his way out Promod took Munna with him.

'I am leaving four of my men here right now. I will send some more as soon as possible.'

'Thanks.'

'I will see you tomorrow, Munna.'

'I want a name, Promod saheb.'

'You will. Soon.'

Promod instructed a few of his men and then got into his jeep and drove away. He knew that this was bad. He stopped at Banjara, an eatery known to be open till late night. But Promod Gupte didn't stop because he was hungry but because he was worried. He went into the manager's cabin and motioned for the manager to get out.

He closed the door of the cabin and dialled a number.

Ruslaan picked up the phone on the other side.

'Kamran says that he didn't see you.'

'He is lying, Promod saheb. He has seen me.'

'You fucking dumbfucks, both you and Murli.'

'Why are you keeping yourself out? We are a threesome.'

'Kamran will have to go.'

Promod hung up and dialled again.

Murli Highway picked up the phone.

'This boy—Kamran—will have to go.'

'I will arrange.'

'Don't fuck up this time, Murli seth.'

'Fuck-ups *happen*, Promod. Let me assure you that fuck-ups *happen* . . . like shit. The boy will be gone by tomorrow.'

Murli Highway hung up.

Actually, how Kamran became Ghalib Danger is not really another story.

A few small stories added themselves up to become his story.

12

It was well past midnight and the crowd outside the hospital was still growing. Munna walked up to Kamran.

'You can go home and rest. The boys will drop you.'

'I can manage.'

'I am not asking. I am telling you.'

Kamran could not protest. He had a fair idea by now that these people were very powerful and it made sense to keep his mouth shut. Three of Munna's men escorted him outside. Kamran could hear murmurs. People were identifying him as the man who had saved Mirza's life. A few hands blessed him subtly.

It made him a bit proud.

They sat in a black Fiat and drove off. Kamran sat in the rear seat with two of Mirza's boy's on either side. Kamran again noticed that they were armed. Throughout the journey, no one spoke apart from Kamran who gave directions to his home. Once they reached Karampura, Kamran got down from the car and started walking. The Fiat waited till Kamran vanished into one of the by-lanes.

Only when Kamran knew that he was alone did he run towards Ruslaan's house. It was very dark and the stray dogs cooperated because they knew Kamran from his night shifts. He reached the house and knocked discreetly.

There was no response.

He knocked again.

Kamran heard some movement and after a moment the door opened. It was Ruslaan's mother. She was very old and had not been keeping well at all. Kamran had woken her up. He stood a little away, in partial darkness, because he did not want her to see the blood stains on his clothes.

'Salaam, chachi.'

'Kamran. What happened, beta? It's so late.'

'Chachi, I needed to speak to Ruslaan. Can you wake him up?'

'Ruslaan left for Surat in the morning. He finally got a nice job there. They gave him a good advance.'

'Ohhh.'

'He has told me that once he settles there he is going to send for me as well.'

'I . . . I am sorry I woke you up. Khuda hafiz.'

'Khuda hafiz, beta.'

Kamran walked away from the door knowing that the mother's heart was going to break very soon. The only reason he had not spoken about Ruslaan to anyone was because he wanted to know his side of the story first.

He had no idea about anyone or anything.

Kamran reached home and got to his loft. He took out some fresh clothes and stepped out again.

He needed to wash off Mirza's blood. He tried but it was quite a task.

Mirza's blood refused to come off.

Mirza Azmat Ali Khan was born in 1936 in Bombay on the same the day his father had landed there with his pregnant wife. They were originally from Sultanpur district in Uttar Pradesh. Mirza's father was an electrician at Bombay Talkies, a movie studio that had been founded a couple of years back. They lived in a chawl.

Mirza became Mirza in the year 1970 and it all started because of a very small piece of land.

Two plots of land sat adjacent to each other in Lower Parel, Bombay. While one was vacant and available, the other had a small chawl. Hafiz Patel who had bought the vacant land figured that this would be the finest premium piece of real estate in this part of town if he could get the residents of the neighbouring chawl to vacate. The owner of the chawl was with him on this so all that they had to do was to get rid of the tenants. He had done this on so many occasions before that he didn't think it would be a problem.

Hafiz Patel had money, muscle and connections. What he ran out of was luck.

The chawl that Hafiz had his eyes on had an occupant who was an electrician with B.R. Film Studios. Mirza had followed in his father's footsteps and joined the same line of work. He was hard-working, honest and was liked by everyone in the chawl. He was a matriculate, which increased their respect for him even more.

Hafiz sent the tenants a proposal which involved a small sum of money and a veiled threat. It infuriated all of them. After a quick chat amongst themselves, it was unanimously decided that both Hafiz and his proposal could go to hell.

The next day a message of refusal was sent on behalf of the tenants, signed by Ratnakar Choudhary, one of the oldest residents of the chawl.

That very evening Ratnakar Choudhary was shot dead.

After this, the residents panicked and started backing off. There was dissent amongst them. A few formed a small group and decided to take Hafiz's money. But Mirza sensed they would lose whatever little they had if no one led them to a fight.

It was then that Mirza stepped up. He asked them to hold for a while and calm down. He offered to meet Hafiz the next day to ask him to reconsider.

Mirza did not sleep for a moment that night. That was the first time he weighed upon words like courage and fear and finally figured that fear is all in one's head.

Mirza understood that he just needed to make himself incapable of fear.

The rest and its mother would follow.

The next day Mirza reached Hafiz's office with a friend of his. The guards would not allow Mirza to meet him. Mirza waited the whole day but nothing happened. In the evening, he saw Hafiz's white Mercedes coming out from the building and crossing him.

He reached the office again the next day. Around evening the guard got a message to let Mirza in. Mirza had worked enough on swanky film sets to know class but this was all too real and intimidating. They were made to stand in the reception for another hour before they were finally ushered in.

They entered to see Patel sitting alone in his room. Mirza had seen no one coming out of the room before they entered and understood fully that Patel had just been trying to look tough.

Mirza and his friend stood in silence. Hafiz lit a cigarette and blew a ring of smoke and announced:

'You have two minutes.'

'I will take one. Seth, please leave us alone. We are poor people with our backs against the wall. We live with what we need. You already have more than you need. There are 143 lives at stake here. Sixty of them are too old to move. I request you with folded hands. Sir, please back off.'

It was an honest request from an honest man. Hafiz took a puff and committed the biggest blunder of his life. He spoke.

'What if I don't?'

Mirza smiled slowly.

'Then Mirza would not like it.'

'Who the fuck is Mirza?'

Mirza shook his head and walked out of the room followed by his friend who was shaking like a leaf because he had never seen this side of him.

Hafiz was perplexed. Mirza had played a simple mind game. He had threatened Hafiz with a name. A name that Hafiz could not put a face to. There was only one question ringing in Hafeez's head.

Who the fuck is Mirza?

Hafiz put all his resources behind this querry. Meanwhile, at the chawl, Mirza's friend turned the incident at Hafiz's office into a legend. People started looking up to Mirza, because of which Mirza started feeling even more responsible for their fates.

It took Hafiz three days to figure out the truth and it pissed him off no end. It was at this point that he committed the second biggest blunder of his life.

Mirza often liked to go to Juhu Chowpatty after work. That evening, after he was through with the day's work at B.R. Studios, he decided to walk down to the beach. Just as he was crossing the bus stand he felt there was something wrong. He turned to see four men running towards him with iron rods, swords and knives.

Mirza knew he had been found out. He ran towards Chowpatty and the men chased him across the beach. They caught up with Mirza after a long run, at the stretch near Holiday Inn. Mirza was unarmed but he fought like a man possessed. He managed to snatch a rod from one of the assailants and fought back. Though he was getting slashed all over, Mirza managed to get two of the men down.

In a quick turnaround the crowd now saw a bloodied Mirza chasing the four goons. After a while, Mirza gave up on the chase and summoned all his strength. He had to survive and the first step in that direction would be a trip to the hospital.

Inspector Ramesh Naik was off duty and happened to be there on the beach that evening with his mistress, Savita. They were sipping cola-flavoured ice *gola*s and Ramesh was devotedly rubbing his elbow at all the right places because Savita was certainly not complaining.

What distracted Ramesh was the sight of a man covered in blood, struggling to walk towards the autorickshaw stand. When the auto drivers refused to take Mirza, Ramesh Naik had to put on hold his most likeable pastime and intervene.

So while Mirza was struggling for his life and asking for help, Inspector Ramesh Naik engaged Savita in the following negotiation.

'Savita, let's continue tomorrow. Have this gola and take care. I love you.'

'Fuck off. Where is the money?'

'Sweetheart, I forgot. I will get it for you tomorrow.'

'You will not get to touch these tomorrow if you don't get my money.'

'This is why I love you. Bye.'

'And do something about your hard-on.'

Ramesh ran towards the autorickshaw stand to help Mirza. He slapped an auto guy and got Mirza inside the rickshaw. He then sat in the driver's seat and they rushed off to Nanavati Hospital.

Ramesh was both amused and intrigued by the fact that Mirza had a smile on his face during the entire ride. On reaching, Mirza refused support and walked into the hospital on his own. He caught hold of a doctor and calmly requested him: 'Doctor . . . Please fix me.'

Mirza was in the hospital for seven weeks and in those seven weeks every conscious moment that he had was spent on working out how to decimate Hafiz Patel completely. The man who helped him in this endeavour was Inspector Ramesh

Naik. On the fifth day of his admission, Ramesh came to visit Mirza.

'Thanks for getting me here.'

'Don't mention. Who were these guys?'

'You are an inspector, Rameshji?'

'Yes. Juhu Police Station.'

'And you don't know who did this to me?'

'I know. The question is, do you?'

'Do you want to be co-owner of a plot of land in Parel?'

For the next half an hour, Inspector Ramesh Naik was in negotiations over a plot worth crores with an electrician who had barely survived an attempt on his life a few days ago.

The next day, Hafiz's seventeen-year-old daughter, Nazia, who studied at the National College in Bandra was kidnapped on the way back home. A van stopped near the college, pulled her in and then vanished in a matter of seconds in broad daylight.

Hafiz Patel and his family left no stone unturned to find her. The entire city of Bombay was turned upside down. No money, no muscle and no connection was spared but there was no trace of Nazia.

Three days went by. No ransom call. No news. Nothing.

When the police, mafia and politicians gave up on Hafiz Patel, he remembered a name: *Mirza*.

It was then that Hafiz came to know through his sources that the man he had got attacked, with the intention of killing him, had actually survived. He found out more details and then rushed to Nanavati.

Mirza and Ramesh, by then, had made their only investment and had got Mirza shifted from the common ward to a VIP room, which had two rooms. One for the patient and one for visitors.

Hafiz got everyone to wait outside as he entered the room alone. Mirza was sitting propped up and was having soup.

Hafiz and Mirza locked eyes and Hafiz felt scared. The body was swathed in bandages and nearly lifeless, but Mirza's piercing eyes were repeatedly saying the same thing.

I had told you. Mirza won't like it.

Hafiz finally dared.

'Is . . . she . . . she . . . ?'

Mirza took his time. He took a sip.

'Yes.'

Hafiz started crying like a baby. He dashed towards Mirza and caught his feet.

'I am sorry, Mirza.'

'Go and get your driver.'

'Sorry?'

'Go and get your driver.'

Hafiz ran out and came back with his driver after a couple of minutes.

'Now what, Mirza?'

'Now I want you to ask your driver to stand in that corner and watch you apologize.'

Hafiz knew from Mirza's tone that there was no use stalling. He signalled his driver to one corner and then caught Mirza's feet.

'I am really, really sorry, Mirza. I swear on my mother I am sorry . . . really, really sorry.'

Mirza took his time. Hafiz started crying and then slumped at his feet. The driver didn't know what to do or where to look. After a very long two minutes Mirza spoke.

'Two minutes is what you were giving me the other day. I have them now. You can leave my feet and ask your driver to wait outside.'

The driver was relieved. He almost ran out. Mirza wiped his face with a napkin. Hafiz was still sobbing. Mirza spoke.

'Your daughter is not going to be home till I go home. As of tomorrow you will initiate the process of transferring the plot next to my chawl to Ratnakar Choudhary's son, Satyam Choudhary. The details will reach your office tomorrow morning.'

'Yes.'

'Every week that I spend in this hospital is going to cost you a building which shall be adjusted against the cost of maintenance for your daughter.'

'Is she okay?'

'Mashallah.'

'Can I see her once?'

'In time and only if you behave yourself.'

'Can I have proof that she is alive?'

'I can send you a finger of hers if you want.'

'I am very, very, very, very sorry, Mirza bhai. Please don't let anything happen to her.'

Hafiz caught Mirza's feet again and cried his heart out. What he didn't know was that his daughter Nazia was hearing everything from the adjoining room. She couldn't speak because Inspector Ramesh Naik was sitting next to her holding a gun.

Mirza was in the hospital for seven weeks and thus built the foundation of his empire from room 404 of Nanavati Hospital.

So, there was a reason why Mirza's blood was not coming off Kamran's shirt that night.

It was of a very different kind.

Na tha kuch to khuda tha, kuch na hota to khuda hota
Duboyaa mujh ko hone ne, na hota main to kya hota

Hua jab gham se yun behis to gham kya sar ke katne ka
Na hota gar judaa tan se to zaannon par dharaa hota

13

Kamran didn't sleep well again that night. Was his premonition that something would go wrong coming true?

The next morning Kamran was ready before everybody else. He called Zeenat and both of them started for Salma's house on the way to Zeenat's school. Hamid saw them leaving earlier than usual and could not help commenting.

'Go on ... Spoil the kid now with all your romantic rendezvous.'

'I am making her sharp.'

'By using her as a courier?'

'You won't understand.'

'Of course. Zeenat, be careful with this chachu of yours.'

Kamran and Zeenat reached the lane adjoining Salma's house. He slipped a note into her pocket.

'Chachu, I am feeling sad. '

'We will go to the market in the evening.'

'I want a new school bag and a new water bottle.'

'What's wrong with these?'

'Nothing. Just that I want new ones.'

'Sure. Now do this carefully.'

Zeenat ran towards Salma's house leaving behind a bewildered Kamran. His love affair was proving very expensive. He was spending more money on Zeenat than on Salma.

Salma was sitting alone when Zeenat entered her room. Salma kissed her and Zeenat handed her the note. Salma looked around and decided she had enough privacy. She opened the note.

Got stuck badly. Don't lose hope, love. Will get back soon. Yours, Kamran.

Salma let out a sigh. She took off the earring from her left ear, wrapped it in her kerchief and put it in Zeenat's pocket. Zeenat kissed her on the cheek and ran away. Salma was a little worried but with her worry also came the firm belief that Kamran would not let anyone or anything endanger her and their relationship.

Zeenat handed the kerchief to Kamran and when Kamran opened it, he felt like a millionaire. He was lost in the moment till Zeenat caught his attention.

'I am getting late for my school.'

'I am getting late for my life.'

'What?'

'Nothing.'

They came out of Karampura when it started raining. Zeenat loved the rain and refused to run into a shelter. Kamran picked her up in his arms and started running towards the school.

A jeep came to halt on the other side of the road. Around five people got down from the jeep and ran towards Kamran and Zeenat, holding swords, machetes and rods.

Mirza in the ICU woke up with a jolt. He whispered that he needed to speak to a man called Munna. When the doctor advised him to take it easy, Mirza caught him by the coat and said, 'Now.'

Kamran was fooling around with Zeenat when he saw the five men running towards him with weapons of different shapes and sizes. He also saw Ruslaan sitting in the rear seat of the jeep.

It was then that it hit him clearly.

This was the premonition.

The shower intensified. It suddenly started pouring. Kamran

gripped Zeenat tightly, turned around and rushed towards the adjacent Byculla flyover. The men chasing him also changed their trajectory. Kamran knew that having Zeenat in his arms would soon be a fatal handicap. Zeenat sensed that something was wrong when the smile disappeared from her chachu's face.

In the ICU, Mirza whispered something in Munna's ears and asked him to hurry.

Kamran was running on the flyover with his assailants close on his heels. They were catching up quite fast, the gap between them narrowing quickly. Kamran threw Zeenat's bag away and put her on his shoulder. She was getting very frightened.

The rain was making it even more difficult. When Kamran realized that the assaulters were breathing down his neck he had no option but to turn and take them on. Kamran was no fighter but he had a courageous heart.

We never know how much courage we are capable of. Rage and love can propel anyone to any lengths.

The fact that Kamran was the one to start the fight took the assaulters by surprise. What was supposed to be a simple hunt for a man was turning into a full-fledged battle. Kamran managed to snatch a sword after taking one of them down and challenged the others with it. It was unsettling because he had Zeenat in his arms, but he had no choice.

Kamran kept fighting till a machete tore through his sides and went right through Zeenat.

Another slashed Kamran across his body. As Kamran saw Zeenat convulsing he didn't care for the fight any more. He screamed as he held her tightly. The assaulters kept hitting him. Kamran shielded Zeenat tightly and took in all the hits and slashes repeatedly.

A shot rang through the air.

The assaulters stopped and saw Munna running towards them with his men. Munna kept shooting at them. The assaulters panicked and ran way.

A couple of Fiats arrived on the scene. Kamran and Zeenat were put inside and rushed to the hospital. Kamran hugged Zeenat tightly all the way, refusing to accept the truth.

Zeenat was announced dead on arrival.

Kamran was taken to the ICU. After four hours, the doctors announced that he was unconscious and would be under observation for the next forty-eight hours.

When Munna updated Mirza on the proceedings, Mirza winced and murmured a curse. He issued a fresh set of instructions. Mirza knew he had to get out of the hospital sooner than the doctor liked.

Munna and his men tracked down Hamid by the afternoon and got him to come to the hospital. Mirza then broke the news himself to Hamid. Hamid had heard of Mirza but was completely beside himself when he came to know about what had transpired.

Hamid saw an unconscious Kamran through the glass bandaged all over with pipes and tubes running all over his body. He became so restless that Munna had to escort him outside.

In the other room, his heart broke when he saw the small lifeless bundle that was Zeenat. That fair face with her eyes closed . . . it seemed like she was sleeping. How Hamid wished she would open her eyes.

Hamid took her in his arms and broke down. He kissed her, hugged her tightly and wailed. In his grief he prayed and hoped that Khuda would melt and give his daughter back to him.

Munna arranged for Zeenat to go home for the last time. His men were assigned roles and he personally monitored all the funeral arrangements. Munna was with Hamid the whole time.

They took Zeenat first to Karampura and the whole mohalla came to a halt. They had known Zeenat since her birth and there was not one soul in the whole place who didn't like her. They went into mourning as if she was their own.

Zeenat's mother was inconsolable. She passed out every few minutes. Reshma brought the bad news to Salma and they both rushed to Hamid's place. A crowd had gathered in front of the house and Salma was shocked to see Zeenat wrapped in a shroud.

It was just that morning that she had brought Kamran's note to her. It was just that morning that she had kissed her. A wave of pain cut through her heart. Zeenat had been her only confidante. Hers was the only face that she wanted to see all the time because Zeenat meant Kamran in one sense. Her knees buckled.

The whole place was drenched in sorrow.

The funeral procession, the *janazah*, culminated at Nariyalwadi cemetery. There was a clear-cut directive from Mirza about the burial and Munna had taken care of every detail.

After the burial, Hamid refused to go back home. He did not want to leave Zeenat alone. He stayed beside her the whole night.

Mirza could not rest either. He was aware that Zeenat's death was a direct result of his survival and so it weighed upon him like a cross.

They will pay with their blood.

Murli Highway received the confirmation over the telephone call from SI Promod Gupte. Promod had been in touch with snitches all day and once he reached the safety of his home he picked up the phone.

'It seems that Kamran will survive.'

'It seems that we are fucked then, Gupte.'

'What do we do?'

'Run, I suggest.'

'How much time will they take to figure out who all are in this, Murli seth?'

'Three days. Maximum four days.'

Murli Highway was wrong. Sitting in the hospital bed Mirza had put together all the pieces in this puzzle.

In the cab, Mirza had seen the look on Kamran's face when Ruslaan had taken out the gun to shoot Mirza.

So Kamran and Ruslaan knew each other.

Kamran had saved his life and how.

So Kamran was not the bad guy.

But Kamran needed to be eliminated so that Ruslaan would be safe so that no one would know who ordered the hit on Mirza.

Hence Kamran was attacked.

Why had SI Promod Gupte not given any police protection to the man who had saved Mirza's life? Was Promod protecting someone? Had he moved over?

Mirza had immediately put Munna on the job of getting Promod into their custody and was waiting for Munna to get back.

Munna picked up Promod right after he finished his call with Murli Highway.

There had always been a list of people who wanted Mirza out of the way and he had always taken care of them. Things had been quiet for a while until this incident. It would take an incredibly brave person or an incredibly foolish one to take Mirza's supari.

While Mirza could not think of anyone that brave he knew of one who was incredibly foolish.

The Highway guy . . . What's the name . . . Something Highway.

Munna entered his room and confirmed:

'It's Murli Highway who took your contract, Mirza saab, and you were absolutely right about Promod Gupte.'

'And who gave my contract to Highway?'

'Promod doesn't know, he says.'

'The shooter?'

'It's Kamran's neighbour Ruslaan.'

'Where is Promod?'

'At our warehouse in Mazgaon.'

'How is the boy doing?'

'He is hanging on, Mirza saab. Big hearted he is. Took them on barehanded. If it had not been for that small girl . . .'

'What a mess!'

Mirza kept silent for some time. Munna stood nearby.

'I want everyone who is involved directly or indirectly to pay for this, Munna. It was my life that they were after. It should have remained that way. The taxi driver or the small girl were none of their business. Promod will go tomorrow morning. I want to see Murli tomorrow afternoon. Ask the doctors to get me discharged tomorrow.'

'Yes.'

Mirza raised his hand. Munna left him alone.

None of the pain he had endured in his life could compare to the guilt he felt for having this three-year-old's blood on his hands. It was definitely the worst thing that had ever happened in his life.

Mirza prayed for Zeenat's forgiveness, unable to prevent his eyes from filling with tears.

Dair nahin haram nahin, dar nahin aastaan nahin
Baithe hain rahaguzar pe ham gair hamen uthaaye kyun

Qaid-e-hayaat-o-band-e-gham asl men donon ek hain
Maut se pahale aadami gham se nijaat paaye kyun

Mirza Azmat Ali Khan remembered his own loss from years ago.

Dil hi to hai na sang-o-khisht dard se bhar na aaye kyun
Roenge ham hazaar baar koi hamen sataaye kyun

14

1970

Rone se aur ishq mein bebaak ho gaye
Dhoe gaye hum aise ke bas pak ho gaye

Karne gaye the usse tagaful ke ham gila
Ke ek hi nigah ki bas khak ho gaye

Mirza kept his word. Hafiz Patel got his daughter back the day Mirza got discharged from the hospital. It had ultimately cost Hafiz seven properties at various locations in Bombay. Inspector Ramesh had hand-picked them after some research.

Hafiz asked Nazia only one question when she got back.

'Did anyone touch you, jaan?'

'No, abbu.'

Hafiz hugged her and completely erased the deal he had made with Mirza from his mind. In those seven weeks Mirza had systematically broken him down so much that relief had replaced anger and every other emotion linked to it.

Mirza was received like a hero in his chawl. That night was the last normal night of his life. He knew that what had started as a personal vendetta was going to explode into something really big. An electrician with seven properties in the city of Bombay is not an ordinary thing. He had got what he wanted. But how was he going to keep it?

95

Mirza felt powerful and that became a matter of concern to him because he knew deep down that from now on things would change. He was not going to lead his life any more, his life was going to lead him now. Soon his story spread and the inevitable happened.

He started getting applications from people in similar situations asking him to bail them out. Inspector Ramesh quit his job in the force and aligned with him. Ramesh also got Mirza some really loyal followers who would lay down their lives for him without batting an eyelid.

Mirza started running his own parallel judiciary. This attracted attention from both the police and the traditional mafia but Mirza kept things straight and simple. He marked his territory and never ventured out. The businesses that he wanted to do were his only concern. He never meddled in other people's affairs and thus earned the respect of the other dons. His peers liked him because in many ways he was old school and not like the upcoming young Turks who would do anything for money.

Usool . . . Ideals were important to him.

All that Mirza wanted besides ruling over a certain part of Bombay was a better way of life for his people.

What kept him confused all his life was which part of the aforementioned thought dictated what in this resolve of his.

Mirza started in real estate and then started dabbling in smuggling gold, silver and electronics. Dubai and Nepal were serving his interests in a big way and Mirza started building his empire. He said a clear NO to drugs and women trafficking.

Whenever his conscience pricked him, Mirza built a school or bought an ambulance or did something nice for his people.

Mirza loved Urdu shayari, or poetry. His favourite was the Urdu and Persian poet Mirza Asadullah Baig Khan, popularly known as Ghalib. Mirza could read and recite Ghalib better than his holy book. He had found layers of wisdom and pain in Ghalib's poetry.

Mirza had also discovered that Ghalib had an answer to any situation one could encounter in one's life. There was a couplet for any strife, any pain, any doubt, anything.

Mirza was thirty-four now and though he made frequent visits to Sakina's he still was a lonely soul. At the brothel run by Badi Bi, Sakina was kept exclusively for Mirza. Sakina was a good singer who had come to Bombay hoping to be a playback singer, but Lata Mangeshkar was ruling the scene then and many were forced to take up alternate professions. Sakina's mother promptly made a choice for Sakina and she landed up at Badi Bi's.

Badi Bi took one look at Sakina and knew that Sakina's mother had screwed up. This girl just needed to learn some *ada* . . . some style. This was a diamond in the rough. She also knew who would value this diamond justly.

The night Mirza heard her sing for the first time, he fell in love with her voice. Sakina was aware of Mirza's reputation and was intimidated from the word go. Mirza heard her sing for a while and then did some singing for her.

On the way out, Mirza instructed Badi Bi, 'No one should touch her.'

'Ji, *janab*.'

Badi Bi smiled. She asked one of her attendants to go shopping for Sakina. This one deserved an investment. Sakina turned out to be one of the most pampered girls at Badi Bi's.

One day Mirza was sitting in his newly made office on Peddar Road, chatting with Ramesh, when a member of the staff knocked on his door.

'Saab, there is a lady outside asking for you.'

'Who?'

'She won't give her name. She just says that it's urgent.'

Ramesh looked at Mirza.

'You want me to check?'

'No, it's okay. Show her in.'

A little later a woman in a burqa entered Mirza's cabin. She did a salaam and Mirza responded politely.

'Salaam. Please sit.'

She sat.

'What can I do for you?'

'Can I speak to you alone for five minutes?'

The voice was silken. Mirza looked at Ramesh who promptly understood what he had to do.

'I will go check what the accounts people are doing.'

Ramesh went and shut the door behind him. Mirza and the woman were left alone in the cabin.

'Tell me.'

'You have to understand that I had to summon all my courage to come today. I have spent days scared about how you will react to this but then thought I have to say what I feel because my anxiety is anyway killing me. I have to confess.'

She took a deep breath.

'Yes?'

'I love you.'

The woman then removed the veil and Mirza was in for a big shock. It was Nazia. Hafiz Patel's daughter.

Stockholm syndrome was still to be named at the time but if the international psychologists' community had been aware of this case maybe they would have named it Nazia syndrome.

'Nazia, what do you mean?'

'One night at the hospital I had a chance to escape. Your guards had dozed off. I stepped out of the room and found you sleeping. Your sheet had come off. I decided to put it back on you. I came near you and saw your face. You were smiling. Maybe you were having a nice dream. And then I saw your wounds. I realized that my father had not done the right thing. I had heard his confession to you. At that moment, I felt your vengeance would be incomplete if I escaped and so I stayed back. I stood there looking at your face till dawn. You will not remember but I touched your lips with mine that night. I fell in love with you and completed your revenge for you against my own father.'

There was a silence the size of a whale. Mirza was stunned.

'But I don't love you.'

'I don't expect you too. You are my *ibadat* now. I don't care.'

Mirza was impressed. Mirza's schooling in poetry enabled him to understand exactly what Nazia meant. According to the Arabic literature, there are seven stages of love.

Hub which meant attraction.

Uns which meant infatuation.

Ishq which meant love itself.

Aqeedat which meant reverence.

Ibadat which meant worship.

Junoon which meant obsession.

Maut which meant death.

Mirza fell in love with Nazia in that moment. He stared at Nazia. She kept looking back at Mirza. He blinked and his eyes filled up with tears. This eighteen-year-old was making his heart pump crazily.

'It is not possible.'

'Of course it is. It even works for you as a business model. You already have half my father's wealth. You can have the remaining half too.'

'How is your father going to take this?'

'That actually is between you and my father. If the day comes that you desire me you will let me know. I am yours in body and soul. If my father decides to get me married to someone else before you realize that you are in love with me I will take my own life.'

'You are what . . . Eighteen?'

'Old enough to understand my destiny. Are you?'

'You have some spunk, girl.'

'I also have a useless heart that beats and bleeds in your name and longing. Shukriya for your time. That you are a kind man I already know; whether I am fortunate enough to receive a small act of your kindness we shall see. Salaam.'

Nazia's eyes filled up. She smiled before she brought the veil back on to her face. Nazia then took in one last glimpse of Mirza and left the cabin.

That night when Mirza went to hear Sakina sing, his mind was elsewhere. Sakina decided to take matters in hand. She came to give Mirza a glass of water and, in a carefully rehearsed ada, her dupatta came off her shoulders.

Ooops! The naturally, unbelievably, beautifully constructed bosom stared at Mirza. Mirza looked at it briefly and then got lost in the words of Nazia.

My useless heart . . .

He got up and left.

For the next few days Mirza let the feeling of love tear him apart. He enjoyed the pain and anguish and knew in his heart that he would never be able to love anyone the way he loved Nazia.

Nazia was coming out of the National College with a group of friends when she saw the white van parked on the other side of the road. It was the same van in which she had been abducted. It had tinted glass and she could see no one inside.

Nazia excused herself from her friends and crossed the road. As she reached the van, the doors slid open. She stepped inside. Mirza was waiting for her inside. Nazia smiled as she sat.

'Salaam.'

Mirza motioned but didn't say anything. Nazia kept staring at Mirza till he blinked.

The door shut and the van sped off. It reached the Centaur

Hotel in Juhu. The couple walked in and headed towards room 1324. Once they entered the room Mirza sat on the sofa. Nazia stood in the middle of the room.

'Sit.'

Nazia sat on the edge of the bed. Mirza looked at her.

'You know what I do, Nazia?'

'Ji.'

'You still want to spend your life with me?'

'Ji.'

Mirza sighed. He got up and walked up to Nazia. Nazia got up. It was her turn to get nervous now. She got weak in the knees as Mirza took her face in his hands.

'We will have our nikaah this Friday.'

Nazia blushed and hugged him tightly. Mirza also responded. They stood in that embrace for eternity.

'You have no idea how I have waited for this moment.'

'I can imagine, Nazia.'

'No, you can't.'

'Really?'

'I have married you a million times in my head and heart.'

Mirza teased Nazia, 'And have you slept with me in your head and heart, Nazia?'

'A million times. Every single time after I married you.'

Mirza kissed Nazia. And of course it didn't stop there.

They left the room after an hour and headed towards the van. Both Mirza and Nazia were glowing with an inner joy. Nazia was unabashed in her conduct with Mirza by her side.

She had loved Mirza with obsession, with junoon, the sixth stage of love.

As they were crossing the lobby of the Centaur Nazia saw a man lurking behind a pillar. The man had his eyes on Mirza and was holding a newspaper with something concealed. Nazia knew enough to understand that something was wrong.

Mirza was tipping the doorman when the man took out the gun and started shooting. Nazia covered Mirza and took all the six bullets on her slender frame. Mirza caught her as she started falling to the floor.

Nazia lay in a pool of blood, with Mirza screaming for help. As people rushed to attend to her, Nazia could not help smiling because she knew that the last and the seventh stage of love was maut . . . death.

Nazia was also smiling because she understood that her purpose in this life was complete. It was not only to love Mirza but also to die for him.

What Nazia didn't know was that the hitman who wanted to kill Mirza had been hired by her own father. Hafiz had not been able to let go after all. He put a gun to his temple and pulled the trigger when he came to know about the tragic irony an hour later.

Mirza's happiest day in life was also his saddest.

Ye na thi hamari qismat ke wisal-e-yaar hota
Agar aur jeete rahte yahi intezar hota

Kahun kis se main ke kya hai, shab-e-gham buri bala hai
Mujhe kya bura tha marna agar ek baar hota

15

1992

Twenty-two years had passed but Nazia's death still haunted Mirza. He knew what loss meant. He had questioned himself every day in those twenty-two years as to what would have happened had he not picked up Nazia from her college. What if they had not gone together to Centaur and what if he had left the hotel alone, before her, that day?

In three-year-old Zeenat's death Mirza again found himself in the dock of what-ifs.

Two rooms away from him that night Kamran came back to his senses for the first time since he had been admitted to hospital and screamed out Zeenat's name. He became so restless and unstable that the doctors sedated him immediately.

Mirza Azmat Ali Khan was discharged the next day. SI Promod Gupte was also discharged that morning in another sense of the word. His body was dumped in the Sanjay Gandhi National Park, Borivali. Murli Highway was picked up from his residence after a fierce gunfight between Mirza's men and his. Munna had himself led the group and Mirza's wish was his command.

They brought Murli to the slaughterhouse as they called it. It was actually a warehouse in Mazgaon but it had seen so many deaths in Mirza's twenty-two-year career that it automatically got that name.

The first killing at the location was that of the hitman who had shot Nazia.

In so many ways everything around this particular incident had had a strange sense of déjà vu. By the time Mirza reached the slaughterhouse his men had peeled the skin off Murli Highway. Murli was hanging upside down with his hands tied and there were two people working on him. Murli was no more his usual black. He was pink and red—literally. The workers were also throwing salt water on him every two minutes.

But in spite of the immense pain, Murli had not given out the name of the person who handed him the supari for Mirza. This business was all about reputation and Murli was not about to lose his.

Mirza was wheeled in by Munna and was in quite a bit of pain himself. But this whole affair had required swift justice and Mirza wouldn't rest until it was dispensed and handed out.

'I am sorry, Mirza saab.'

'No, you are not. You are just begging for your life.'

'I want to buy my life back with all that I have, Mirza saab. Everything that I have, that my family has, every single rupee, every property, every asset, everything is yours if you spare me.'

'Who wanted me dead, Murli?'

'It's seriously a lot of money, Mirza saab. I will also give a cut . . . half the cut of everything that I ever make in my life till my death.'

'Who wanted me dead, Murli?'

'You know I can't say that. I can compensate but I can't give you the names.'

'Are you aware that a three-year-old is dead and buried somewhere because of you?'

'I can do something for her family.'

'No, you bastard. You can't. No one can.'

'Isn't there anything that . . . ?'

'I will kill you even if you give me the name, Murli. And I will also promise you that the death I will give you, if you do not give me the name, will be a million times worse than you can ever imagine.'

'I . . . can't . . . my reputation . . .'

Mirza signalled to Munna. He could hear Murli begging for his life even as his car pulled out from the warehouse.

Mirza's men worked on Murli till he passed out. Then they would revive him and work on him some more. Murli's threshold of pain got redefined with every single passing moment. He became delirious but the workers waited for him to come to his senses. They did that through the night.

The sight of blood and flesh was so excruciatingly unbearable that after some time the workers themselves started getting nauseated.

But Murli Highway had a reputation he believed in and even as his lifeless body was thrown out of a moving van at Chowpatty he had not given out the name of the person who had given him the contract.

The early-morning joggers saw the gruesome sight of a badly mutilated body. They couldn't bear to look at it. Murli's right hand . . . little finger . . . twitched and then froze.

Mirza had kept his promise. His last thought before passing out was this—was it even possible to inflict such a degree of pain?

Over the next few days, Kamran had to be sedated every time he came to his senses. Finally, on the fourth day, doctors decided to break the news to him. Kamran, who had a notion of what was coming and was hopelessly in denial, finally gave up. He couldn't move or stand. He just lay in his bed and spent hours crying in the memory of the little one.

Zeenat's smile tore him to pieces and his failure to protect her, to save her, made him want to take his own life. And he would if he could. Kamran only survived because his condition was so bad that he could not even do that.

All the hospital expenses were being taken care of by Mirza and the doctors were instructed to spare no cost.

Munna would monitor his condition and report the progress to Mirza every evening.

Hamid came to see him on the fifth day. A few others from the mohalla also accompanied him. Hamid's tears had dried up. He ran his hand over Kamran's head and smiled.

'How are you feeling, beta?'

Kamran broke down helplessly.

'I am so sorry, mamu. I tried . . . I . . . tried and failed. I do not want to live.'

Hamid hugged him.

'Ssshhh. Shut up. I have lost enough. Shut up.'

'I tried, mamu . . . really.'

'I know that, beta. I know.'

Both sat silently till the visiting hours were over.

Kamran went in to rehab and because of his sheer will and tenacity managed to get discharged from the hospital in three weeks. Munna came to get him discharged. He then dropped Kamran at Karampura.

As Kamran walked towards his home he started feeling the jitters. He reached the house but could not summon the strength to go inside. A crowd had started gathering. His mami rushed out and caught him by his shirt and got hysterical.

'You took her that day with you, Kamran. Just get Zeenat back for me.'

'I am sorry.'

'I don't care, just get my Zeenat back for me.'

Hamid had to intervene. He caught his wife and took her inside. Kamran could not help breaking down himself. He rushed out of the mohalla.

It was raining heavily when he reached the Nariyalwadi cemetery. He found Zeenat's grave after a bit of looking around. He knelt and ran his hand over the small mound. Kamran then spent the next few hours apologizing to Zeenat and begging for her forgiveness.

And he would do this once on that day of every month for the remaining part of his free life.

It was beginning to get dark and was still raining when Kamran stepped out of the cemetery. There were two vehicles parked on either side of the exit. Hamid was waiting for him on the left side of the exit and Munna was waiting for him on the right.

It was actually a zero-conflict situation as Kamran walked towards Munna.

They drove past Hamid who understood that it would be a while before he would see Kamran's face again.

Kamran reached Mazgaon docks in Munna's car. They reached the desolate far end of the dock. The sky was grey and gloomy and the rain was beating down heavily. The car came to a stop and Kamran got down. There was another car parked ahead of him and Mirza was standing outside. A man was holding an umbrella for Mirza. Munna motioned Kamran. Kamran walked towards Mirza.

After his tenth step towards Mirza, Kamran saw a gunny bag placed in the middle of the stretch. There was somebody inside because the bag moved every once in a while. Kamran reached Mirza who was staring at the bag.

Mirza turned and held Kamran by his shoulders.

'I will not demean your brave act by a simple word like 'thanks'. I can never repay you enough. If you ever figure what I can do for you let me know. Mirza will not think twice. That, Kamran, is for you.'

He pointed towards the gunny bag, which started moving again.

'My boys will clean up the mess once you are done. Keep well.'

Mirza sat in his car and drove off. Munna motioned to one of his boys who went and opened the knot on the gunny bag.

And out fell Ruslaan, the not-so-sharpshooter.

The moment he saw Kamran, he started pleading but the man who had opened the knot quickly shoved him back and tied the knot again. Munna handed Kamran an iron rod.

Kamran took it and for the next fifteen minutes or so went berserk. With each blow the blood became a spot and then spread and trickled away in the rain. The air was heavy with muffled groans and agonizing screams. Kamran's wounds opened up again but there was no stopping him.

His rage was extreme. Life ebbed out of Ruslaan by the seventh minute but the next eight minutes were spent by Kamran to release his angst.

The gunny bag had become a red pile of lifeless pulp by the time Kamran was through. Even a toughened criminal like Munna was left cringing at the sight.

Kamran dropped the bloodied rod and walked out of the dockyard.

That night around nine, Kamran entered Karampura again. From a distance he saw Mohsin's house lit up with *mirchi* lights in readiness for Salma's wedding. Kamran went to Reshma's place and knocked on her door. She was shocked to see Kamran standing there.

'Hi.'

'Hi.'

Kamran had tears in his eyes but he smiled in desperation. Asking for favours was not in his nature. Reshma made it easy for him.

'Go and stand near the overbridge. I will see what I can do.'

'Th . . . Thanks, Reshma.'

'Shut up, Chikne. Go now.'

Kamran headed for the overbridge. Reshma went inside her house and spoke to her younger brother.

'Ajju, I will be back in an hour. Lock the door and keep awake.'

She quickly put on a dupatta and rushed out.

That evening, Salma had come to know that Kamran had been discharged from the hospital. She knew that Kamran would definitely come to meet her. She was both longing for and dreading this moment.

The moment she saw Reshma, Salma knew that Kamran had come to see her.

Koi mere dil se puche tere teer-e-nimakash ko
Ye khalish kahan se hoti jo jigar ke par hota

Ye kahan ki dosti hai ke bane hain dost naseh
Koi charasaz hota, koi ghamgusar hota

16

Kamran stood away from the lamp post near the overbridge as he did not want to be seen. It seemed like he had been waiting for an eternity.

When he saw Reshma approaching him, with Salma at her side, Kamran felt overwhelmed. It was the same for Salma. She was looking stunning in her red-and-green salwar-kameez and had covered her head with a dupatta. Her heart started pounding as she stood face to face with Kamran.

'Sorry but you guys have just fifteen minutes.'

Reshma walked away.

Their eyes welled up with tears. Salma started sobbing. She stretched out to touch Kamran's face. Kamran noticed the fresh henna on her hands.

'There is mehndi on your hands, Salma . . .'

Salma embraced Kamran tightly.

'What could I do, Kamran? Ammi found the last note that you had written to me. There was a huge ruckus, Kamran. Abbu just wouldn't listen and expedited the whole thing. And after what happened to Zeenat . . . without you by my side . . . what could I do, Kamran?'

'Are you willing to come with me this moment, Salma? Now!'

'My parents will kill themselves, Kamran. I could not live up to your expectations . . . Let me just live up to theirs.'

'This is not right, Salma.'

'I know. But what could I do?'

'You could kill yourself.'

'I thought about that a thousand times, Kamran, and believe me I would have if it would have solved the problem but my death would also mean my parents' death.'

Kamran held her tightly.

'Then why did you come here, Salma?'

'I wanted to see you one last time. I wanted to hug you for the last time.'

'Through now?'

'No. Kamran, do me a favour. Never ever forgive me. I want to be in your heart even if it's by way of hatred.'

Kamran took her face in his hands.

'I am an illiterate, Salma, but I am not a fucking idiot. What forgiveness and what hatred and which heart are you talking about? I have no heart left any more. Salma, I suggest you leave before I fucking decide to kill either you or your parents myself. Just get going and don't turn back on your way home or else I swear I won't have just one fucking murder in my destiny.'

Salma looked into Kamran's eyes and immediately understood that the man had changed. This was a totally different Kamran. One that was actually capable of killing.

She had let him down.

Salma hugged him once again and refused to let go. In her heart she was hoping that she could take away some of the bitterness and find a glimpse of the man that Kamran had been.

'Kamran, I love you. And I will always love you.'

Kamran did not answer. There was nothing to say. He let go after some time and looked her in the eye.

'Pray that you never cross my path, Salma, and hope your god listens to you this time around.'

Kamran took off the earring from her left ear. He saw her for one last time and then turned and walked off. Salma was left standing and sobbing, ruing her wretched destiny.

She looked at his receding figure till he was lost in the darkness.

Kamran came out of Karampura to find Munna and his black Fiat waiting for him again. Mirza had instructed him to be available as a service. Whether Kamran availed of it or not was Kamran's call.

'I . . . I . . . have nowhere to go.'

'No, you have. Sit.'

Munna took him to a one-room-kitchen flat in Mahim. It was sparse but neat. Munna left him after handing him the keys and an envelope. Kamran opened the envelope to find some cash there and a chit of paper with a telephone number on it. He looked around the flat. There was a bed, a small almirah and a television set. His medicines were lying on a small table near the bed. A telephone was sitting on a wall mount.

He opened the almirah to find his clothes from Hamid's place stacked in there. All his other belongings were also in there. Kamran felt even lonelier.

It was as if the world had decided that it didn't want anything do with Kamran Ali Khan any more.

He lay down on the bed and passed out after a while.

Kamran was a wreck for the next six days. Ruslaan came to haunt him in his nightmares. He had fever most of the time. A boy came to give him his breakfast, lunch and dinner. A woman came in every morning to clean the place. No one spoke to him. They just did their bit and left.

On the seventh day Kamran felt better. He had not had any nightmares the previous night. He had slept well and woken up fresh. He spent the next few hours thinking. By evening he was clear about the next two steps he should take in his life.

The first was a telephone call. Kamran called the number that Munna had left in the envelope. Someone took the call on the other side.

'Hello. Can I speak to Munna bhai?'

'Who's that?'

'Kamran.'

'Hold on.'

Kamran waited for some time. Munna came on the line.

'Hello, Kamran.'

'Hello, Munna bhai.'

'How are you feeling now?'

'Better. I needed a favour.'

'Of course. Tell me.'

'I needed to meet Mirza saab for ten minutes.'

There was a long pause.

'Let me call you back in five minutes.'

The line went dead and Kamran kept the phone down. He wondered if he had asked for too much. The telephone rang inside of five minutes. Kamran picked up the phone. It was Munna on the other side.

'Be ready. Someone will be there to pick you up in half an hour.'

'Thanks, Munna bhai.'

'It's okay.'

Kamran got ready and went downstairs. About twenty minutes later, a Fiat arrived to pick him up. There were two people sitting in it. They were the same guys who had dropped him on the first night. Kamran sat inside and the car left for Mirza's place.

Mirza Azmat lived at Barqat Mahal. But you could sense his presence the moment you entered Chisti Nagar. It was like a country within a country. As soon as the black Fiat entered the mohalla, people started making way for it and it was not out of fear but respect. Bystanders were looking inside the car and

Kamran noticed that a few actually smiled at him. He remembered the crowd that had come to inquire about Mirza in the hospital. They placed him. He placed them.

Kamran's car reached the mansion. Armed guards were standing outside it. Kamran got out and looked at the guards. There was a sense of respect and admiration in their eyes. The guards didn't frisk him and just waved a salaam. Kamran responded as Munna stepped out and led him inside the mansion.

The white-and-blue structure was a testimony to Mirza's life. It looked old yet solid, and had an old-world charm about it. Kamran crossed more armed guards, more people on the way to the terrace.

Mirza was lying stretched on an easy chair in the centre of the terrace. Munna asked Kamran to wait. He then went and whispered something in Mirza's ears. Mirza waved and Munna relayed the wave to Kamran. Kamran walked up to Mirza and Munna left them alone.

'Salaam alaikum.'

'Wa'alaikum salaam. Sit.'

'I am okay, Mirza saab.'

'I said sit.'

Kamran sat down on the chair opposite Mirza. Mirza removed the small towel from his head and propped himself up.

'You will have some tea?'

'I don't mind.'

Mirza raised his hand and someone somewhere ran to get some tea for them.

'How have you been?'

'Getting better, saab.'

'So you have figured out what you want from me?'

Kamran was taken aback for a moment but he quickly collected himself.

'Ji.'

'So what is it, Kamran?'

'I want to work for you, Mirza saab.'

It was now Mirza's turn to be taken aback. The tea arrived. As soon as the attendant left, Mirza started.

'Why?'

'My earlier life is finished for me, Mirza saab. Some of it lies buried in a cemetery and some of it lies buried in my memories. It is all over for me there. Now I want to start from scratch, saab. The world that I lived in didn't suit me, Mirza saab. So now I want to create my own world.'

'I can get you a taxi or a new job.'

'My hands are drenched in blood.'

'I did that for you because I felt that it would purge you of your rage.'

'And I thank you for that. I live with no regret or remorse. I am at peace now. Really.'

Mirza smiled and murmured:

Dost gamkhwari mein meri sai farmayenge kya
Zakhm ke bharne talak nakhun na badh jayenge kya

'Do you understand shayari?'

'Not at all, saab. Never understood one couplet.'

'You want me to do something about the girl?'

'Which girl?'

'Your girl.'

'In all humility Mirza saab there is nothing that you can do that I can't in her case. She gave up on me and the matter is over.'

'It's never over. Think again, Kamran. I have promised you that I won't say "no" to you so think really carefully what you wish for.'

'I have thought long and hard, Mirza saab. I really want to work for you.'

'What do you know about our world?'

'Nothing. But I am a fast learner, Mirza saab.'

'That I can see.'

Mirza started contemplating. Experience told him that Kamran had already moved over to this side. If he shunned Kamran then he would look for an alternative on the wrong side of the law. Immoral moral responsibility and his word to Kamran made him accept Kamran's request.

'Don't be under the illusion that this world is going to be nice to you either, Kamran. We don't know which is worse here. Life or death.'

'Ji, Mirza saab.'

'Call up Munna tomorrow morning. He will have something for you.'

'Shukriya, Mirza saab.'

'Khuda hafiz.'

'Khuda hafiz.'

Kamran got up and went. Mirza shook his head.

> *Vo firaaq aur wo visaal kahaan*
> *Vo shab-o-roz-o-maah-o-saal kahaan*
>
> *Dil to dil vo dimaag bhi na raha*
> *Shor-e-saudaa-e-khat-o-khaal kahaan*
>
> *Aisaa aasaan nahiin lahuu ronaa*
> *Dil mein taaqat jigar mein haal kahaan*
>
> *Fikr-e-duniyaa mein sar khapaataa hun*
> *Main kahaan aur ye bavaal kahaan*

And so Kamran joined Mirza's gang in the middle of 1992.

The pir who had prophesized that the world would be at his feet had seen this day in his destiny.

17

Present Day

Kamran snapped back to the present as soon as the van entered the court compound. They had reached the sessions court in Sewri. Through the netted window, Kamran saw again the sea of reporters and newscasters waiting for him in reception. They went berserk the moment they spotted the convoy.

'Fucking jokers.'

SI Kanitkar was acting irritated but was actually excited because he would be all over the television channels the moment he stepped out of the van. He would also be in the next day's newspapers as the guy leading Kamran to the court. The wife had especially bought him a new shirt for the momentous occasion.

The van door opened and Kanitkar led the procession from the front. He got Kamran down and cut through the crowd. The police made sure that the path was cleared. While he was doing his duty diligently, Kanitkar also ensured that the inevitable photo-op was not missed.

They entered the premises and went straight to the waiting room. It was a bare room with just a bench, a chair and a table . . . A posse of cops stood vigil outside the room.

Kamran was to wait for his turn.

Police Commissioner Nitish Kumar was also waiting for his turn at the chief minister's residence. His wait was shorter though. The personal assistant (PA) ushered him into the study soon enough, where the chief minister was sitting watching an anchor screaming her lungs out on the television.

'Good morning, sir.'

'What good morning, Nitish? I am told this Kamran will walk a free man today.'

'He has a very good chance, sir. If he does, he will definitely run away to a country with which we do not have an extradition treaty.'

'And what have you thought about it?'

'Nothing, sir.'

The chief minister knew that Nitish was an honest officer who had very little tolerance and always spoke his mind.

'We are off the record here, Nitish.'

'Sure, sir.'

'We had him for five years. We should have nailed the bugger.'

'We would have, sir, had it not been for our very own home minister. The truth of the matter is that the one before you, sir, and the one before me are the ones responsible for this situation, sir. In the last four years Kamran's case has been weakened systematically. Lala who was to depose today was shot by someone this morning.'

'Someone?'

'I know it's Kamran's man. But I cannot prove it.'

'What's the CBI doing?'

'They are laughing at us.'

'How come?'

'We charge-sheeted Kamran. The CBI got him arrested and fought for two years with the French government to get him extradited. They successfully did their job and now they are laughing at us because we have not done ours.'

'And?'

'Sir, if Kamran walks then all the international law enforcement agencies will be laughing at us. Also sir, once Kamran is out, there are two things in the offing. A small bloodbath and resumption of his illegal activities.'

'It amazes me that you have still chosen to do nothing about it, Nitish.'

'Sir, you can ask your PA. I had called up four times for a meeting.'

The chief minister fell silent. He knew exactly why his PA had chosen to ignore the message.

'I want you do something about this, Nitish.'

'Sir, home minister Joshiji won't . . .'

'Fuck Joshi.'

'Great, sir.'

'This is a fucking hardened criminal and everyone is aware of that. If the law bends and he gets out then it is a slap on our faces.'

'It will be, sir.'

'So what can you do about this, Nitish?'

'Sir, the last three links of the underworld are Farookh Khitkhit, Yakub Mental and Kamran Khan. Khitkhit is invalid. Mental is in Dubai and we often use him for our own dirty work. If we manage to take Kamran out then Mumbai will be relatively underworld free.'

'How do we take out Kamran?'

'There is a long list of people who want him dead. Everyone will suspect the Mumbai Police but no one will have any concrete evidence against us.'

'And do you have someone in mind to carry this out?'

'Avinash Sharma. He was an SI with us. Currently on suspension, sir.'

'For?'

'Sir, a fake-encounter case. An inquiry is on. He will come

out of it. Kamran and he have a history. He was the one who
got Kamran caught in France.'

'Why will he do this for us?'

'Kamran's boys killed Avinash's wife, sir.'

In the waiting room Kamran was just beginning to get bored
when his lawyer Vidya Rai entered with her two assistants. One
male and one female. Vidya was around thirty-eight years old
and had fought for Kamran since the start of his case. She
didn't like small talk besides many other things.

'Hello, Vidyaji.'

'Hello.'

'You are late and I was just wondering whether you forgot
about me.'

'I don't forget hearings and I am not late; you are early.'

The male assistant walked up and thrust a bunch of papers in
front of Kamran and gave him a pen. Kamran started signing
on them. On the second signature, Kamran slipped a phone in
the assistant's hand. The assistant quietly put it in his pocket.
On the third signature, Kamran could not help himself.

'So what are my chances like today, Vidyaji?'

'Why? You are facing any problems in there?'

'You sound irritated. Still worried about your kid's admission?
Right?'

Vidya looked at her female assistant. The assistant blushed
and felt like digging a hole and going inside it.

'You let me know, I will try making a few phone calls and . . .'

'Your "few phone calls" have got you here, Kamran. If you
happen to walk today then my one single piece of advice would
be to stay away from phones for the rest of your life.'

'I will remember that.'

'By the way thought I should tell you that Bashir Lala who

had seen you killing Mirza and was the key witness for the prosecution was shot dead this morning by some unidentified gunman.'

'So what you are telling me is that Lala will not be able to make it?'

The signatures were done.

'They will call you in some time.'

'Okay, I will hang around here then.'

Vidya walked out of the room shaking her head.

Around the same time Commissioner Nitish Kumar was stepping out of the chief minister's bungalow, dialling a number on his cell.

Suspended officer Avinash Sharma was a ghost of the man he once was. The daredevil uncompromising police officer was now reduced to a perpetually abusive alcoholic who trained newly employed personnel of Triple Securities on the Juhu Versova Link Road footpath. He was in the middle of such a training session. There were twelve new security people who were starting out that day in various buildings of the area and they were now being given a crash course in how to conduct themselves while on duty.

'. . . And the thing is that while you fuckers have no idea about the word security and most of you guys will be the first to run in the face of any danger but still the fucking residents of this city will entrust you fuckers to keep them safe in their nice, cute-looking housing societies. They don't fucking know or care that you have just landed this morning at the Chhatrapati Shivaji Terminus and have been trained for just fifteen minutes on this roadside. It just so happens that the fucking residents of this city are more fucking dumb than you guys and so they will fucking hire you guys and you fuckers will get fucking paid for sleeping on the job. Motherfucker number three in the second row . . . stand straight or else I will fu . . .'

His phone rang. The scared group sent a collective thanks to the heavens. Avinash looked at the display and his hangover disappeared. This was the call he was waiting for.

'Hello, sir.'

'Hello. We are good to go, Avinash.'

Avinash felt the blood rushing through his veins.

'Thank you, sir.'

'Don't use yourself. Hire a hand.'

'Sir.'

'Do you have someone?'

'Yes, sir.'

'I hope this will get you back, Avinash.'

Avinash kept silent. *Back? Fuck knows.*

'Call up Bhonsle and tell him what you want. He will make arrangements.'

'Yes, sir.'

Nitish hung up. Avinash knew he had to act fast. There was hardly any time left in hand. Avinash turned back to the group and delivered the closing.

'You fuckers have to identify who the fucking secretary of the society is . . . Who the fucking chairman is . . . Who is who in the society. Then just be fucking extra-sweet to them and their families. Stand up and fucking salute when they pass by. The rest of the people in the building . . . you can fucking ignore. All you motherfuckers, you are now fucking ready to protect the Mumbaikars from the any sort of fucking danger. Go fuck yourselves.'

That was dismissal for Avinash. Once the group scrammed away, Avinash took out his phone and dialled a number. A couple of rings later someone answered.

'Hello . . .'

'Call up Bhonsle and tell him what you need. I will be there to see you in some time.'

Avinash then called up Bhonsle.

'Hello, Bhonsle saheb. The boy will call you. Give him whatever he needs.'

Avinash hung up. He didn't need a confirmation. It was an instruction and it had to be followed. He walked up to his bike and started it. There was only one word running in his head.

Finally.

Avinash Sharma hurried towards the Siddhivinayak temple.

In a waiting room of the sessions court in Sewri, Kamran Ali Khan, however, was revisiting the words of his lawyer Vidya Singh . . .

'By the way, thought I should tell you that Bashir Lala who had seen you killing Mirza and was the key witness for the prosecution was shot dead this morning by some unidentified gunman.'

> *Ragon mein daudte phirne ke ham naheen qaayal*
> *Jab aankh hee se na tapka to phir lahoo kya hai?*

> *Chipak raha hai badan par lahoo se pairaahan*
> *Hamaree jeb ko ab haajat-e-rafoo kya hai?*

18

1992

It had been two months since Kamran had joined Mirza but all he had been doing so far was turning up at Barqat Mahal in the morning, spending the entire day hanging outside and then retiring in the evening. He was in a group of five boys who were all his age. Though Kamran was a greenhorn he was respected and liked because of what he had already done. Once in a while, Munna would call the boys and send them on an errand or something, but not Kamran.

In those last two months he had been asked to do absolutely nothing. Once he reached his flat, the only thing Kamran could do was either mull over his past or watch television. To break the monotony, he would sometimes go to the movies in the evening.

But he was essentially a loner. He was good-natured but aloof and since virtually everyone at Mirza's knew his story they let him keep to himself. Over time Kamran picked up legendary stories about Mirza.

Most of them started with 'You know what happened once . . .'

In two months, however, even the stories started running out. Kamran decided that he had had enough. He caught up with Munna one evening when they were calling it a day.

'Munna bhai . . .'

'Yes, Kamran. All okay?'

'Can I talk to you for a moment?'

'You are. Go on.'

'Munna bhai, I need some work. I will go crazy otherwise. I can't just sit around on my ass and not do anything. You ask of everyone besides me.'

'You drink?'

'Rarely?'

'Is it rare today?'

'Can be.'

'Come then.'

Kamran went with Munna to his house in Mahim, which turned out to be quite close to where Kamran lived. Munna first took him to his flat where he introduced him to his wife, Rajjo, and his two baby girls. They were around Zeenat's age and Kamran stayed away from them. Munna noticed his discomfort and led him to the terrace after instructing his wife to send them drinks.

It was a nice, cool night and a couple of drinks later it became even nicer.

'So Kamran? Don't like what you are doing?'

'I am doing nothing.'

'What do you want to do?'

'I want to do some stuff.'

'What would you like to do? Kill . . . rob . . . what?'

'I want to learn from you.'

That got Munna silent. He lit a cigarette and offered one to Kamran. Kamran also lit one.

'How did you join Mirza saab?'

Munna tried to evade the question.

'It's sort of a long story. Some other time.'

'You don't give me work . . . don't give me a story.'

'Stop sulking. And you didn't hear it from me.'

Munna took a deep drag and started.

'My father was an inspector in the police. There was an incident where Mirza saab was badly injured and my father, Ramesh Naik, had rushed him to the Nanavati Hospital. My father sort of saved his life and Mirza saab gave him an offer to start this business. My father quit the force and they became partners. I must have been around ten then. One day Mirza saab was coming out of Centaur when a man pulled out a gun and fired six rounds at him. A woman who happened to be with Mirza saab threw herself at him and saved his life at the cost of hers. Mirza saab was distraught. He knew that there was a snitch that had ratted on his location. He gave my dad the responsibility to find out who it was. My father found there were six people who knew exactly where Mirza saab was at that time on that day.'

Munna poured another couple of drinks for himself and Kamran. While Kamran struggled, Munna gulped it in one go.

'It took my father about three hours to figure out who the culprit was. But here is the catch. My father had a younger brother called Jagan whom he had helped get a job in Mirza's gang. As it turned out, the snitch happened to be his very own loving brother. My father took him to Mazgaon docks and they spent a lovely evening together, much like this. After they had quite a lot to drink, my father shot him dead.

'The next morning my father told Mirza saab the truth and excused himself because he had to go for his brother's funeral. A few days later Mirza saab asked my father why he hadn't saved his brother. My father smiled and replied that their friendship came in the way. It felt just.'

Munna sighed deeply.

'They worked together and built all this. I was fourteen when I was arrested for the first time. When my father died a few years ago I took his position. I didn't have to join Mirza saab. I was born into this. I inherited this.'

There was something about Munna that impressed Kamran that night. Maybe it was his honesty or maybe it was the impending tragic coincidence about which Kamran had a premonition.

'You will be with me from tomorrow onwards.'

'Thank you, Munna bhai.'

They started drinking again. After a while Kamran couldn't resist.

'Can I ask you something?'

'Sure.'

'Why did Mirza saab never marry?'

'That, my friend, you will have to ask Mirza saab himself.'

Mirza's family had requested him a million times to get married but he had never relented. He took care of his extended family like his own. He was there for weddings and funerals and any such occasion that warranted his presence but beyond that Mirza was a loner.

He did continue going to Badi Bi's though and Sakina had grown old with Mirza but that was that. A few ghazals . . . a few drinks . . . a few adas.

Make love . . . take money. Mirza kept this part of his life very simple. Once, in a rare moment of awkward intimacy, Sakina shared with him her failed dream of playback singing. Mirza called top music director Vikramjeet at his residence.

'How are you, Vikramjeet bhai?'

'I am good, Mirza saab. Order?'

'Your sister wants to sing a couple of songs in your next film.'

'Of course. Please send her tomorrow to my studio.'

'Thanks, Vikramjeet bhai.'

That night after her singing, Sakina went an extra mile or two to thank Mirza.

On Nazia's death anniversary, he would have a private prayer meet and give alms. In fact, that was the reason Mirza had gone alone to Haji Ali Dargah on that fateful day when he had bumped into Kamran.

Hue mar ke ham jo ruswa, hue kyon na gharq-e-dariya
Na kabhee janaaza uthata, na kaheen mazaar hota

Usay kaun dekh sakta ke yagaana hai wo yaktaa
Jo dooee ki boo bhee hotee to kaheen do-chaar hota

Rag-e-sang se tapakta wo lahoo ki phir na thamta
Jise gham samajh rahe ho, ye agar sharaar hota

The next day onwards, Kamran went wherever Munna went. Munna made him his shadow and Kamran stuck with him. Very soon Kamran became aware of the city's underworld.

There were three major stakeholders in the underworld at that time. Mirza Azmat, the old hand, and two relatively younger Turks, Farookh Khitkhit and Yakub Mental. There were others as well but they were all actually working for one of these three factions. While Farookh and Yakub always crossed the lines in their businesses, Mirza kept himself in check. Mirza didn't crave money and power too much because he had learnt the hard way that they were never enough. He was content with what he had.

Farookh and Yakub, however, were greedy for power and this evidently led to clashes between them and Mirza. On the face of it, they showed respect for Mirza but how they wished he were gone. Mirza would not allow the trafficking of women and drugs in the areas he controlled and would also not allow either Farookh or Yakub to do such businesses there. And this pissed them off no end.

Of all the illegal businesses that Mirza had, Kamran was most interested in extortion, which was also ironically called protection fees. It was generally targeted at anyone who was making good money or spending good money. There were builders, businessmen, industrialists, film financiers and producers who were expected to cough up money to one bad guy so they could be protected from the other bad guys.

What got Kamran interested was that doing this business required an investment of just one rupee.

The cost of a telephone call.

Kamran would hear Munna make threats on the phone and then recover huge sums of money. He would go with him for collections and see the petrified faces of the guys coughing up large amounts. Sometimes it would require more than a telephone call and the responsibility for firing the warning shot soon fell upon Kamran.

Satish Bhai Jhunjhunwala, the owner of Pritam mills, had had a great turnover that year. He was also spending lavishly. This caught the attention of Mirza's gang which maintained a regular roster of people they could potentially target. Individual files were also made for each name on the list.

These files held comprehensive facts and figures about the person. Right from their businesses to their traits . . . the person's strengths and his weaknesses. Their most intimate and dark secrets would be there. Stuff that even their dearest ones might not be aware of.

Mirza would listen once his men were ready with all the information. Then, after evaluating the 'merits' of the operation, he would give the go-ahead and approve the extortion.

The calls were generally made at night. Night is dark and a faceless voice in the dark threatening you with death was a great first step. It meant that the target would lose sleep, fear taking over.

But it so happened that Satish Bhai was a bit drunk when Munna called him and so the fear factor didn't quite actually set in. It was 11 p.m.

'Hello.'

'Hello.'

'Is that Satish Bhai?'

'Speaking.'

'I am calling on behalf of Mirza saab?'

'Who Mirza?'

'Mirza Azmat saab.'

'Yes, tell me.'

'Mirza saab has requested two crore.'

'What?'

'By the end of this week.'

'I will not give any money.'

'Thank you.'

'I will not give any money.'

Munna disconnected. He knew at once that this would not be easy. Kamran could also feel it. Munna sensed that Satish Bhai would file a formal police complaint first thing in the morning.

'This bugger will go to the police tomorrow morning. He has the balls to ask, who Mirza?'

'So let's pick him up tomorrow morning first thing, Munna bhai.'

'What?'

'We do not have the time to threaten him. If we fire a shot he will still go to the police. Bhai, I read the note. Satish Bhai goes to Chowpatty for his morning walks. We can pick him up tomorrow morning and then he can pay his own ransom.'

Munna was surprised at the speed with which Kamran came up with the solution.

'I will be back in some time.'

Kamran knew that Munna had liked the plan but something as big as this would always need clearance from Mirza himself.

Mirza heard the plan and asked Munna, 'Who thought of this?'

'Kamran.'

'What do you think of it?'

'I think it's great, Mirza saab. The kid has got it right.'

'Do it then.'

Munna and Kamran planned the whole thing. They decided that only two of them would carry out the operation.

Just the two of them and a gun.

The next morning when Satish Bhai was returning to his car after his morning walk he felt something poke him. It was a 9-mm in Kamran's hand. Satish Bhai saw it and froze. Kamran had covered his face with a piece of white cloth. A Maruti Omni screeched to a halt right in front of them. The door slid open. Munna, who was driving, had also covered his face. Satish Bhai walked in without a fuss. The Omni started. Kamran who was sitting with Satish Bhai in the rear seat spoke first.

'Bhai, do we kill him here and now?'

'Hang on.'

Satish Bhai knew that he would be dead if he didn't open his mouth.

'I will pay.'

Munna and Kamran didn't respond.

'I will pay today.'

Munna and Kamran still didn't respond.

'I am sorry for yesterday night. I know about Mirza saab. I want to say sorry to him.'

'Bhai . . . Is now good?'

'Hang on.'

'Arre baba, I am saying sorry and I am paying you two crore. What now . . . hold on, what are you guys doing?'

'It was two crore yesterday when I called you, Satish Bhai. Now that we had to come to meet you, the rates have changed. It's going to be five crore now.'

'Bhai, you mean that if he agrees then we will not kill him?'

'Hang on.'

'Please take me to a phone.'

'Sure.'

'But, bhai, you promised me that I would get to kill someone today.'

'Hang on.'

Munna and Kamran played their parts to perfection. Satish Bhai was taken to a phone at a desolate location. He spoke to his wife for forty-nine seconds. A few hours later a couple of trunks were dropped at Barqat Mahal. Munna got a call from Barqat Mahal saying that the count was fine.

Around 1.25 p.m., Satish Bhai was dropped in front of his house.

On the way back, Kamran was pleased as Punch.

Five crore rupees' return on a one-rupee investment through a telephone call.

19

The Satish Bhai Jhunjhunwala case became the world's worst-kept secret. For the next few days, the stock of the Mirza gang shot through the roof. The daring act was for everyone to see. With awe came admiration. Everyone was trading opinions.

No negotiation, nothing.

Just picked up the guy.

A five–six-hour job.

What pluck!

Only two guys.

I hear that one of them was a first-timer.

They say it was his idea only.

What fucking daring?

This is how it's done?

WOW!

It also caught the attention of Commissioner of Police Sandeep Nath. Sandeep had only a couple of months of duty left. He called Joint Commissioner (Crime) Amar Shinde in desperation.

'Amar, I want a fearless young guy with balls.'

'Sir, you heard of this kid named Avinash Sharma?'

'The one who slapped MLA Sharma for catching him by the collar of his uniform?'

'Sir, Avinash actually did worse than that.'

'Really?'

'Yes, sir. He locked him in a cell and then got the MLA stripped. Avinash then took a hawaldar's danda and beat the

MLA till his bottom was red as a baboon's. Avinash also called for a camera and clicked pictures of the bottom before sending the MLA home.'

'Nice.'

'You want him, sir?'

'Send him.'

'Sure, sir.'

A couple of hours later, SI Avinash Sharma landed at Commissioner Sandeep Nath's office.

'Have a seat, Avinash.'

'Thanks, sir.'

'Did you hear about the Satish Bhai Jhunjhunwala case?'

'Yes, sir, and Satish Bhai is denying the kidnapping obviously.'

'Avinash, I have only a few months left to retire. I used to believe that I have managed to keep crime under check but this incident has proven me wrong.'

Avinash kept silent. Sandeep took out a file and put it in front of Avinash. Avinash opened it to find just three postcard-size photographs in there. Nothing else. A name was scrawled on each photograph.

'That's Farookh Khitkhit, Yakub Mental and Mirza Azmat. I want these three.'

'Okay, sir.'

Avinash put the photographs back inside and looked at Sandeep. Sandeep, expecting a reaction or a question, finally got one after a long moment.

'Do you want them in any particular order, sir?'

Sandeep was stumped.

'Not really.'

'I will take your leave, sir?'

'Good luck, Avinash.'

'Thank you, sir.'

Once Avinash had left, Sandeep picked up the phone and dialled JCP Amar Shinde's number. He had a pertinent question.

'Is this Avinash crazy or what?'

That was the effect Avinash Sharma had on people around him. An incorruptible, dynamic young officer whose only passion was to serve the force and cleanse the city. His wife, Preeti, used to say that Avinash was actually married to his job. She happened to be his second wife.

They had a good life but all that was going to change soon.

Kamran had been given a good bonus for the Satish Bhai incident. He sent the money immediately sent to his mother. In the message box of the money order he wrote: *Dear Ammi, Inshallah I am coming home this Eid. Love, Kamran.*

In the meantime, Munna had told one and everyone that this was Kamran's brainchild. Kamran started getting closer to Munna and his contributions by way of ideas became very important. Soon, Kamran started taking care of administration in Mirza's gang. Munna was happy that he had a good ally in Kamran.

It was Kamran's idea that instead of bribing cops for information on a tip basis they should actually keep them on a payroll. Debase their integrity so they could actually be Mirza's eyes and ears.

It was because of this foresight of Kamran's that he received information on a cop named Avinash Sharma who he heard was digging into all the old cases related to Mirza Azmat.

Within a fortnight of his meeting with Sandeep Nath, Avinash had accumulated enough evidence to arrest Farookh Khitkhit, Yakub Mental and Mirza Azmat. Warrants were issued against their names on a Thursday night and Avinash had everything in place. But everything was kept under wraps and Avinash was playing his cards close to his chest.

Early Friday morning, a jeep, a big police van, a posse of

twelve officers and constables and an informer proceeded towards Dharavi, where Yakub Mental stayed. Dharavi was one of the largest slums in the world and Yakub stayed in the heart of its 1.7 square kilometres. The city was still waking up and Avinash had chosen the time for precisely that reason.

The informer asked them to stop. The van could only go so far. Ahead was a maze of narrow lanes and by-lanes. The informer mumbled something in Avinash's ears and then ran off. Avinash was in plain clothes. He asked two of his uniformed officers to accompany him and the rest were asked to stand near the vehicles.

Avinash entered the slum with his gun in hand. The people who had woken up froze on the sight of a man walking with a gun followed by a couple of cops. There were a dozen of Yakub's men standing outside his building. Avinash waved his gun at them and entered the building that the informer had told him about. He went to the second floor and knocked on the door. A little later a man opened it. Avinash put the gun to his head and asked for Yakub. The man was flabbergasted. He just pointed to a direction. Avinash entered the flat and went inside the room.

Yakub was in a lungi and a banian having his morning tea.

'Who the fuck are you?'

'Let's go.'

'Fuck off right now. On the way out give your name and the name of the station where you are posted. Your *hafta* will reach you. And fucker don't fucking disturb me like this ever again.'

Avinash lunged forward and gave Yakub Mental a tight slap.

'Mental! If you abuse me again I will shoot you in your balls.'

Yakub was infuriated but didn't want to take the chance.

'You have entered my den. Fine. But how do you think you are going to get out?'

'In style, you pimp. In such style that people are going to tell their kids not to become someone like you when they grow up.'

Yakub stuttered.

'Yo . . . you are making a huge mistake.'

'If I am making a mistake then why the fuck are you shaking like a leaf?'

Avinash lunged at Yakub and had him in a headlock. Avinash then put a gun to Yakub's head and led him downstairs.

Yakub was still dressed in a lungi and a banian. Avinash dragged him through the lanes. His men could only look on as their boss was subjected to this humiliation. The entire slum stood and watched as Yakub was led to the van and pushed inside. Many in admiration for Avinash.

No one dared to stop Avinash. As they headed towards the jeep Avinash asked an officer, 'Bhonsle, this Farookh Khitkhit lives close by . . . right?'

'Yes, sir. Heera chawl.'

'Let's pick him up on the way.'

'Sir.'

They proceeded towards Heera chawl and a constable got fidgety.

Kamran was sleeping in his flat when the telephone rang.

'Hello.'

'It's me here.'

'Yes.'

'Mirza saab will be arrested inside an hour.'

'What?'

'Yakub Mental and Farookh Khitkhit are down.'

The line went dead. While Avinash was arresting Farookh Khitkhit, Head Constable Wagh had slipped away to make that telephone call to Kamran. Wagh knew the next stop would be Mirza's and so decided to play the spoilsport.

Kamran quickly called up Munna and apprised him of the situation.

'Are you sure about this, Kamran?'

'Why don't we wait for an hour to find out?'

Munna wanted to scream but then controlled himself. Kamran started again.

'Munna bhai, I think this is very well planned. Yakub Mental and Farookh Khitkhit are already down. It's a Friday and they will automatically have custody over the weekend. I suggest you take Mirza saab and go someplace safe. I will be there as soon as possible.'

'Okay.'

Kamran hung up. Munna dialled a number.

'Munna here. Give Mirza saab the phone. Tell him it's urgent.'

The servant took the cordless to Mirza who had just woken up.

'Hello.'

'Mirza saab . . . Kamran has received a tip that the police are on their way to arrest you.'

'Are you sure?'

In his head Munna repeated what Kamran had told him.

Why don't we wait for an hour to find out?

'Yes, Mirza saab. I will be there shortly to pick you up. Please be ready.'

'Okay.'

Munna hung up. He was at Barqat Mahal in twenty minutes and supervised the escape. From the route Avinash had taken, there was only one way he could enter the mohalla. Munna got that lane crammed with carts, taxis and other vehicles. This meant that Avinash and his team would have to walk the last seven hundred metres which in turn meant that Mirza would get more time to escape. Munna also got a vehicle ready. There would be four of them travelling, Mirza, Munna, a driver and a help.

Kamran reached Barqat Mahal to see Mirza boarding the car. Though he had been in the gang for some time, Mirza had never spoken to him barring that one occasion. Mirza noticed him and called him over.

Mirza was in the rear seat of the car. He signalled for a moment of privacy. Mirza and Kamran were left alone.

Mirza whispered something in Kamran's ears and Kamran was left stunned.

Mirza then called for everyone else and the vehicle sped off. Kamran watched it disappear and then headed inside Barqat Mahal. He went to the first floor and dragged a chair next to Mirza's chair and sat down. Mirza's words were still ringing in his head and he couldn't help smiling.

Avinash and his team landed in an hour. Avinash arrived on the first floor and caught hold of a servant.

'Where is Mirza Azmat?'

'I don't know.'

Avinash was about to slap him when Kamran's voice boomed.

'Mirza saab has gone for a walk.'

Avinash noticed the back of a man sitting on a chair on the small open terrace. He walked up to Kamran.

'Stand.'

Kamran stood up and faced Avinash.

'What did you say?'

'I said Mirza saab has gone for a walk.'

'Where?'

'Don't know.'

'When will he be back?'

'Don't know. Maybe Monday. Maybe Tuesday. It all depends.'

'On?'

'The weather in the city.'

Avinash understood that the man was playing him. Kamran was looking him in the eye. Avinash smiled.

'Bhonsle! Take this slab of meat and put him in the van.'

'Bittu! Make some tea for me. I will be back soon.'

Avinash and Kamran were still staring at each other. Kamran's response got Avinash shaking his head. He turned to leave as Bhonsle caught Kamran's arm and led him downstairs.

Kamran came out of the building to see a huge crowd gathered. He kept smiling throughout that seven-hundred-metre walk to the police van. Kamran wanted this moment to register in public memory for ever. He wanted this event to become a legend.

He was no ordinary fall guy. He was Kamran Ali Khan and he didn't give a fuck about the police and the law.

Kamran looked at the people who had lined up on both sides of the lane and his message was loud and clear.

Mirza Azmat is safe and no one can touch him as long as Kamran is around.

The look on their faces acknowledged the fact. Men, women and kids were looking at him in admiration and respect. This was a signpost moment in his life.

Baazeechaa-e-atfaal hai duniya mere aage
Hota hai shab-o-roz tamaasha mere aage

Juz naam naheen soorat-e-aalam mujhe manzoor
Juz waham naheen hastee-e-ashiya mere aage

Hota hai nihaan gard mein sehara mere hote
Ghisata hai jabeen khaak pe dariya mere aage

20

Kamran entered the van to see two very scared looking men sitting inside, surrounded by cops. One of them was in a kurta-pyjama while the other was in a lungi and a banian. Kamran had never seen them in person but had seen them in photographs. Also, he remembered Head Constable Wagh's tip-off.

The van started for the police station and Kamran looked around. Everyone looked glum and tense. Kamran started humming a hit number from the film *Deewana*. It kept him busy for a while but once he was through with the song, he started getting bored again. Kamran made eye contact with a cop.

'All well at home, saheb?'

The cop turned his face away. Kamran waited for a while and then started again.

'Once there was this guy whose wife passed away. He was in mourning but still managed to give her a good farewell, cremated her and did all that was due. In the evening he bade everyone goodbye, took a long shower and made his first drink of the evening. Suddenly there was thunder and lightning streaks flashed in the skies for a minute. The man raised his glass and murmured, "So she has finally reached."'

Farookh Khitkhit and Yakub Mental stared at him. A couple of cops also looked at him briefly. Kamran waited. A giggle started somewhere, followed by another and then another. It became a laugh, followed by another and then suddenly there was laughter all around.

The van resembled a group going for a picnic.

'That's better. We are not going for a fucking funeral, are we?'

Kamran then addressed Farookh and Yakub innocently.

'By the way, just out of curiosity, between the two of you who is Khitkhit and who is Mental? Also, who the fuck gave you guys names like that?'

The cops had a bigger laugh at this barb. Farookh and Yakub were not amused but they certainly were in awe of Kamran's guts.

At the police station, Kamran was put in a cell alone. A little later, Avinash arrived accompanied by Kambli. Kambli was huge and intimidating and was known in the entire department for his gruesome tortures. If there was a canary that was not singing then Kambli was the go-to guy.

They stood outside the cell, stared at Kamran for a while and then started the conversation.

'Kambli?'

'Sir.'

'You see this chap?'

'Sir.'

'I have a feeling this chap knows where Mirza is but he won't open his mouth. Plus he has some attitude problems. How much time would you need to make him cooperate?'

'Sir, half an hour . . . One hour tops.'

'Good. I don't need any injury marks on him. Start.'

'Sir.'

As Avinash turned to walk towards his cabin he overheard Kamran saying, 'Kambli saheb, before you start I suggest you call your wife and kids and tell them you won't be home for the next few days.'

That made Avinash smile.

Kambli was a true-blue sadist. All he ever thought of was torture. He would think about torture while having food, while having a shower, while getting a haircut, while on his way to office, while on his way back, while making love. The moment Kambli saw an object, his mind would start thinking about how to put it to good use.

Extracting confessions or information from the toughest of criminals was his life and nothing else mattered.

Kambli today was a happy man. At last there was a challenge in life in the form of this rookie. Kambli was sick of guys pissing at his sight or confessing to everything inside of four minutes.

Kamran opened his shirt on his own, the moment Kambli stepped in with his attendant. What Kambli saw amused him no end. Kamran's bare body was full of scars. Kambli felt really happy.

Good good good. He is tough. Good good good.

Kambli got his attendant to hang Kamran upside down and started working on him. He did the imaginable and the unimaginable but Kamran had prepared himself for it.

All through the journey to the police station while Kamran was humming and cracking jokes, he was also bracing himself for the worst pain imaginable. He was aware that the human body had its own limitations and tends to break down before the spirit and that bit of awareness helped him.

Kamran summoned memories of Zeenat and Salma. He reminded himself that there was nothing that could be more painful than this cumulative loss.

An hour later Kambli went into Avinash's cabin.

'Sir, I will need another couple of hours.'

'I need no marks on him, Kambli.'

'Sir.'

Another couple of hours went by. Kambli entered Avinash's cabin again.

'Sir, I need more time.'

There was a hint of defeat in Kambli's tone. Avinash knew then and there that Kamran would hold on. On the way back to the cell, Kambli stopped by his table and made the telephone call that Kamran had suggested he make earlier.

'Listen. Something has come up in my duty. I won't be home tonight.'

'But I have already made dinner now.'

Kambli hung up and formed a theory.

Women, actually, are the biggest torture.

Kambli then went and let out his ire on Kamran. The soles of Kamran's feet were whacked for an infinite amount of time. They worked upon him the whole night and didn't let him sleep.

Farookh and Yakub on the other hand were completely cooperative. They made their confessions and told the authorities whatever they wanted to know. They were sharing the cell and Farookh was full of praise for Kamran.

'The kid's got daring, Yakub. Made Mirza escape . . . took control.'

'Fucker is an idiot.'

'Where does Mirza get these boys from?'

'What's fucking special about him?'

'Took the fall. That's special. Not like our boys who kept on looking while we walked towards the van. And he is definitely better than your boys who could have at least got you changed into something decent after your arrest. Mark my words, he will become something one day, Yakub.'

'What become something? He will be singing by tomorrow morning.'

'Want to bet?'

'Sure.'

Kamran did not open his mouth on Saturday morning. He didn't on Sunday morning nor on Monday morning.

Yakub Mental lost three big bets to Farookh Khitkhit.

Officer Kambli lost about four kilos in those three days.

On Monday morning, Munna arrived with a lawyer and Kamran was released on bail. While he looked completely okay from the outside Kamran could barely walk. On the way out of the station, he noticed Kambli resting on his chair drenched in sweat. Kamran smiled and could not help himself.

'What's up, Kambli saheb? Looking a bit tired today morning.'

Kambli was so tired that he just ignored the comment.

Munna and the boys took him home. Kamran had secured another level of respect in their eyes. In the evening, Kamran received a surprise visit from Mirza Azmat. Kamran was sitting in the middle of the room with both his legs in a bucket of hot water. The phone rang and one of the boys took the call and there was a flurry of activity in the flat. Someone opened the door and Mirza entered the flat.

Kamran was surprised and he tried to get up in respect. Mirza waved his hand.

'Keep sitting.'

A chair was brought and Mirza sat in front of Kamran. Everyone went out of the room, leaving Mirza, Kamran and Munna inside.

'How are you feeling?'

'Great, Mirza saab. I am fine.'

'Really?'

'Yes. This time I had fun, Mirza saab. I realized that I could be useful. That's a good feeling, saab.'

'What do you want, Kamran?'

'This is what I want, Mirza saab. This life.'

'Do you think you are ready, Kamran?'

'Mirza saab, I know that you will tell me when I am ready.'

'I think you are ready.'

Kamran skipped a beat.

'Munna, call the boys.'

Munna called everyone inside and Mirza made the announcement.

'Kamran will take care of the film and construction lines from now on.'

The crowd would have exploded had it not been for Mirza's presence in that room. Mirza got up and this time let Kamran get up. Mirza hugged him.

'You could not be good and if being bad suits you then so be it. Maybe you are destined to doom. So enjoy it while it lasts.'

'Ji, Mirza saab.'

> *Qatra dariya mein jo mil jaaye to dariya ho jaaye*
> *Kaam achchaa hai woh, jiska ma'aal achcha hai*

> *Hamko ma'aloom hai jannat ki haqeeqat lekin*
> *Dil ke khush rakhne ko, 'Ghalib' yeh khayaal achcha hai*

Mirza walked out, followed by Munna. The words stayed with Kamran. The crowd finally broke into cheer. Kamran's broken body had no respite from the hugs of his gang members.

As Munna opened the door of the car for Mirza to get in, Mirza turned to him.

'You remember, Munna, that day when we were about to flee from Barqat Mahal I suddenly called for Kamran?'

'Ji, Mirza saab.'

'I whispered something in his ears.'

'Ji.'

'I told Kamran the exact location where we were going. I told him that we were going to be at my Aligarh farmhouse for the next three days. He knew exactly where we were hiding, Munna.'

Munna looked surprised.

'I am telling you all this in case you are wondering why I have become so generous to Kamran.'

'Ji.'

Mirza sat inside the car. They drove off.

Kamran barely took a couple of weeks off to recuperate since he now had so many much-desired responsibilities. Mirza's parting lines came to haunt him. He asked one of the boys to get some Ghalib stuff for him. Cassettes, books, something, anything.

About four years ago, in the year 1988, Sampooran Singh Kalra, also known as Gulzar, had written and directed a television series for Doordarshan called *Mirza Ghalib*. It was a very fine piece of work with Naseeruddin Shah playing the genius poet. The music of the series was done by Jagjit Singh, who also sang the ghazals along with his wife, Chitra.

Kamran's boy got him the twin audio cassette pack of the series and Kamran got hooked on to them in a big way. It was non-stop Ghalib *shayari* for the next week.

Kamran didn't understand one single ghazal fully but it still left an impression on him. He knew that he was dealing with a master and for some unexplainable reason he found a lot of solace in his work.

He found out that Ghalib also worked in mysterious ways.

The moment Kamran got back on his feet, he sent a couple of bouquets for Avinash and Kambli. Kambli obviously didn't find this funny.

For the next few weeks, Avinash tenaciously went after Farookh Khitkhit and Yakub Mental. He brought their businesses to a grinding halt, leading to both of them doing the rounds of the court on one pretext or the other.

But Avinash could do very little about Mirza. Kamran made sure they were extra careful in their dealings. Kamran instructed the boys to get an office in Khar. It was outside Avinash's jurisdiction so even if he was on Kamran's tail he could not bite at it all the time.

Kamran requested Mirza to be at the opening of the new office. All illegitimate businesses need a legitimate front.

Kamran's ironically was named ALL OKAY Investment Company.

Mirza Azmat opened the office that would be the starting point of Kamran's businesses. It was a nice professional set-up with a staff and the works. Kamran had three cabins in there. One each for Mirza, Munna and himself. Kamran was completely aware that Mirza and Munna would not be regulars but he still felt that this was right.

When Commissioner Sandeep Nath retired, Farookh Khitkhit and Yakub Mental were completely in check but now there was a new pain in the ass and the pain had a name.

Kamran Ali Khan.

21

Nafrat ka gumaan guzare hai, main rashk se guzaraa
Kyon kar kahoon, lo naam na uska mere aage

Imaan mujhe roke hai jo khinche hai mujhe kufr
Ka'aba mere peeche hai kaleesa mere aage

Khush hote hain par wasl mein yun mar naheen jaate
Aayee shab-e-hijaraan ki tamanna mere aage

Kamran grew from strength to strength in the next few years as the city went through its own share of strife in late 1992, early 1993.

Emotions were running high and hatred and enmity was being bred. Politicians romanced the underworld and Farookh and Yakub, who were otherwise having a bad time, were suddenly back in the reckoning. Seeds of the biggest upcoming illegitimate business—terrorism—were being sown.

Mirza stayed away from all this. When rioters were burning the city, Mirza's locality didn't simmer and there was not one single casualty. The Hindus and Muslims stayed calm. Even if they had strong religious opinions, they kept them to themselves. Kamran saw contingents of leaders, both religious and political, come to meet Mirza and then walk away dejected after the meetings.

Mirza would just excuse himself saying that his hands were

already soiled with blood. Kamran started getting telephone calls offering him great opportunities if he left Mirza. He would attend to them . . . laugh and disconnect. The offers kept upping, and Kamran's laughter kept getting louder.

Then the 1993 blasts happened. Farookh and Yakub made a killing—literally. Mirza stayed away again. His instruction to his entire team was to take it easy. In the underworld too, you are as good as your last Friday. Farookh and Yakub had Black Friday on their side. Mirza was not playing.

While Farookh's and Yakub's stocks shot up, Mirza's stocks fell. Mirza waited for things to cool down and then called on Kamran one evening. Mirza, Munna and Kamran got down to a closed-door meeting.

'How is it going, Kamran?'

'All fine, Mirza saab.'

'The offers coming your way . . . are they any good?'

'Yes, Mirza saab.'

'Tempting enough?'

'No.'

Mirza smiled and took a moment.

'Let's get back some momentum, Kamran. People have started forgetting about us.'

'As you wish, Mirza saab.'

'Who's hot in construction right now?'

'The Dhamanis and the Jasjeet Group, Mirza saab.'

'Are they in our territory?'

'No. In Yakub's. But I think we should not care about that, Mirza saab.'

'Why shouldn't we?'

'Mirza saab, we are not into everything that the others are and I think we should not let others be where we are.'

Mirza just looked at Munna but didn't react.

'Film line?'

'Laxmi Arts has had a great year and Farookh's people have been calling him. Sharma has not caved in as yet though.'

'Offer him protection from Farookh.'

'Ji.'

'Let's gain some ground now.'

'Ji.'

'Munna . . .'

'Ji, Mirza saab?'

'What did you tell me . . . What do the kids call him?'

'Ghalib Danger! Mirza saab.'

Kamran went red.

'Why?'

'He keeps listening to the same Mirza Ghalib ghazals and shers on that cassette player of his over and over again. And after the Jhunjhunwala case and the arrest they were dying to give him a name in any case.'

'Who gave him this name?'

'Mushtaq bhai, who is sick of Kamran asking him the meanings of those verses.'

'Call Mushtaq.'

Mushtaq was Mirza's driver. Someone called out his name and Mushtaq quickly rushed to where Mirza was sitting.

'Ji, saab?'

'Why Ghalib Danger, Mushtaq?'

Mushtaq started stammering incoherently. Mirza couldn't understand a word.

'Relax. Why Ghalib Danger?'

'Saab, Kamran keeps listening to Ghalib all the time and keeps pestering me for meanings. The boy is dangerous and so the surname saab.'

Mirza smiled. He looked Kamran in the eye and asked, 'You like Ghalib?'

'Trying to like, Mirza saab. I can't seem to understand him though. Most of the time it goes over my head.'

'You have to be patient with Ghalib. You have to court the poetry, listen to it again and again, fall in love with it and only then have a chance of understanding it completely. It's like how you would treat a woman. The only difference being that Ghalib, of course, won't let you down.'

'Ji.'

'All the questions of life are answered in Ghalib's poetry, Kamran. He has left no emotion unexplored, no riddle unsolved. Ghalib not only left his poetry to this world but he also left behind a handbook for catharsis.'

'Ji.'

Mirza then heaved a sigh and complimented him.

'Nice name. Do it proud.'

'Ji, Mirza saab.'

Kamran took his leave. Mirza knew that Kamran was basically old school, where both Need and Greed had a threshold. He wished in his heart that Kamran would remain the same in his core. In one sense, Kamran reminded Mirza of himself and that's the reason Mirza had taken a particular interest in him.

Kamran valued Mirza and his words because he knew that Mirza understood him like no one else would.

Underneath Kamran's hard, stony exterior was a man who could still not bury his past. Once a month, in the dead of the night, Kamran would go to Karampura alone and knock on the door of Ruslaan's house. He would hand Ruslaan's mother some money saying that he had happened to be in Surat and Ruslaan had asked him to hand this money over to her.

Kamran could not forget his uncle Hamid and his family either. He never visited them but he kept a tab on them through Reshma. Whenever Hamid and the family would face a crunch, help would arrive in mysterious ways. Hamid soon saw a pattern and quickly understood the source but he ignored the knowledge because he wanted Kamran to forgive himself.

Once in a while Kamran would also pay a visit to Zeenat's grave. His wounds never healed. Whether it was deliberate or not, Kamran had kept his angst intact. It was his belief that it would be useful later.

Kamran kept promising his mother that he would come soon to meet her but never did. He kept increasing her allowance and instructed his friends to make sure she was keeping well. But he didn't want to see her because she would know that he had changed the moment she saw him.

His soul was as scarred as his body.

He did keep his word to his friends and called them over to Bombay in installments. They were in awe when they saw what their Kamran bhaiyya had achieved. But they weren't aware of the price that Kamran bhaiyya had had to pay for all that he had.

'The blouse as well as the choli will have to come down, Tamanna.'

Tamanna was shocked.

'Some more cleavage and some more navel. The men— bastards—love navels and yours is a lovely little pit of immense promise. Mark my words, Tamanna, that cute navel of yours will take this whole city by storm. Baby, it will be the new Gateway of India.'

Eighteen-year-old Tamanna couldn't make any sense of this. It was her first day at the dance bar Sapphire and she was trying on her costume. A lehnga-choli had been picked for her and Razia, her guardian, was initiating her into the job. According to Razia, customers would watch her, ogle her, desire her, and shower her with money but not touch her. She didn't know what was in store, but could only hope that Razia's assurance would hold true.

All that you have to do is sway. Fuck rhythm, just sway. The rest will be taken care of by the itchy lust of the customers and that wonderful navel of yours.

Tamanna was born in Jamshedpur and cruel circumstances had landed her at Sapphire. She had been a bright student, but her very bright future had been nipped in the bud due to some extraordinarily tragic events.

Kamran used to visit Sapphire every now and then. A top-end dance bar, Sapphire was the seat of unbelievable action in the history of this city's nights. Khushi was the queen at Sapphire and she and the other girls there ruled over the corrupt, the sick, the rich and the super rich. The powerful became powerless and legends were made every night.

For instance, the record books state that a man once blew up Rs 93 lakh on a girl in one night. And that was just to pay for her to dance. The man did not touch her even once on the floor. He just instructed nine men to keep showering currency on the girl. He had been involved in a stamp scam or some such thing and his ill-gotten wealth had found its way to Sapphire.

The bar itself had a very basic set-up. A stage was set up in the middle and bar girls would dance on the stage to Hindi film tracks under psychedelic disco lights.

At a premium, and if you were very, very important then a private dance could also be organized for you upstairs. It all depended on the client and the kind of service he wanted and the price he could pay.

The city's underbelly was perpetually hungry for any vice.

Kamran would once in a while go to Sapphire with his boys. They would sit in one corner and drink. Kamran would never shower money on any particular girl. He would just leave a generous tip for everyone.

That evening too was just like any other evening. Kamran and the others were parked in one dark corner; the usual business of dancing and the showering of currency was on.

Khushi was burning the floor. True to her name, she was making people happy. A foreign cricket player, a world-record holder, was in the house and Khushi took it upon herself to represent her country and bring him to his knees. The player was a bit drunk and soon started making a fool of himself while Khushi kept egging him on.

Kamran was watching the circus with amusement.

And it was that night, one moment, that his eyes caught a face in the crowd of background dancers behind Khushi. Tamanna was in a corner swaying without any sense of rhythm or grace. She was out of place. Kamran noticed her and for some strange reason his interest lingered.

Khushi went for a costume change and the floor was given to the background dancers. Kamran noticed that the girl in the corner stayed in the corner. He realized the quirk. He was sitting in one corner. She was swaying in another.

A little later Khushi returned in a provocative red lehnga-choli and went for the kill. By the time she retired for the night the word happiness had been redefined. The cricketer sent word that he would like to have a private moment with Khushi. Khushi sent word back that she was very tired and would wait for his next visit.

The cricketer was stumped. What he didn't know was that times had changed and this was the new ada. Bar girls generally worked upon you for months before letting you sleep with them.

Kamran, whose reputation always preceded him, called for Razia who promptly came up to him.

'Salaam, bhai. All well?'

'Who was the girl in the right corner?'

'Tamanna. She is new. Her first day today, bhai.'

'I want to meet her.'

'Of course. Please give me a moment to arrange it.'

Razia was gone.

Tamanna had already changed into a salwar-kurta when Razia entered the room. She shooed all the other girls away and locked the room from the inside. Razia then rushed and hugged Tamanna tightly.

'Mashallah, you are so lucky. You are so blessed. I am so blessed.'

'What happened?'

'You have caught the eye of Kamran bhai. He wants to meet you in private.'

'But you told me that no one will . . .'

'Arre idiot, do you even know who Kamran bhai is?'

'I do not want to meet anyone. I want to go home.'

'You will find it burnt before you reach there if you don't listen to me.'

Tamanna started crying. Razia caught her by her shoulders.

'Listen carefully. They call him Danger bhai. He is ruthless but also very generous. Just meet him. He will not force himself upon you, that I can assure you. We get all sorts. He just wants to talk.'

'What if he does force himself on me?'

Razia summed up her own life.

'Sweetheart! Virginity is extremely overrated. I will send him now. Change back to the lehnga-choli and don't forget what I said about your navel.'

22

Kamran entered the room, led by Razia. Tamanna had changed into a lehnga-choli and was standing, again, in a corner. She had covered herself with a dupatta much to Razia's disappointment.

Kamran sat on the chair.

'You need something sent, Kamran bhai?'

'My drink.'

'Of course.'

Razia called out to her helper. An attendant arrived and Razia asked him to get the bhai's drink.

'Bhai, she is very decent . . . comes from a very good family. Just that . . .'

'I am not sure if I asked you.'

'Of course not. Bhai, your drink.'

The attendant had got Kamran's drink. Kamran took the glass and cleared his throat. Razia closed the door behind her and left. Kamran looked at Tamanna who was feeling really scared. Kamran lit a cigarette.

'Sit.'

Tamanna sat.

'What is your name?'

'T-t-t-t . . . Tamanna.'

'Your real name?'

Tamanna didn't know what to do. Kamran got up and dragged his chair next to hers. Tamanna recoiled.

'First day, I hear?'

'Y-y-y . . . yes.'

'Where are you from?'

'Jamshedpur.'

'Scared?'

Tamanna nodded. Her eyes welled up with tears. Kamran took out his kerchief and threw it on her lap.

'I like your face so I will give you a tip. Be strong or else this city will feast on you. And these tears . . . I suggest you leave them at home when you leave for work. I will stay here for the next twenty minutes and then leave. The world will look at you differently when you step out of the room. My advice to you is to just play along. Now, switch on the TV and push up the volume.'

They watched *Antakshari* on Zee TV for the next twenty minutes. After twenty minutes, Kamran finished his drink and left a stunned Tamanna behind. On the way out he tipped Razia generously.

'You are very large hearted, bhai.'

'This girl . . . Razia . . .'

'Don't worry, bhai. Don't worry at all.'

Kamran left Sapphire that night with a good feeling.

Mirza's clout had increased. Kamran was getting very active on the extortion front. After the Jhunjhunwala incident, people always paid up—sooner or later. But some negotiation was always involved. Cellular services had not started as yet and every threat and deal was done on the MTNL landline.

Film financier and producer Surinder Sharma had been stalling his payments for a long time and the news reached Kamran. Kamran was sitting in his cabin when Babloo came in.

'Bhai, that Surinder Sharma has been stalling for the last four weeks. He disconnects our calls, bhai.'

'Where is he right now?'

'At the studio, bhai.'

'We have someone there on the floor?'

'Chote is there, bhai.'

'Get Chote to call me.'

Chote from Qasimgarh had arrived in Bombay about a year ago to join Kamran. In that one year, Chote had fallen in love with Hindi movies. He used to watch a film every day. The ones he liked he watched again and again. Chote had a Funai VCP and a wonderful collection of movies. His favourite was *Sholay*. In moments of extreme pressure, Chote would imagine himself in a thriller movie.

Someone relayed the message to him and he called up Kamran.

'Haan, bhai . . .'

'Chote! Is Sharma there on the floor?'

'Yes, bhai. He is on the floor.'

'What's his status right now?'

Chote filled him in on the details and Kamran listened to him very carefully.

'You carrying a piece?'

'Yes, bhai.'

'Look at your watch. Three minutes from now I want you to fire a shot in the air right there on the studio floor.'

'Okay, bhai.'

Kamran hung up and ordered, 'Give me Sharma.'

Babloo dialled a number and gave the receiver to Kamran. A peon picked up the phone.

'Hellooo . . .'

'Give the phone to Sharmaji. Tell him it's Danger calling on behalf of Mirza saab and if he asks you to lie tell him that you won't because then not only am I going to come there and talk to him but I will also have a nice little chat with you.'

There was silence and Kamran heard the sound of the receiver being kept down. Kamran looked at his watch. Sharma wanted to stall again but on hearing the threat proceeded to take the call.

'Hello, Danger bhai . . .'

'Hello, seth.'

'What seth, Danger bhai? I am so stuck with this production, what do I say? It has already gone over budget. I needed fifty dancers for this song today but the heroine is dancing alone on the set. The caterer didn't send the food today, bhai, and the lightmen didn't turn up because I could not pay them last week. There are no lights on the set today, bhai. I don't even know if what we are shooting is going to get exposed. Please have patience na, Danger bhai.'

'Seth, I want you to listen to something.'

'What?'

'Ssssshhhh . . .'

Kamran was looking at his watch and Sharma was wondering what was happening. Chote looked at his watch. The three minutes were up. Chote took out his gun and fired a shot in the air. A stunned silence followed and everything went silent. Sharma's heart skipped a beat and his pulse doubled.

'Did you hear that, seth?'

'Y-y-y-y . . . yes.'

'That was me. Don't lie to me because I am right next to you, seth. I know that you took delivery of your brand-new white Mercedes yesterday. I know that there are seventy-five dancers dancing with your heroine on your set today. There are foreigners also in there. The food is excellent and so is the lighting. There is Diwali on your set, seth, so do not bullshit me.'

'S-s-s . . . s-s-sorry, Danger bhai.'

'Now there are three things that I want you to do, seth.'

'I am listening, Danger bhai.'

'Firstly, keep two crore ready by tomorrow. Babloo will call you and tell you how we will collect it. Secondly, once the copy of your film is ready send a print to us. We will need it for piracy.'

Sharma was too shocked to react.

'And, bhai?'

'And?'

'You said three things, Danger bhai . . .'

'Oh yes. Thirdly, seth, I want some tips on how to invest in this movie business. I quite like it.'

Sharma needed a chair and a glass of water immediately.

Incidents like these became stories that spread like wildfire. The film industry was shocked at this unbelievable negotiation and it brought Kamran to their attention. Kamran's roster soon had financiers, producers, actors and suppliers. He had an amazing network where any spike in income would be relayed to him without delay. He had access to any information that he wanted on these guys. It could come from their drivers, their production guys or sometimes their best friends.

Many in the film industry stopped flaunting their wealth.

Kamran's next trip to Sapphire was in a couple of months. Khushi still led the pack but Tamanna had caught up rather fast. She was still in the corner but now she was not obscure or innocuous. When Khushi went for a change and the floor was thrown open to the background dancers, Tamanna took over like a seasoned pro.

Khushi started having a tough time claiming the floor back. When she complained to Razia and threatened her, Razia told her who Tamanna's patron was. That was enough for Khushi to shut her trap and scurry away.

Danger bhai had that effect.

That evening as Kamran watched Tamanna dance without inhibition, he knew that she would be trouble. And Kamran liked trouble.

Once the night was through, Razia led Kamran bhai to Tamanna's room. Drinks were served and they were left alone.

'Sit.'

Tamanna sat. Kamran again dragged his chair next to hers.

'How are things here?'

'Thank you very much.'

'So it's good?'

'Yes.'

'You are a quick learner.'

'You helped me. I am thankful for that.'

'Don't have to be. Like I said, I like your face.'

Kamran pulled out a visiting card and gave it to her.

'It has my number. Call me when you feel like it. I repeat—when you *feel* like it.'

Kamran scanned Tamanna. Her sweet face and her fair body. The curves that were getting more and more interesting with every passing day.

This is fucking trouble, Kamran.

'What soap do you use?'

'Llll . . . Lux.'

'That bar of Lux has the best destiny in town.'

Tamanna's heart raced. Kamran's was also picking up. The room felt like a sauna.

'When are you coming next?'

'Never.'

'Why?'

'Because I am also trouble, Tamanna.'

Kamran got up and went. Tamanna was left gaping.

That was Ghalib Danger's last trip to Sapphire.

> *Zulmatkade mein mere shab-e-gham ka josh hai*
> *Ik shamma'a hai daleel-e-sahar, so khamosh hai*
>
> *Deedaar, waada, hausla, saaqee, nigaah-e-mast*
> *Bazm-e-khayaal maikada-e-bekharosh hai*
>
> *Daagh-e-firaaq-e-sohabat-e-shab kee jalee hooee*
> *Ik shamma'a reh gaee hai so wo bhee khamosh hai*

Builder Praveen bhai had no option but to call Kamran. The phone call was brief and urgent.

'Please, Danger bhai. Please drop in today at my site whenever you feel like. I want to show you something. Please bhai.'

At Praveen bhai's Juhu site, a building was on the verge of completion but there were no workers around. Praveen bhai was sitting alone in his office and the moment he saw Kamran's car he rushed out to receive him.

'Danger bhai, I am so glad you came.'

'I had no choice, Praveen bhai. Your persistence got me here. Tell me?'

'Firstly, what will you have?'

'A couple of penthouses.'

Praveen bhai went white. Kamran enjoyed his reaction for a moment.

'Relax, Praveen bhai. I was just kidding. Tell me why I am here.'

'Your office called. They wanted two crore.'

'You want to give more?'

'Please . . . This way. Yakub Mental called yesterday. Himself. Abused me to his heart's content and asked for three crore. When I said that I have to give you money as well he hung up and sent his boys in the evening and they came and did this.'

Praveen bhai pointed out to Kamran more than a dozen bullet holes on the wall of the lobby.

'Danger bhai! I am in a mess. Nobody turned up for work today. You want money, Yakub wants money, the BMC wants money, the corporator wants money. On top of this, the consumers say that we ask for a lot. What do I do, Danger bhai?'

'Let's go to your office.'

They entered Praveen bhai's office.

'Babloo, dial Yakub's number!'

Kamran sat while Babloo dialled the number. Once it started to ring he handed the receiver to Kamran.

'Hello.'

'Hello, is Mental there?'

'He is out. Who is this?'

'This is Ghalib Danger. I will now speak in Yakub's language so that you understand it better. If you guys call builder Praveen bhai even one more time, then I will personally come and pay you motherfuckers a visit. You fired a dozen yesterday and it felt good, right? You don't have a fucking clue what good means to me so tell Mental to keep his phone off the hook and stay away from Praveen bhai because otherwise Danger won't like it. Did you hear me?'

'Yes.'

'So why the fuck are you still holding the phone? You should be warning your fucking boss, you idiot.'

Kamran hung up and turned to Babloo.

'Babloo, ask a few of our guys to hang around here till the matter is absolutely cool. Ask the contractor to get his guys to start work from tomorrow. They also have to make up for today. Praveen bhai, all will be fine from tomorrow. You can relax now.'

'Thanks, Danger bhai. Thank you very much.'

Praveen bhai was relieved. The colour was back in his face. Kamran started walking out towards his car but Praveen bhai still wouldn't let go.

'Have something na before you leave, Danger bhai. Please.'

Some people just don't know when to stop. Kamran stopped and pondered. He looked at the building.

'Praveen bhai.'

'Ji.'

'You know that I joked about the couple of penthouses but now I seriously feel that I am beginning to fall in love with that corner one over there.'

Kamran was pointing to the top floor in the right wing of the building. Praveen bhai followed Kamran's finger.

'P-p-p-p . . . penthouse.'

'Sea view?'

'Y-y-y . . . yes.'

'It's booked?'

'Y-y-y . . . yes.'

'Who owns it?'

'You.'

The next few years were full of negotiations like this.

23

Kamran was looking at the new cell phones that had just been launched by Nokia. Cellular services had recently been launched in the country and Kamran knew that this piece of technology was going to take business to the next level.

Kamran had four telephone instruments on his table—red, white, black and blue. But soon these small little Nokia beauties would replace the four bulky instruments on his table. A home-grown engineer was explaining how it worked to him.

Kamran was just beginning to understand the concept of different countries having different SIM cards and how one could use this to beat the police phone-tapping network when Babloo knocked on the door.

'Bhai, there is a boy outside asking to meet you. He says you know him. Bhai, his name is Chintu.'

Kamran tried to remember who Chintu was but couldn't.

'Bhai, he has been waiting for the last one hour. What do I do?'

Kamran excused himself and stepped out of his cabin. Babloo pointed to a fifteen–sixteen-year-old kid standing in the reception. The kid smiled on seeing Kamran and Kamran then recognized him in an instant.

The kid from Haji Ali Dargah who had seen him wait for Salma for three straight days had not changed much except for having gotten taller.

Kamran was suddenly sucked into his past. He gathered himself quickly and signalled for Chintu to follow him to an empty room. Once inside, Chintu hugged him, and Kamran felt very awkward.

'Salaam, Kamran bhai.'

'Salaam. How have you been?'

'I knew it was you from the photos.'

Once in a while Kamran's mugshot would find its way into a local newspaper. Sometimes in connection with a crime and sometimes in connection with a philanthropic affair.

'Sit. How are you doing, Chintu?'

'Bhai, you have become such a big man. I just wanted to see you.'

Kamran knew that this was not true. With time his intuition had sharpened and he could spot lies easily.

'Bhai . . . bhabhi still comes.'

'She is not your bhabhi, Chintu.'

'Sorry.'

'You will always remember that.'

'I will, Kamran bhai.'

Chintu got scared. This was not the man he had known back then. The tone and the eyes had changed.

'Bhai, all this looks very nice. I am very happy for you.'

'What do you want, Chintu?'

'Nothing, bhai.'

Kamran kept looking at Chintu and Chintu finally blurted out.

'Bhai, I want to join you.'

Kamran got up and with his left hand picked Chintu by the collar. He then slapped Chintu with such force that Chintu blacked out for a moment and his ears started ringing. Kamran made him sit. Chintu started crying.

'You need money?'

'I want to join your gang.'

Kamran raised his hand again and Chintu hid himself with both his hands.

'I will kill you if you say that again.'

Kamran took out some money from his wallet and shoved it into Chintu's pocket.

'Why, Chintu? I didn't want to become me, you idiot. You have your whole life ahead of you. Pick an honourable career and pursue it. I am there for you . . . any time. You need anything . . . tell me. You just have to let me know.'

Chintu looked at Kamran for a long time. After a while he got up and took the money out of his shirt pocket and put it on the table. He then cleaned his face with the sleeve of his shirt and walked out of the room.

Kamran knew this chapter had not ended.

The Tamanna chapter had not ended either.

A few days after the Chintu incident, Kamran was busy fixing a cricket match between India and Pakistan, when his red telephone rang. Only four people had that number. Mirza, Munna, his mother back home and Tamanna.

Kamran picked up the phone.

'Hello.'

'Hello. It's me.'

It had been more than eight months since the night at the Sapphire, but Kamran remembered it as it were yesterday.

'How have you been?'

'You didn't come?'

'I had told you.'

'But I still kept waiting. Every evening. Every single evening.'

'Where are you?'

'I am calling from a PCO near my home.'

'Go home and wait. My driver will pick you up in half an hour. Bye.'

'Wait. How will he know where I live?'

'He knows.'

Kamran hung up. He called for his driver and instructed him to pick up Tamanna.

The driver picked her up from her house in Andheri East and drove her to Juhu. Praveen bhai's building was complete and had full occupancy. Tamanna was taken to the penthouse on the right wing of the building.

She went in and was told that bhai would come soon. It was a huge place and had a great view. The sea lay spread out before her. A few minutes later the door opened and Kamran walked in.

'Hello.'

'How are you, Tamanna?'

'My name is Sonia.'

'Nice name.'

'Thanks.'

'What are you doing here, Sonia?'

Sonia looked at Kamran.

'I want to do whatever you want me to do.'

They kept looking at each other. Kamran was looking for a sign to know if she meant what she said. Sonia kept looking at him in the hope that he really understood what she had said.

Kamran kissed her and she reciprocated with equal passion. The action shifted to the bedroom and when Sonia took off her clothes Kamran realized that he had been wrong about her.

Sonia was not trouble.

Sonia was evil.

Sonia was a succubus.

Parveen bhai's lavish penthouse and all the rooms were finally put to good use.

Kamran woke up in the morning to find Sonia staring at him, her face glowing. She smiled.

'What happened?'

'Nothing.'

'What happened, Sonia?'

'I now know what happiness is.'

Sweetheart, you now know what sex is but I will not break your illusion for now.

'Great. Come here. Mornings are even better for some more happiness.'

Kamran was incapable of love and Sonia was falling hopelessly in love with him. But they were both happy, obviously because it meant two totally different things to them. Kamran was in it for the sex. Sonia was in it for love.

It was the perfect relationship.

Kamran gifted Sonia a cell phone. That gave them access to each other any time. They spent a lot of nights together. Sonia never demanded anything from Kamran except for his time. And she never complained on the nights when Kamran couldn't make it. But she would let out her pain through her performances on those occasions by treating her body as a useless chunk of meat that had no worth. If Kamran didn't wish to be with her that night then nothing mattered. It was disgusting and humiliating but in some weird sense it was also therapeutic for Sonia.

She knew that Kamran didn't feel for her the way she felt for him. Still, she didn't stop investing in the relationship. So what if Kamran only wanted her body for now?

Some day . . .

Once in a while Kamran's heart also wanted to have a quick chat about Sonia but he would quietly and quickly strangulate that moment.

One night, Kamran woke up in the penthouse to find Sonia missing. He walked into the hall and found Sonia standing near the balcony, crying. He went and held her. She hugged him and broke down.

'What happened?'

'My father . . . he . . . passed away.'

In that one moment Kamran realized he nothing knew about Sonia. He made her sit and comforted her through the night. Though Kamran didn't say much, he was sure that Sonia was feeling better that he was by her side.

The next morning Sonia left for Jamshedpur to attend to her father's last rites.

Farookh Khitkhit and Yakub Mental were sitting together at Yakub's place. They were sick of Kamran's regular encroachments on their businesses.

'This fucking Kamran is getting too big for his boots, Farookh bhai.'

'Agreed. I called Dubai and they also don't understand. Bhai screamed at me saying that I should handle these trivial matters on my own or else make way. Fucking asshole is fucking destroying our reputation.'

'Let's meet Mirza and have a chat.'

Mirza called Kamran that evening at Barqat Mahal.

'Farookh called. He and Yakub want to have a chat.'

'Ji.'

'This will turn ugly. Are you prepared to pay the price?'

'Ji, Mirza saab.'

The chat was fixed at Mirza's Mazgaon office. All the concerned parties were there. Only three people were sitting— Mirza, Farookh and Yakub. Munna and Kamran were standing behind Mirza.

'Mirza saab, your boy keeps entering our areas by mistake all the time.'

'Yakub, both you and I know that Kamran doesn't do that by mistake. We have a proposition. You guys do all sorts of businesses everywhere and we are just into smuggling and protection. What I propose is that you guys do whatever other businesses you want but leave these two businesses exclusively to us. We will give you a share of them to compensate though.'

'That is not fair, Mirza saab.'

'If I were you I would choose my words more carefully, Yakub.'

'Sorry, Mirza bhai. I didn't mean that.'

'I know exactly what you mean. Listen carefully, both of you. If we join hands, it will be a win-win situation for us all. And if we don't, this will be painful for all of us but especially for you guys.'

'Mirza saab, you are threatening us?'

'Assuring you, Yakub. Threatening, if you recall, has never been my style.'

'But what makes you sure that Kamran will be better than us?'

'Yakub! He protected Praveen builder from you, right? My simple question to you is can you protect Praveen builder from Kamran?'

Yakub kept silent. Mirza continued.

'Think about it and let me know in a couple of days. Khuda hafiz.'

Yakub and Farookh got up and went.

'Munna, tell the boys to be on standby. This is going to be very ugly.'

'Ji, Mirza saab.'

'Kamran, be careful. You have become important enough to be killed.'

'Ji, Mirza saab.'

Farookh and Yakub were travelling back together in Farookh's white Mitsubishi Lancer.

'What the fuck does this fucking old Mirza think of himself?'

'True, Yakub bhai.'

'The old fuck thinks that that chap of his is Rambo?'

'True, Yakub bhai.'

'This is fucking enough. Fuck respect. He can't have his way.'

'True, Yakub bhai.'

'Arre, what true? You kept your mouth shut the whole time as if you were fucking paralysed.'

'What could I say? You were already asking the right questions. Would it make sense for me to just repeat whatever you were saying?'

'This fucking Kamran and this fucking Mirza . . . they both will have to fucking go.'

'True, Yakub bhai.'

After the meeting Kamran was sure that his life and Mirza's were in grave danger. He also knew that in a situation like this allegiance was the first casualty and loyalty was the first thing up for sale. Kamran instructed his boys to be on alert and keep their eyes and ears open for any untoward signs.

Munna was about to enter his building when he heard his name being called.

'Munna bhai!'

Munna turned to see a man standing behind him.

'Bhai, Yakub bhai wants to speak to you about yesterday's meeting.'

The man pointed to a van standing on the other side of the road.

'And he expects me to sit in the van alone and go to meet him?'

'Ji, bhai. It's important and he said you could bring your piece with you. No one will stop you. If you are not carrying yours then he asked me to give you mine, but he has requested you to trust him on this.'

The man took out his gun and offered it to Munna. Munna looked at it and then raised his shirt to show that he was carrying his.

Munna then walked towards the van and looked inside. It was empty. The man who was talking to him sat in the driver's seat and looked at Munna.

Munna stepped into the van and shut the door behind him.

> *Rahee na taaqat-e-guftaar, aur agar ho bhee*
> *To kis ummeed pe kahiye ke aarzoo kya hai?*

> *Bana hai shaah ka musaahib, fire hai itaraata*
> *Wagarna shehar mein 'Ghalib' kee aabroo kya hai?*

24

The van stopped outside Rose, Yakub's dance bar near Khar. This was a loud bar and was quite different from Sapphire. Here the clientele was from the middle class and the service was mediocre. Munna stepped out and was led inside. He crossed the crammed floor, which had garish dancers gyrating to loud Hindi film songs.

Munna was led into Yakub Mental's private lounge and, of course, the first thing he noticed, apart from Farookh Khitkhit, was that Yakub had kept the good-looking dancers on this floor.

Some were serving their clients, some dancing for them or sitting close to them. Yakub and Farookh got up the moment Munna arrived at their section, which was basically a three-sofa set-up. Farookh and Yakub were sitting on one sofa, each with a woman by his side. Yakub hugged Munna and requested him to sit. The moment Munna sat, Yakub signalled for the women to vanish. A voluptuous waitress entered the section to serve them drinks. Munna could not ignore her when she turned to him.

'Ice?'

'Yes.'

'How many cubes?'

'Two.'

She smiled and bent down, revealing her cleavage and making

Munna wish he had asked for more than just two ice cubes. Once she made her exit Yakub started the proceedings.

'Munna, I will come straight to the point.'

'Will appreciate that, Yakub bhai.'

'We like you very much, Munna. We like you because you stand for loyalty and hard work. We feel that if Mirza saab's business has survived till today it is not without your good hand.'

Munna sipped his drink.

'We also feel that Mirza saab has changed. How else could he ignore what all you have done and bestow his affection on that taxi driver? Construction and film line both? The least he could have done is give both you guys an equal share. Ever since that asshole entered the market he has been doing whatever he feels like. That fucker thinks we don't know that it's his boys who are constantly tipping that cop Avinash about us.'

Munna had another sip. He knew this was true.

'As it is, our business is a bit tight and then Mirza saab proposes this fucking unreasonable offer. You think that's fair?'

Munna started to laugh.

'What happened?'

'The fucking irony, Yakub bhai . . . the motherfucking irony.'

'What irony?'

'When Mirza saab was shot at by one of Murli Highway's boys, I had a hunch that it was either you or this Farookh bhai. Even today I am sure it was one of you but I can't prove it. Anyway, the thing is that the thorn that's actually pricking you guys in the ass is a direct result of that failed attack. And that, Yakub bhai, is the motherfucking irony. Kamran alias Ghalib Danger, who you so badly want to eliminate, is actually the creation of either one of you guys.'

Yakub looked at Farookh and realized the truth but he quickly came back to the point.

'Fuck that, Munna.'

'Yes, let's fuck that, Yakub bhai. I will have another drink and you will tell me what you want from me.'

Yakub signalled for service. The same waitress appeared.

'Ice?'

'Yes.'

'How many cubes?'

'Five.'

Munna was preoccupied till she was through.

After she left, Yakub continued, 'We want you on our side, Munna.'

Munna took the glass and emptied it.

'Go on.'

'We want you to take over.'

'Mirza saab is like my father.'

'He didn't act like one to you, Munna. You know that. It's time Mirza saab and Kamran both went. It's time you got what was rightfully yours. Munna, listen carefully. Sooner or later this will happen because we want it done and Dubai wants it done.'

Munna eyes went moist. He shook his head and wiped his eyes.

'What's the plan?'

'There is none. Now that you are with us the plan will take shape. We will take down both Mirza and Kamran in one go.'

'Mirza saab!'

'What?'

'You said "Mirza", Yakub bhai. Never ever fucking take his name in front of me without respect.'

Munna looked into Yakub's eyes with a demand for an apology.

'I am sorry.'

'Good.'

'Understood. I will call up Mirza saab tomorrow and tell him that both Farookh and I agree to what he had proposed. That will cool them down and make them complacent. We will meet again on Friday to have a little chat. Meanwhile, we would like you to have this gift. It's a *nazrana*.'

Yakub signalled and a man appeared with a briefcase and laid it on the table. It had a numeric lock. Yakub looked at Munna.

'111.'

Munna leaned forward and rolled the digits. He opened the briefcase to find it stacked with Rs 500 notes. There was also a manila envelope. Munna opened the envelope to find some court-stamped papers related to some property.

'What's this, Yakub bhai?'

'There is this hotel that we are building in Bandra West. There are three owners—Farookh, Yakub and Munna. That's your share, Munna. Congratulations!'

That very night, Kamran was meeting Sonia for the first time after she had come back from Jamshedpur. He entered the penthouse to find her waiting. They hugged each other. They sat for a long time without actually talking, Sonia clinging tightly to him.

'I will make a drink for myself.'

Kamran got up and made a drink and went to the balcony. It was dead silent and the waves were lapping gently against the stones. Sonia joined Kamran and kissed him on the shoulder.

Kamran suddenly remembered something from another life.

'What's your story, Sonia?'

This was the first time that Kamran had asked Sonia about her life. She smiled and let out a sigh.

'I lived with my father, mother, a younger brother and a sister in Jamshedpur. My dad was a government servant and we were a happy family. I had just completed my tenth and was very good in studies. One day, my father and my mother had gone to visit a relative. Dad used to ride a Vespa scooter. On their way back, a drunken truck driver jumped a signal and hit them sideways. My mother died on the spot and my father was seriously hurt. The doctors at the hospital tried their best but they could only do so much. After multiple surgeries he survived but the damage was done. I for my part was thankful that he was at least alive. Soon, our savings evaporated. Debts started accruing. Dad's colleagues, his friends, our relatives . . . People started disappearing one after another. My younger brother and sister were rusticated from their schools for non-payment of fees. It was the same for me as well. Our situation worsened to the extent that we were soon struggling for a square meal.'

Sonia's voice cracked. Kamran put his arm around her. She continued.

'One day an aunt in our locality called me to her home. She told me she had seen my younger sister asking the neighbours for food. I died that day, Kamran. I died.'

Kamran felt sorry. This was also the first time Sonia had ever addressed Kamran by his name.

'I went home and slapped her and then ended up crying the whole night. I realized that I had to do something quickly. I went to the same aunt and told her that I needed to earn. She gave me some money and asked me to wait till the next week. Someone called Razia was coming from Bombay and she could give me work. The rest, I believe, you know.'

'It takes a very brave girl to do what you did, Sonia.'

'It takes a very cruel destiny to do what I did.'

'How are your brother and sister?'

'I have put them in boarding school. My only dream now is that they become real big in life.'

'And what about yourself?

Sonia looked at Kamran. She tugged at his shirt button and shook her head.

'I am too scared to dream.'

She smiled but Kamran knew that it was a feeble attempt to be heroic. Sonia then asked Kamran, 'What's your story?'

Kamran started laughing. He gulped down his drink.

'Don't have a brother or a sister and was not into studies at all. In short, there is no story here, Sonia.'

Kamran kissed her and they headed towards the bedroom. Sonia knew that Kamran was lying because good or bad, interesting or dull, everyone has a story.

That night Praveen bhai's penthouse saw passions of a different level altogether.

For the first time that night Sonia felt that Kamran wanted a piece of her heart as well.

For the first time Kamran acknowledged that he was screwed.

> *Nuktachi hai gham-e-dil usko sunaye na bane*
> *Kya bane baat jahan baat banaye na bane*
>
> *Maein bulata to hun usko magar ae jazbaa-e-dil*
> *Uspe ban aaye kuch aaisi ke bin aaye na bane*
>
> *Bojh woh sar pe gira hai ke uthaye na uthe*
> *Kaam woh aan padha hai ke banaye na bane*
>
> *Ishq par zor nahin hai yeh woh aatish 'Ghalib'*
> *Ke lagaye na lage aur bujhaye na bane*

'Ice?'

'Yes.'

'How many cubes?'

'Seven–eight.'

It was Friday night and, as decided, the meeting between the three was on. Yakub, Farookh and Munna clanked their glasses. Yakub started.

'This is a good one, Munna. This is a really good one. We are going to threaten Avinash, taking Kamran's name. Just phone calls to his residence and messages and stuff. Then we wait to take down Mirza saab and here is where you are going to come in, Munna. You will identify the best moment for us to take him down. You will have to just make that one phone call. We then take down Avinash and then the Mumbai Police will take down Kamran. What do you say?'

Munna took a sip.

'Who does the thinking for you guys?'

'Why?'

'Because this is actually good.'

Farookh smiled and waited for Yakub to acknowledge him.

'Farookh came up with this actually.'

'Well done, Farookh bhai.'

'Thanks.'

Farookh Khitkhit's cell rang and the display said *Mohabbat calling*. The colour drained from his face and he disconnected the phone. Munna sighed deeply.

'Fifteenth of this month, Yakub bhai. Be ready for the date and be on standby for my call.'

'Awesome.'

'I need another drink.'

Yakub signalled. She came.

'Ice?'

'Yes.'

'How many cubes?'

'Fill up the whole glass.'

The next day, Avinash's wife, Preeti, was cooking in the kitchen when the telephone rang. She asked the maid to keep an eye on the gas and picked up the receiver.

'Hello.'

'Hello, madam.'

'Who's this?'

'This is your husband's death calling. Please ask him to keep away from Mirza saab's business and mind his own.'

'Who is this?'

'Unless he urgently wants you to be a widow.'

The caller hung up, leaving Preeti shivering. Inspite of Avinash anticipating this situation and asking her to mentally toughen herself for something like this, Preeti could not remember his words and stood shaken for a while.

After a bit she dialled Avinash's number.

'Hello.'

'Avi, where are you?'

'On my rounds.'

'Can you come home?'

'What happened?'

'Please come home right away.'

'What happened, Preeti?'

'I . . . I got a call.'

Avinash reached his home and held Preeti who started to cry the moment she saw him.

'Preeti, some spineless idiot will give you a threatening call and you will start to cry?'

'I am scared. Who is this Mirza?'

'Tell me exactly what the caller said?'

Preeti told Avinash every word she could remember. Avinash recalled a face from his past.

'I know who it is.'

Kamran was sitting in the office when Babloo knocked.

'Bhai, there is a woman outside asking for you.'

'Who?'

'Khushi from Sapphire.'

Kamran was surprised. He motioned Babloo to send her in. A few moments later, in walked happiness.

'Salaam bhai.'

'Salaam.'

She waited for Babloo to close the door behind him.

'What can I do for you?'

'Bhai, I need fifty lakh.'

'Great. So what can I do for you again?'

'You can watch this.'

Khushi removed her dupatta. Covering her breasts was a small brown packet. Khushi offered the packet to Kamran. Kamran took the packet and looked inside.

There was an unlabelled VHS tape inside the small brown packet.

'It's a very nice film, bhai. You will make millions. I just want my fifty lakh.'

Khushi then calmly put the dupatta back on and smiled.

25

MLA Pramukh Joshi was slated to become chief minister of the state of Maharashtra some day. He was a family man with two kids and lived in a joint family with his father and mother. He was known to be honest and a people's person. A dynamic leader, Pramukh Joshi had fought for public causes on numerous occasions quite successfully.

The state elections were round the corner and Pramukh Joshi was leading the party's campaign. The prospects were looking amazing.

That is until now.

When the VHS tape given by Khushi played back Kamran could not believe his eyes. It was a hidden camera recording MLA Pramukh Joshi having an orgy with some foreigners in what on the face of it looked like Bangkok. He was completely naked with just Santa's cap on his head. In the badly edited footage, Pramukh was first seen playing hide-and-seek with Asian girls and then doing some really kinky stuff as Santa Claus.

The bad audio quality still gave away what he was mouthing.

'I am the bad Santa! I am the bad Santa! I am the baddest Santa!'

The tape then had Pramukh in action. It was a twenty-three-minute compilation of Pramukh's colourful secret holiday in Bangkok last Christmas. The common public, however, at that time had been wishing him a speedy recovery because they'd been told that he had gone abroad for a gall bladder operation.

Kamran took the tape out and turned to Khushi.

'How did you get this?'

'His bodyguard got this made. On Christmas night, the minister suddenly wanted to have Chinese. The bodyguard quickly arranged for the shooting. Nice film na, bhai?'

'Who is this bodyguard?'

'Forget him na, bhai.'

'You have copies?'

'Just another one, bhai. I will give it on payment.'

'The bodyguard has anything else?'

Khushi did a slight tilt of head and smiled. On cue the dupatta slid down.

'I have but I am not sure if you are interested.'

Kamran spotted the tell. It was supposed to distract him. Kamran got up and walked over to Khushi. Khushi stood up.

'The bodyguard likes you, doesn't he, Khushi?'

Khushi was stunned. She quickly covered herself with her dupatta.

'It's a dangerous game you guys are playing.'

'He wants me to quit this line, bhai. We plan to run away.'

'You guys are way over your head here.'

'How, bhai?'

'Word gets out, Khushi. In this world, eventually, word gets out.'

'We have it covered, bhai. You will please give us a window of a couple of days after the payment. We will be out of the country before they know who's behind it.'

Kamran was impressed.

'This is all your planning, right?'

Khushi blushed and nodded.

'My bodyguard is tough but a little slow, bhai. His only virtue besides being great in bed is that he listens to me.'

Kamran apprised Mirza of the situation. This was big money and he wanted to keep Mirza in the loop. Mirza gave his consent and asked Kamran to keep this just to himself. Munna was also to be told only when the right time came.

The bodyguard collected the money, all of it, the next day. Both the copies of the tape were now with Kamran. He kept them in a safe in the office.

This was an investment that could come really handy in future.

Preeti was mentally prepared when the second telephone call came.

'Bhabhi, why don't you make Avinash saheb understand? He is unnecessarily inviting trouble. He will be shot needlessly.'

'Why don't you speak to him directly, bhaiyya? He just doesn't listen to me any more.'

She banged the phone down and felt really good. Both Preeti and Avinash had a good laugh over this phone conversation that evening.

The next day Kamran was picking up Sonia from her new one-bedroom flat in Lokhandwala Andheri West, when his cell rang. It was Babloo.

'Bhai, there is this cop Avinash who has landed at the office.'

'So?'

'He wants to talk to you?'

'Get him some tea, coffee. I will be there shortly.'

'He wants to talk now.'

'Get him on the line.'

After a brief silence Avinash came on the line.

'Hello.'

'Avinash saheb. How are you?'

'Why are you calling my home, Kamran?'

There was a pause. Kamran couldn't understand.

'Sorry?'

'That you will really be if there is one more fucking telephone call from your end. My phone was tapped this time around and the call came from one of your landline numbers. This is a warning, Kamran, so be very, very careful before you dial my number again.'

'Hang on one sec . . .'

But Avinash had already disconnected the line. Kamran was surprised at this new development. He figured that someone in his office had turned rogue but who and why was something he just couldn't get his head around. Sonia entered the car and saw him worried.

'What happened?'

Kamran quickly gathered himself and smiled.

'Nothing.'

'So what's the surprise?'

Kamran remembered that he had promised Sonia to tell her his story. At least a part of it.

Kamran asked his driver to drive by Karampura.

They spent the whole day together and Kamran filled Sonia in on details that he had never shared with anyone. He spoke about his past and Zeenat. The only person that he didn't speak about was Salma. Kamran was not sure if he was ready to share anything about Salma as yet.

Sonia knew that somewhere in the jigsaw was one missing piece but chose not to question Kamran about it. She had seen his passionate and wounded side. There had to be a woman there somewhere. There was always a woman.

She was not inquisitive.

The answers would come in good time.

The next day was the fifteenth of the month.

Mirza had woken up very early. He always used to on that particular date. It was Nazia's death anniversary. Munna had noted that Mirza would always go alone every year on that particular day and that's the reason he was up early too and pacing his rooftop holding his cell phone and waiting for a call.

Yakub Mental was in turn waiting for Munna's call. His stomach signalled for the pot. Yakub decided to wait for some more time. There was no reception in his loo.

Mirza stepped out of Barqat Mahal. He waved for everyone to just leave him alone. They did. Mirza spotted Mushtaq cleaning his taxi.

'How are you, Mushtaq miyan?'

'As-salaam alaikum, Mirza saab. All well with your blessings.'

'Wa'alaikum as-salaam. Can you drop me to the Mahim dargah?'

'Of course, Mirza saab. Please sit.'

Mushtaq quickly opened the door and Mirza sat inside. Mushtaq then ran over and sat in the driver's seat.

'Anyone else coming with you, Mirza saab?'

'No, it's just me today, Mushtaq. Let's go.'

Mushtaq started his taxi.

In the adjoining building, a man dialled a number on his cell. Munna's cell rang on the terrace.

'He's left in a cab, Munna bhai. Mahim dargah, he said.'

Munna disconnected and dialled Yakub.

'No more tea for me. Hello.'

'He has left for Mahim dargah. He will there in twenty-odd.'

'Okay.'

Munna disconnected. Yakub quickly dialled another number.

'Mirza will be at the Mahim dargah in about twenty minutes. And please, for the love of God, do not fuck it up.'

Yakub hung up and dashed towards the loo. The boy serving him tea rushed out of the room and ran towards the back of the building. Once there, he looked around, took out his cell and dialled a number.

Kamran was sleeping when his cell rang. He took the call on the third ring.

'Yes, Raju.'

'Bhai, Mirza saab is in danger. They want to finish him off near Mahim dargah in about twenty minutes.'

Kamran couldn't believe this. He got up and dashed towards the door. Sonia was surprised but Kamran left her with only one instruction.

'Get ready . . . take a cab . . . go home and stay put. I will call you.'

The elevator was on the ground floor so Kamran took the stairs. The very next minute he was inside his Fiat, driving towards the dargah.

Kamran was clocking no less than eighty. He took out his phone and dialled Mirza's cell phone. It kept on ringing in a room at Barqat Mahal. Mirza was not carrying it because he wanted no distractions. He unstrapped the gun that was kept under the driver's seat.

Mirza got down from the cab and took out some money for Mushtaq. Mushtaq shook his head.

'Mirza saab, this taxi is mine because of you. I can't accept this.'

'Keep it, Mushtaq. You know that I don't like to hear no.'

Mirza smiled. Mushtaq took the money and thanked him. Mirza walked towards the dargah of Hazrat Makhdoom Ali Mahimi.

The Mumbai Police and the Mahim dargah share an amazing relationship. It is believed that the Hazrat's residence used to be the place where the Mahim police station stands today. In fact, a room in the police station contains a steel cupboard that has the saint's personal belongings. It's called the Makhdoom Baba room. It's opened once every year to the public.

Another legend has it that when the saint was dying, it was a police constable who gave him water from his cap.

Mirza was already halfway to the mazaar when a black van arrived and four men got out.

A group of children flocked to Mirza and Mirza stopped and took out some money for them. The group of four walked casually towards Mirza.

In the meantime, Kamran stepped on the gas but the machine had its own limitations.

Mirza got away from the kids and proceeded towards the steps. The group of four men reached Mirza and one person took out his gun, which had a silencer attached to it. In a smooth, orchestrated effort Mirza was shot at five times by the man while the other three covered him. There was no sound, just five little ticks.

As Mirza fell, the four turned around and started walking back towards their van. As they walked their separate ways, passers-by were shocked at the sight of blood oozing from underneath Mirza's white Pathani and a crowd quickly gathered around him.

Kamran had finally reached the area by that time. He quickly got out of his car and started running towards the dargah. His eyes were searching everywhere for Mirza. On the way he unknowingly bumped into the man who had a gun with a silencer tucked in his back.

Kamran stopped when he saw a small crowd ahead of him. He feared the worst and rushed towards them. Kamran tore through the swarms of people only to see Mirza gasping for breath and completely covered in blood.

He picked Mirza in his arms and turned his face over. The moment Mirza saw Kamran he smiled.

'Just hang on, Mirza saab. Someone call an ambulance. Do it now!'

'Kamran . . .'

'Call the ambulance please.'

'Kamran . . . easy. Don't scream. We are in a dargah.'

'Mirza saab, nothing will happen to you. I will get you to the hos . . .'

Kamran tried to get up. Mirza caught him.

'Kamran, listen to me.'

'Mirza saab . . . please . . .'

Mirza grimaced in pain. His body writhed in pain as he struggled to speak.

'Kamran, my time has come . . . I know it . . . I was to die on this date . . . Twice my death went back empty-handed . . . Once because of a girl . . . and the next time . . . because of you. But today I know.'

'Please don't say that, Mirza saab.'

'Kamran . . . I asked you the . . . other day if you . . . were ready to pay a price . . . for what you wanted and you said yes.'

'Not this, Mirza saab . . . not this.'

'But the price is never . . . for you to decide, Kamran.'

Kamran started crying. Mirza moaned in pain.

'These kids today . . . they don't even know where to shoot someone. Look at this mess. It's going to be very agonizing.'

'Mirza saab, please don't go.'

'Will you . . . do me a favour, Kamran?'

'Please don't do this, Mirza saab.'

'Make it easy for me . . . Kamran.'

'No, Mirza saab.'

'Please make it easy for me, beta . . . Do your name proud.'

Kamran hugged Mirza tightly. He was sobbing like a baby. Mirza was in tremendous pain. Kamran heard the police siren coming from a distance. He finally let go of Mirza and stood up, wiping his tears and taking out his gun. Mirza smiled, closed his eyes and mumbled, '*Inna Lillahi wa inna ilaihi raji'un.*'

Mirza then opened his eyes and looked at Kamran. Kamran had stopped crying. The police siren was getting closer.

Kamran shot Mirza twice in the heart.

Mirza went still.

He died with a smile on his face. He chose to go the way he had arrived.

Kamran got down and folded Mirza's hands. He closed Mirza's eyes and walked off.

> *Mauj-e-khoon sar se guzar hee kyon na jaaye*
> *Aastaan-e-yaar se uth jaayain kya?*
>
> *Umr bhar dekha kiye marne kee raah*
> *Mar gaye par dekhiye dikhlaayain kya?*
>
> *Poochchte hain woh ki 'Ghalib' kaun hai?*
> *Koi batlao ki ham batlaayen kya?*

26

Kamran sat in his car and broke down. The police cars arrived and the cops rushed towards the crime scene. He forced himself to start his car and sped away. Once safely away, he took out his cell and dialled a number.

Munna was surprised to see Kamran's name flashing on his cell. Yakub had just informed him that the job was done, so he wondered why Kamran was calling him at that moment.

'Hello Kamran.'

'Munna bhai . . . He is gone . . . Mirza saab . . . is gone.'

Munna was stupefied at Kamran's knowledge of the incident. Still, he feigned ignorance.

'What!?!!'

'They shot Mirza saab at the Mahim dargah.'

'Are you out of your fucking mind?'

'Bhai, it's true. I was there. Mirza saab is gone.'

'Oh God!'

Munna kept silent. Kamran waited for him to say something.

'Where is he?'

Kamran choked.

'Still at the dargah. I had to leave because the cops had landed.'

'How did you know that he was going to be at the dargah?'

'My mole at Yakub's told me.'

'Where are you now?'

'Just left Mahim.'

'Go straight to Barqat Mahal. I will meet you there shortly and keep this to yourself.'

'Ji.'

Kamran disconnected the line. Munna scrolled down the last-dialled list and stopped at Yakub Mental. Yakub was relaxed and through with his morning ablutions when his cell rang.

'Yes, Munna.'

'There is a fucking mole in your house. Kamran called from the dargah. He knows that you ordered the hit.'

'Fuck.'

'Yes.'

'Does he know about you?'

Munna wondered if Yakub was actually Mental.

'No. I have asked him to go to Barqat Mahal. I am meeting him there in some time.'

'You will have to take him down, Munna. It has to happen today.'

'Take care of the mole immediately and stop taking my fucking name when you receive my calls, Yakub bhai.'

Munna cut the phone. A tense Yakub replayed the events of the morning again and again. On his fourth recap, he remembered that Jamal was serving tea when Munna had called him with the news that Mirza was on his way to the dargah.

Yakub also remembered that he had mentioned Mirza's name in front of Jamal. Yakub cringed and slapped himself on the head.

I am such a big chutiya.

Yakub came out of the room and looked around for Jamal. His boys got up on seeing him. Yakub went around and finally spotted Jamal in the kitchen. He was busy cutting vegetables inside. Yakub looked around and found a sledgehammer lying among some other stuff. He picked it up and went inside the kitchen.

Yakub Mental came out after four minutes drenched in blood and pulp.

Kamran ignored his cell phone for the fourth time. It was an unidentified landline number and Kamran was in no mood to talk. On the fifth time, Kamran got irritated and pressed the green button.

'Who is this?'

A voice laughed and then spoke:

'Ghalib bhai! How are things?'

'Whoever this is, call me later.'

'So you also want to die today, you idiot? Come right away to Dagdi Chawl and ask for kholi number seven.'

'Who is this?'

'I am the guy who turned Kamran Khan into Ghalib Danger. Disconnect the fucking phone and turn the car around.'

Kamran slammed the brakes and his car screeched to a halt. He tried to place the voice but failed. He tried desperately to look for an answer but drew a blank.

But there was something in that voice and the tone that told Kamran that he could trust it.

The man had said, 'So you *also* want to die today itself, you idiot?'

Kamran turned his car around and headed towards Dagdi Chawl.

On arriving, he stopped at the entrance of the slum. He got out of his car and started walking. People were just starting their day. Kamran went to a small paan shop and asked for kholi number seven. The shopkeeper gave him directions and he headed towards the shack.

He found the place and knocked on the door. Kamran entered the shack. It took him time to adjust to the low light inside.

A man stood near the window in anticipation. A young girl was helping him wear his shirt, buttoning it up for him.

Kamran, of course, didn't know the young girl but Munna did. This was the ice-cube girl who had caught his undivided attention at Yakub's bar. She went inside the kitchen, leaving the two alone.

The man who was standing didn't have a right hand. There was just a stump. His entire face and body were full of scars. His skin was covered in black and a weird pink. He looked at Kamran and came near him. As their eyes locked, the man scratched his head with the stump and started laughing.

'That father figure of yours is finally fucking dead.'

Kamran kept staring at him.

'What was the name of that little girl? Ahhh . . . Zeenat! Right?'

Kamran went up and caught the man by the collar.

The man smiled and then advised Kamran, 'Don't waste your anger on me. Preserve and conserve it because you will need lots of it very soon, Kamran.'

Kamran let go of the collar.

'The name used to be Murli Highway. Now people call me Murli Loola.'

Murli chuckled, then turned away and walked towards the window.

'What's the story?'

'The story? Here it goes. Murli Highway used to rule the Bombay–Goa highway once. Mirza was a powerful man and he had two arch-enemies: Farookh Khitkhit and Yakub Mental. The two wanted whatever Mirza had. They wanted Mirza dead but they also knew that even if a slight hint got out about what they were thinking then the two would be slaughtered. This is where Murli Highway enters the scene. Farookh and Yakub know that they are in safe hands and that matters will remain absolutely discreet.'

Murli scratched his head again.

'Murli's boy Ruslaan shoots Mirza but Mirza is saved by a taxi driver. He survived because of you. Mirza hunts Murli down and peels off the skin from Murli's entire body but Murli doesn't open his mouth. Murli is left for dead with just half a breath on him at Marine Drive. Then a miracle happens. Murli survives. He loses one hand but he survives. It takes him ten months to recover. His business in the meantime is taken over by Farookh and Yakub. When Murli goes to claim what is rightfully his, Yakub kicks him in the backside and abuses him. Farookh calls him worthless and abuses him too. When Murli reminds them that he can still reveal the truth, the two remind him about his daughter, Laxmi.'

Murli Highway started crying.

'They had taken my daughter and Yakub had given her a job in his bar. When I begged them to let her go Yakub asked me to be thankful that he had not got her sold. Laxmi still works there and, you know what, she is the one that's made our meeting possible.'

Murli wiped his face.

'She told me what Yakub and Farookh are up to again and she also told me the name of the person who was going to deliver Mirza Azmat to them.'

Just then Kamran's cell rang and the display read *Munna Bhai*. Kamran figured.

'Munna!'

Murli acknowledged it, one hand repeatedly beating his thigh. Kamran's eyes welled up.

He received the call: 'Bhai.'

'I have reached. Where are you?'

'I am stuck in traffic bhai. Will be there shortly.'

Kamran disconnected. His voice broke as he asked, 'You could have saved Mirza saab? You could have told me all this before and I would still . . .'

'Who better than you to know what wrath, rage and vengeance is, Kamran? Ruslaan or I were not the ones truly responsible for Zeenat's death. Kamran, we were just instruments for Farookh and Yakub.'

Murli shook his head violently.

'That day I had begged Mirza for my life. I had offered him everything for my failure. This was business. I offered him every fucking thing that I owned and every fucking thing that I would earn for the rest of my life. But he didn't listen. In our world the machinery of revenge stops only with someone's death. My revenge with Mirza is complete and I am doing you two favours. Firstly, I am saving your life and secondly I am giving you the guys who killed Mirza—Farookh, Yakub and Munna. Do what comes naturally to you.'

'What do you want, Loola?'

'I want my daughter back, Kamran. I have not seen her smile in years. And I also want a promise in lieu of saving your life.'

'What?'

'Yakub should be kicked to his death.'

Munna at Barqat Mahal was sure. He quickly dialled Yakub's number.

'Kamran knows, Yakub bhai.'

'How?'

'I don't know that but Kamran knows.'

'Let's hunt him down. You send some boys to his penthouse. I will send some to the office.'

'Yakub bhai, go back to the original plan as well. Let's take Avinash out. In case Kamran escapes us, let the police hunt him down.'

'You are right. I will ask Farookh to coordinate that.'

Kamran came out of the slum and started his car. He knew that he had to act fast. He called up Chote, his most trusted man.

'Yes, bhaiyya.'

'I want you to go and open the office right now. I will be there in fifteen minutes.'

'Okay.'

Kamran then called Hussain bhai. Hussain bhai was a master forger and when it came to fake passports, or any illegal document, Hussain bhai was the go-to guy. Hussain was particularly fond of Kamran. Once, Hussain had wanted to do a Film-stars' Nite in Dubai but the film stars were not agreeing. Kamran had then stepped in and arranged everything. The film stars were very happy to attend after that.

That morning, Hussain bhai picked up the phone on the third ring.

'Hello, Hussain bhai.'

'Kamran, what am I hearing?'

'It's true, Hussain bhai.'

'Ya Khuda!'

'Hussain bhai, I have to run. There is going to be a huge mess.'

'When and where?'

'Today itself, to Dubai.'

'Come to my place.'

Kamran disconnected and then called Sonia.

'Hello.'

'Mirza saab is dead, Sonia. They shot him dead.'

'God.'

'I am going out of town.'

'Why?'

'They are coming after me.'

'Who?'

'All of them.'

'I want to come with you.'

'No.'

'Kamran, I want to come with you wherever you go.'

'Sonia! Don't do this.'

'Please don't leave me here. I will not be able to live.'

Kamran had not anticipated this complication.

'I might not return for a long time, Sonia.'

'Doesn't matter.'

'Might not return for a very long time.'

'Doesn't matter. I just want to be with you.'

'Sonia . . .'

'Don't leave me. If you feel anything for me . . . anything, then please don't leave me.'

Kamran sighed deeply.

'Be ready. I will call you in some time.'

Kamran disconnected and dialled Hussain bhai again.

'Hussain bhai, there are two of us.'

The man on the bike outside Avinash Sharma's building saw Avinash and his wife, Preeti, coming out. He immediately took out his phone and dialled a number. Farookh Khitkhit's cell rang.

'Bhai, he and his wife just came out. He is in plain clothes.'

'Tail them.'

Avinash was in plain clothes because he was taking Preeti to the Lotus Nursing Home. There was good news in the offing and Avinash was taking Preeti for her first regular check-up. In all the excitement, Avinash didn't notice the two people on the black bike tailing his jeep.

Avinash reached the nursing home and the couple went inside to meet Preeti's gynaecologist.

'Bhai, they are inside.'

'How is the weather?'

'Nice, bhai. Little traffic. Less people. It's bright and sunny, bhai.'

'Have some tea. As soon as he steps out take him out.'

'Okay, bhai.'

Farookh disconnected. This was promising to be a great day.

Kamran landed at the office to find Chote waiting for him. The news of Mirza's death had spread like wildfire. As Kamran walked inside, Chote asked, 'Bhaiyya, what's this happening?'

'Someone wants a war.'

'Why?'

'Why not?'

> *Maze jahaan ke apnee nazar mein khaak naheen*
> *Siwaay khoon-e-jigar, so jigar mein khaak naheen*
>
> *Bhala use; na sahee, kuchch mujhee ko raham aataa*
> *Asar mere nafas-e-be asar mein khaak naheen*
>
> *Hamaare sher hain ab sirf dillagee ke 'asad'*
> *Khulaa ki faayda arz-e-hunar mein khaak naheen*

27

Kamran entered the office, followed by Chote.

'You carrying your piece, right?'

'Ahh . . . No, bhai. I left it at home.'

'Idiot. Did I give it to you to keep it at home?'

'Sorry, bhai.'

'Keep this and stay put here.'

Kamran handed Chote his gun and walked towards Mirza's cabin. He went inside and opened the safe. The VHS tapes from Khushi were inside there. He took the tapes and headed towards his own cabin.

He took out a briefcase from under his desk and opened it, emptied all its contents on to the desk, replacing them with only the VHS tapes. He then opened his own safe and took out all the cash, jewellery and other papers. There was also a gun in there with a couple of boxes of cartridges. He started putting what he needed into the briefcase.

At the Lotus Nursing Home, Avinash and his wife stepped out and headed towards their parked jeep. A bike revved and crossed them. The pillion rider shot some six bullets at Avinash and the bike then disappeared into the adjoining lane.

Avinash had reacted on the first shot itself. He shielded Preeti and took her down with him. He lay there for a moment, before getting up. Avinash had heard six shots but was surprised to see he had been hit only twice.

The other four had all hit Preeti and she lay on the ground writhing in pain. Avinash quickly picked her up in his bleeding arms and ran towards the nursing home.

Chote saw the two vans stop on the other side of the road. He rushed to Kamran who had already shut his briefcase and was preparing to exit.

'Bhai, they are here.'

'How many?'

'Two vans. Bhai, I will stop them. You take the rear exit. They don't know anything about it.'

In the face of so many threats to Kamran, Chote had designed an emergency exit for the day when matters went out of hand.

Chote realized that today was that day. Kamran was caught in a dilemma. It was not in his nature to turn his back this way.

'Bhaiyya, I am telling you, please go.'

'Chote, don't you fucking die on me.'

'Bhaiyya, I didn't come to Mumbai to die. Don't worry about me. It's important that you move now.'

'Keep this.'

Kamran handed Chote the second gun and the boxes of cartridges.

'Just what I needed. I will call you the moment this gets over.'

Kamran heard a shot ring in the air. Chote pushed Kamran towards the emergency exit. They went to the last cabin on the floor and started to push the steel almirah that covered the hole. It was essentially a hole made in the wall that led to a small tunnel that in turn opened into the adjoining alley.

Chote and Kamran moved the almirah completely. A couple

of more shots got fired. Once Kamran was in the tunnel, Chote covered it back with the almirah.

Chote then picked up his guns and smiled.

It was just like in the fucking movies.

Chote, the hero, then walked back towards the entrance where all the villains had gathered.

Kamran came out of the alley and boarded a taxi. He heard a string of shots that announced Chote's arrival.

Preeti succumbed to her wounds shortly and Avinash was rushed into the ICU soon after. This incident instantly mobilized the entire police force.

Sonia picked up the phone on the first ring.

'Hello.'

'I will be there in ten minutes.'

'I will see you downstairs.'

Kamran picked up Sonia from below her building and they headed towards Hussain bhai's place.

Hussain bhai had his set-up in Santacruz East. It was close to the international airport and he was both on and off the radar of the Mumbai Police. 'On' because they knew that he was really, really good. 'Off' because he had helped the police on numerous occasions.

Though everyone knew about Hussain bhai no one could ever pin a charge on him.

Kamran paid the fare and warned Sonia before stepping out of the cab.

'You will have to move very fast. They know me very well here and everyone is greedy for a tip today.'

Kamran had put on his shades and entered the lane leading

to Hussain bhai's house, followed by a very brisk Sonia. It was a small walk but Kamran was tense till the time Hussain bhai opened the door and let them in. Hussain bhai was surprised to see Sonia with Kamran but didn't feel like probing the matter further.

'It is all over the news. They are saying that they suspect you killed Mirza saab?'

'And what do you think?'

Kamran looked at Hussain bhai. Hussain bhai was a master forger with a very keen eye.

'It's all cock and bull.'

'Thanks, Hussain bhai.'

Hussain bhai waved and called for his man.

'Firdaus!'

A man arrived. He was exactly like Hussain bhai.

'That's Firdaus. He will help you.'

Kamran was surprised. Firdaus took them inside and started the job.

Back at the office, Chote looked at the box. He had just four more bullets left. Chote looked in the direction of the chatter and guessed that there would be at least five or six villains left. He looked down at himself. Though he had been shot at thrice himself, he couldn't help smiling.

This is like fucking Sholay man!

Chote looked in the direction of the kitchen. Not visible from where Chote was were two gas cylinders next to each other. He knew that one was about three-fourths full while the other was completely full.

In an extremely heartfelt, honestly dramatic moment Chote closed his eyes and muttered, 'Sorry, bhaiyya.'

Chote then got up and walked towards the kitchen. The

villains were bewildered because Chote was walking across from them. They started shooting at him but Chote just ignored them and kept walking towards the kitchen. He took a couple of more hits on the way but managed to get inside.

Once inside, Chote disengaged the connected cylinder and threw it outside. He then took the second one and threw it out too. The villains finally understood what the hero was up to and decided to run but it was too late.

The hero Chote took out his gun and fired at the cylinders. No one knew which cylinder burst first but the whole office blew up to bits, pieces and smithereens.

The last sad little thought that had crossed Chote's mind was:

Who will fucking know what I just fucking did man?

Kamran dialled Chote's mobile but it was switched off.

Firdaus had taken Kamran's and Sonia's photographs and had made fresh identities for them in one hour.

They were now Mr Ibrahim Ali and Mrs Ferozi Ali.

Kamran then sat with Hussain bhai and opened his briefcase. Apart from the tapes, he put everything out on the table. Hussain bhai then took a pad and put a piece of carbon paper between two sheets. He listed the amount of cash and the valuables that Kamran was carrying and arrived at a total valuation.

Hussain bhai tore a copy for Kamran and also tore a thousand-rupee note. He kept one portion for himself and gave the other to Kamran.

He also handed Kamran a piece of paper with some telephone numbers on it.

'Rizwan will be there at the airport to receive you.'

'Okay.'

Hussain bhai then asked Kamran and Sonia to get ready. They were to leave for the airport in half an hour.

Half an hour later, Kamran emerged from Hussain bhai's house in a completely different avatar. His hair was coloured and he was wearing specs and sporting a moustache. Sonia was wearing a burqa.

As Mr and Mrs Ibrahim Ali sat in Hussain bhai's car, Hussain bhai couldn't help remarking, 'It was a great idea that you got her along, Kamran. It should be a cakewalk.' Sonia looked at Kamran.

Munna was furious. He was at Yakub's place and they had just got news that Kamran had managed to escape. Farookh was worried too.

'You have no idea how big a fuck-up this is.'

'Don't worry, Munna. He will be hunted down. My guy tells me that the entire police department has been instructed to shoot him down the moment they spot him. No questions asked. There is *nakabandi* everywhere. Railway stations, airports, national highways, all exits have the police looking for this guy.'

'You don't know Kamran, do you?'

'I don't want to.'

'And how did your boys fuck up, Farookh bhai? They killed the poor woman instead.'

'They shot at the cop but apparently she got in the way.'

'You guys are one piece of work.'

'You are fucking overreacting, Munna.'

'Yakub bhai, I really hope so. Because you have no fucking clue what Kamran did to Ruslaan.'

'Who the fuck is Ruslaan now?'

Munna shook his head and for a fleeting moment regretted joining hands with these guys.

When Hussain bhai reached Sahar international airport, he dejectedly saw that the place was teeming with cops. As they got out of the car, he hugged Kamran.

'Khuda hafiz, Kamran.'

'Khuda hafiz and thanks, Hussain bhai.'

Hussain bhai left. Kamran fetched a trolley. He was carrying a big suitcase and Sonia a handbag. They entered the airport and crossed the first barrier without any problem. Once inside, Kamran's stomach started fluttering. There were cops everywhere.

They proceeded towards the airline counter trying to look nonchalant. But every single moment felt like an eternity. At the counter, they presented their tickets and passports and the lady behind it started going through them industriously.

Kamran looked around and smiled at Mrs Ali in the burqa. They made small talk while the airline representative scanned everything and stamped their tickets. Kamran checked in his luggage. The representative then thanked them for being patient and returned their tickets and papers.

Kamran and Sonia had crossed the second barrier.

They headed towards the immigration check.

It was Sonia's first flight ever and she was thankful that she was in a burqa because she was so obviously in awe and bewilderment that they would have been caught the moment they entered the airport.

Kamran reached the immigration check and froze.

Right in front were members of Mirza's gang standing with the Mumbai Police. They were scanning each and every face going through.

Kamran chose not to tell Sonia about this. They got in the queue and got chatting.

They kept smiling through their conversation, though it was anything but cheerful.

'I had warned you against this.'

'But I like this. I just like that I am here next to you.'

'You are the dumbest thing that I have ever seen in my life.'

'Hussain bhai, by the way, was complimenting you on this smart move of having me alongside you.'

'You are not nervous?'

'I am more happy.'

Kamran let Sonia go ahead of him. While the immigration officer checked her passport and visa, Kamran kept looking straight at her, just like an extremely concerned husband would. Not more than four feet away stood Mushtaq bhai, the cabbie that had dropped Mirza Azmat at Mahim dargah that morning.

Mushtaq bhai had been inconsolable. He was the last one to see Mirza alive from their mohalla and was regretting not waiting for him to return. Mushtaq bhai obviously didn't know that it wouldn't have made a difference.

Mushtaq bhai recognized Kamran the moment he laid his eyes on him. There was word that Kamran had killed Mirza Azmat but Mushtaq knew that this was not true. Mushtaq knew Kamran very well. After all, he was the one who had given Kamran his new name. Mushtaq looked at Kamran for a brief moment and then let his eyes drift to another face in the crowd. The cop who was following his gaze was confused for a moment, but decided not to question the matter, since Mushtaq hadn't had a strong reaction.

Sonia walked through and it was now Kamran's turn. He went and gave his passport to the officer. After a moment of review, the officer stamped it and handed it back to him. As Kamran walked through, his eyes met Mushtaq's.

Mushtaq saw Kamran's innocence in his eyes and refused to
identify Kamran. Kamran walked through.

When the flight to Dubai took off, Kamran looked at the
coastline and wondered when he would be back.

Kamran believed that he had some seriously unfinished
business left in Mumbai.

28

Present Day

Another person who had stayed glued to the television set since morning was Chintu. Though Chintu, the kid from Haji Ali, was now a grown man, his name had stuck. A lot had happened to him since the day Kamran had slapped him at his office. Chintu's lukewarm desire to join the underworld had transformed into a full-fledged mission that day.

He had started looking for small jobs. He had age on his side and Mumbai never disappoints you if you are tenacious. Chintu started as a runner but soon got a gun in his hand. And with the gun came some more confidence.

Chintu soon became a *dhamki*, or warning. That is, if you needed to warn someone and not kill them, the likes of Chintu would do it for you. They would ring the warning shot— literally. They were the most important cogs in the extortion machinery.

The most important phase in Chintu's life came in 2009. He had graduated to become a hitman and his first hit was the notorious corporator Shivam Shukla, in Kurla. It was a *dahi handi* event on the occasion of Krishna Janamashtami and the corporator was the one who had organized it. A group of Govinda players entered the compound.

Chintu had entered with the team and the crowd. The formation of the pyramid started. Shivam Shukla was sitting on the dais with some guests. People were throwing water on the pyramid and cheering the effort. Music was blaring out of the big speakers. Everything was religiously chaotic.

He had sneaked behind the dais which was completely empty. A thin white cloth served as a backdrop of the dais and that was the only thing that separated Chintu from the corporator.

Chintu saw Shukla from behind the sheet, but couldn't shoot because the corporator's chair might just save him. Chintu knew that the first kill was always very important. It would be the basis of his reputation. He knew that he had to be patient. After all, he had chosen the best team.

But the team didn't know they had been chosen. They went about the pyramid formation; after many slip-ups and near failures they closed in on the gap.

One more guy.

Chintu got ready.

Corporator Shivam Shukla was excited.

A man reached the top of the pyramid and slipped slightly. There was a collective gasp that cut through the loud music. The man regained his footing and got up. At last he stood and became the top of the pyramid.

Corporator Shivam Shukla also got up in excitement and gave Chintu the opportunity he was waiting for. Chintu shot him four times in the neck and the head and vanished before the corporator hit the ground.

Chintu had chosen the right team indeed. The case was given to an officer who was on the verge of getting suspended because of erratic behaviour, corruption and alcoholism. Avinash Sharma. Still very sharp in spite of these minor vices, he investigated the case and tracked Chintu down and was about to arrest him when his suspension was invoked.

Avinash called Chintu at the Adarsh bar in Andheri West to have a chat.

'I know you killed that Shivam fellow.'

'Sorry, sir.'

'Sorry for what, you motherfucker? For killing him or for the fact that I know?'

'I do not have any clue what you are talking about, sir.'

'You know Talreja? The guy who gave you the money to bump off the corporator.'

Chintu knew he was finished and looked down at the floor.

'I don't want to arrest you.'

Chintu looked up.

'I was suspended today and I am not putting anything on you. Say thank you.'

'Thank you, sir.'

'Good. But I will need you to do things for me. Does that suit you?'

'Yes, sir.'

'Good. Finish the drink and scoot.'

Chintu gulped down the drink and got up and left. Avinash celebrated his suspension till the wee hours of the morning. He remembered each and everyone from his past and regretted that he hadn't shot Kamran dead at La Chapelle. Kamran got extradited but the very law that Avinash had so much faith in became the preferred tool to defer his punishment.

The day Kamran managed to choose the resort prison Taloja, Avinash gave up on the law and the uniform and began to wait patiently for his turn.

And, finally, it had come.

Avinash Sharma parked his bike and walked into the building called Shraddha Niwas in Prabhadevi. He climbed to the first floor and rang the bell. A moment later, Chintu opened the door. Avinash walked inside the room and looked around. The flat was sparse and the TV was on. Newscasters were talking about Kamran and the moment Avinash saw his picture his anger returned.

'You spoke to Bhonsle?'

'Yes, sir. He delivered the package himself.'

Chintu pointed to an open brown parcel lying on top of a table.

'You got what you wanted?'

'Yes, sir.'

'It's got to be done today.'

'Sure.'

'You do this and then you will never ever hear from me.'

'Okay.'

Avinash was so excited that he forgot the most crucial detail in the entire exchange and Chintu had to ultimately ask, 'Who are we talking about, sir?'

Avinash looked at him and realized the lapse. He turned to the TV screen and pointed to it.

'Kamran Ali Khan.'

Chintu could not believe it.

'You mean Danger bhai?'

'Or Ghalib Danger or whatever the fuck he is called.'

Chintu stood there quietly.

'Any issues?'

'No, sir.'

'You should be leaving for the sessions court then.'

Avinash walked out of the flat. Chintu shut the door behind him and sat on a chair.

After a few dead minutes he suddenly started clapping and laughing maniacally. The design and tapestry was amazing. Kamran and Chintu bumping into each other at the Haji Ali Dargah years ago.

He was the kid who used to serve tea to Kamran.

He was the boy who wanted to join Kamran bhai's gang.

He was the one who was slapped by Kamran, who was humiliated and shown the door.

Now he was the one that was chosen to eliminate Kamran.

This was a godsend. All the hard work that he had put into his career had led him to this.

Chintu got up and started getting ready.

Sewri Sessions Court, Mumbai

'Sir! It's time.'

Kamran snapped back into the present. It was Vidya Rai's assistant. He got up and walked out of the waiting room. The media downstairs woke up again. He turned briefly to the cameras.

Kamran smiled, sending a coded warning to the people who were following him on television.

Farookh Khitkhit in Mumbai skipped a beat and stopped swinging.

Yakub Mental in Dubai lit a cigarette and inhaled deeply.

At the entrance of the courtroom, Kamran was seriously frisked by the security. Kamran entered the courtroom and walked over to his seat. Over the years, Vidya Rai had taught Kamran how to conduct himself in the courtroom. How to sit, when to stand, how and when to speak. Vidya had tutored Kamran and Kamran had made her proud by being an attentive student.

The judge was yet to arrive. Kamran's gaze wandered lazily over the pile of papers and photos spread on Vidya's table. A photograph of Sonia peeped at him from the clutter. Vidya caught Kamran looking pensive.

'Nervous?'

Kamran smiled.

'Extremely. Vidyaji, you never told me about my chances today?'

'Why leave the jail? What are you going to do if you get free?'

'Arre, what are you saying? There is a tonne of work I have got to settle.'

'Try not to return immediately.'

'Will try.'

'Why did Sonia betray you, Kamran?'

Kamran sighed deeply. In all these years Vidya had never asked Kamran this question. That she was asking it today was a great tell. He was going to be a free man today in her opinion and curiosity had got the better of her.

'That is precisely what I want to know and once I know I will give you a call and let you know.'

'I know that you have tried to track her and have failed, Kamran.'

'Failed so far, Vidyaji. Things change.'

Judge Balwant Mehra entered the room and everyone stood up. Kamran stood up but his mind was clearly drifting to another place. The judge asked everyone to sit. The case was announced and the judge started reading the allegations, charges and the cases against Kamran.

'Please wake me up when it gets to the verdict part.'

'Sssssshhh!'

Kamran's mind went back in time for an answer to the question that Vidya had asked a little while earlier. Kamran had seen her barely a few times after his arrest and that too only during the trials in France. She had never visited him in jail either there or here. Sonia had traded his arrest for her freedom and had testified in court against him. That hurt Kamran the most.

Kamran tried to track Sonia after his extradition but she had just vanished. There was no news of her anywhere. Kamran tried tracking her all the way to Jamshedpur but she had simply left no trace. Sonia was just off the radar. Kamran had unknowingly taught her too well.

While in jail there was not one single day that Kamran had not thought about why Sonia gave up on him. It baffled him. She had risked her own life for him when they were on the run. Kamran's mind went back to the day they landed in Dubai.

Rizwan was there to receive them. By the time they reached their new residence in Bur Dubai, it was late at night. It was a nice two-bedroom apartment facing Deira. Hussain bhai had taken care of everything at short notice in a very impressive way.

Rizwan gave them a small tour and explained what needed to be explained in terms of the driver, servants and other services. Rizwan also gave Kamran a new cell phone. Kamran handed him the torn thousand-rupee note.

'Bhai, I will be here tomorrow morning at eleven. If there is anything that you need then I am available on phone all the time. My number is saved there on your phone. *Tesbah ala kheir.*'

'*Shabba khair.*'

Kamran and Sonia were finally left alone with no clue of how the future would pan out but they were too drained to think about it and just collapsed. Life on the run had just begun for Kamran.

The next morning, Rizwan was there exactly at eleven. Kamran sat with him alone in the drawing room.

'Bhai, it's not going to be safe here for you in the long run. Hussain bhai also feels that sooner or later they will try again to take you out. The Mumbai Police believes that you are the one who ordered the hit on Avinash's wife. She is dead, bhai. The cop is still in the ICU. They have launched a manhunt for you. Furthermore, Munna has taken over completely. After Chote's death, a few more guys from your village were hunted down. They have clearly thought this one through, bhai.'

Kamran agreed that they had.

'How many people know that I am here?'

'Just me. The staff here thinks that you are my elder brother from Hyderabad in India. You are on a holiday here for a few weeks with your wife. But it will be very difficult to keep it this way for long.'

'What do you suggest, Rizwan?'

'Europe. Bhaijaan, you have to live to fight another day.'

They kept on chatting and Kamran began to realize that there were very few options left for him.

Sonia woke up in the morning to see Kamran missing. She rushed to the drawing room to find him staring at construction sites on the barren desert land. Dubai was becoming a popular business destination and buildings were coming up in full swing. Sonia came and hugged Kamran from behind and kissed him on his arm.

'I will have to go, Sonia.'

'We will have to go.'

'I have to be on the run. It's going to be very difficult.'

'We will have to be on the run. It will be very easy.'

Sonia's grip tightened on Kamran's arms. Kamran could make out that her voice was about to break.

'You have your brother and your sister. You have a responsibility, Sonia.'

'You have one too. You know that I love you.'

'Same here but I . . .'

Kamran stopped, realizing that he had just confessed. Sonia looked at him in surprise. Kamran looked back at her.

Hell!
They spent that day and night completely secure in that feeling.

> *Mat pooch ke kya haal hai mera tere peeche?*
> *Tu dekh ke kya rang tera mere aage*

> *Sach kahte ho, khudbeen-o-khudaaraa na kyon hoon?*
> *Baitha hai but-e-aainaaseemaa mere aage*

> *Phir dekhiye andaaz-e-gulafshaani-e-guftaar*
> *Rakh de koi paimaanaa-o-sahba mere aage!*

29

'Sonia, I will ask you one last time. Are you sure about this?'

'More than anything else.'

'I hope you don't regret this.'

'I am sure I won't regret this.'

Kamran knew this wouldn't go any other way. A part of him actually didn't want it to go any other way. A big part of him, that is. Kamran hugged Sonia. The first rays of the morning sun peeped out from behind the clouds.

It was a good morning.

After breakfast Kamran asked the driver to take out the car. He put his and Sonia's papers in a brown envelope and sealed it. He then put on the get-up that had helped him escape from India. On the way out, Kamran asked Sonia to stay in the house, telling her that he would be back by the evening.

Kamran went downstairs and sat in his car, a black Mercedes. He was on his way to the Gold Souk where Rizwan was already waiting. Kamran got out of his car and they walked into a gold shop. The people there wished Rizwan and him with the knowledge of his fake identity.

On the way towards the cabin Rizwan confided in Kamran.

'Inside is Aziz bhai. He knows you by the name on your passport and is going to help you with everything. I will wait outside for you.'

'You can come inside, Rizwan. No issues.'

'Bhaijaan, the less I know the better it is.'

Rizwan opened the door.

'Aziz bhai, this is Ibrahim bhai. Please let me know if you people need anything.'

Rizwan shut the door from outside.

The two men inside the cabin greeted each other and sat down. Aziz was there as a consultant. For the next hour or so the men talked about which would be the safest place for Kamran to relocate to.

Kamran decided upon France. Aziz smiled. It was a good choice because it would be easy for Kamran to lose himself in the crowd there.

'When would you like to leave?'

'How fast can you make me leave?'

'It will take me a minimum of five days.'

'Great. Here are our passports and papers.'

'Okay. Ibrahim bhai, let me run you through our services again. I will arrange for your visa and all the other relevant documents. I will make sure that you and your wife are received at the airport and taken to a safe place.'

'That will do.'

'I will keep Rizwan updated. Salaam.'

Aziz got up and left. Rizwan came into the cabin.

'Bhaijaan, all well?'

'All well.'

'You need something?'

'I need to make a call to India.'

'Of course. I will make sure nobody disturbs you.'

Aziz had barely stepped out of the shop when his cell phone rang. He looked at the display and received the call hurriedly. It was from India.

'Salaam alaikum, Yakub bhai.'

'Wa'alaikum salaam, Aziz. How are you?'

'All dried up, Yakub bhai. Just got my first couple of clients in months today. Business is bad, Yakub bhai.'

'Listen, there is this fucking situation that has come up.'

'Tell me, bhai.'

'Mirza's boy, that . . . Kamran . . . Danger . . . whatever is absconding. There is word that he might have or will eventually fucking run off to Dubai. I want you and your boys to keep your fucking eyes and ears open. I want any information on this bastard.'

'Sure, bhai.'

'Great.'

'Can I ask a question, bhai?'

'Ask.'

'Who got Mirza, Yakub bhai?'

'Who the fuck do you think had the balls?'

'I knew it was you, Yakub bhai. What a score . . . Mashallah . . . What a great score!'

Kamran was waiting for the phone to be answered on the other end. After a long series of rings a lady picked up the phone.

'Hello!'

'Hello. I would like to speak to MLA Pramukh Joshi.'

'He is in a meeting. Who is this?'

'That's not important. Go into the meeting and tell him that someone called regarding an amazing holiday offer to Bangkok this Christmas for him and his family. I will call him again in exactly ten minutes and I expect him to take the call or I will have to pass on the same offer to the chief minister.'

Kamran disconnected the phone.

Pramukh Joshi was discussing development policies for women in rural parts with a delegation when his secretary barged into the room and put a slip of paper in front of him. It had the following bullet points:

- *A man called wanting to speak to you.*
- *It's regarding a Bangkok Christmas holiday package.*
- *If not interested he said he will pass on the offer to CM.*
- *Will call back in 10 mins.*

Joshi glanced at the chit and suddenly felt depleted.

He addressed the head of the delegation: 'Shantiji, I have always looked at women as equals. Why equal? I think they are superior. I will have a look at your demands and make sure that they are all met by Christmas this year.'

'Sir . . . why . . . Christmas, sir?'

'I meant Diwali.'

'Thank you, sir.'

Joshi then got rid of the delegation. He personally saw them off to the lift. He then shut the door and ran to his desk, glancing at the chit again and hoping that maybe the words would have changed but of course they hadn't. They were still the same four very threatening lines.

Joshi dialled his receptionist.

'Transfer the call when he calls next.'

'Yes, sir.'

Joshi started perspiring. All the obvious questions started popping into his head but he had no answers.

Kamran delayed his call deliberately by another five minutes or so. It was just to break the MLA down a bit more. MLA Joshi had to suffer five more agonizing minutes before the phone rang again.

'Sir, it's him.'

'Put him through.'

'Hello, Joshi saab?'

'Speaking.'

'Sir, this is regarding the Bangkok Christmas holiday package offer.'

'What about it?'

'It's an amazing offer. You get to play Santa Claus again, sir.'

'Who . . . who . . . are you?'

'Sir, I wanted to come personally and meet you but due to certain unavoidable circumstances I will have to ask you to come to Dubai.'

'Dubai?'

'Yes. I have a video presentation that I would like you to see here to get an idea of the holiday offer. I will see you the day after tomorrow in Dubai. You will be travelling alone, sir. We will have dinner together and you can go back the next day. Now if you will kindly give me your cell phone number I will text you your hotel and pick-up details, etc.'

'But I won't be able to make it day after.'

'Trust me, sir. You can and you will. The number, sir?'

MLA Pramukh Joshi gave Kamran his cell phone number.

'I will call you tomorrow, sir, and take down the flight details. Have a good day, Joshi saab.'

Kamran hung up. Joshi felt shockingly helpless. The person who had organized his secret tryst to Bangkok, P.A. Sharma, had died in a road accident a few months back. Sharma had taken a lot of secrets with him so how did this one get left behind?

Was the dead P.A. Sharma behind this?

MLA Joshi cancelled all his meetings and spent the whole day wondering how to solve this situation. He couldn't come up with anything and couldn't afford to share his problem with anyone either. He had no option but to call his receptionist and arrange for a ticket to Dubai for the day after the next.

Kamran called him again the next day and exchanged pick-up and hotel details in lieu of Joshi's flight details. It all went very smoothly. Joshi landed in Dubai and Rizwan was there to receive him. They didn't speak one word on the way to the hotel. MLA Pramukh Joshi was booked in the Ocean Superior King at the Jumeirah Beach Hotel.

Kamran, as always, understood what service was. A good service was also a gentle reminder of your clout. Joshi was promptly checked in without any fuss.

Inside his beautiful sea-facing room Joshi saw a gift-wrapped envelope kept on the bed. He tore open the envelope and found a VHS and a note.

The note said: *Marhaba Joshi saab! I will see you in the evening for drinks and dinner. Till then you can rest or enjoy this movie. Regards.*

Joshi took the VHS and rushed to the player and TV. He put it inside and then saw himself playing Santa Claus in a movie that he had not known he was the star of.

Joshi kept forwarding the tape. It looked funnier and was more embarrassing in the fast-forward mode.

Kamran was getting ready for dinner when Sonia walked in. She stood near the door. She could always sense Kamran's business mode.

'You will be late?'

'A bit. Don't wait for me. Have your dinner and go to bed.'

Sonia walked up to Kamran and started buttoning his shirt. She ran the back of her hand against his shirt and smiled.

'Keep calm.'

'I am always calm.'

'Take care.'

'See you.'

On the way to the Jumeirah Beach Hotel Kamran remembered what Mirza had once said to him.

Never rush into revenge.

Kamran couldn't help smiling. The evening was beginning to look very pleasant.

Kamran knocked on Joshi's room and waited. Pramukh Joshi opened the door after a while and was shocked. He knew the face. He knew what had lately transpired in the underworld. Kamran motioned for him to go in. He then closed the door behind him and walked into the room. Kamran shook Joshi's hand and introduced himself before sitting down on the sofa with the sea as the backdrop.

'Kamran Ali Khan.'

'I . . . know.'

'This will save a lot of time.'

MLA Joshi sat opposite him.

'Joshi, sorry to have troubled you but I am a little pressed for time and hence I had to call you over.'

'No problem.'

'Did you manage to see the film?'

'Y . . . Yes.'

'I would like you to do something for me, Joshi. I don't need your money or anything. I just need your good offices.'

'I don't understand.'

'I want you to wipe out Farookh Khitkhit and Yakub Mental. I want you to take special care of Munna. Not kill them but kill their businesses. You are tipped to become the next home minister, Joshi. I want the police force and the law to strip them of all power and all reputation. I want them in a certain state, Joshi, and I want you to be my proxy.'

Joshi was surprised. This was not what he had expected.

'You don't want anything else?'

Kamran smiled. Some people just don't know when to stop. But that day Kamran let go.

'That's it, Joshi. That's it.'

'Oh.'

'Let's have dinner. Would you like to go to a really nice happening place or have room service?'

'I prefer room service.'

'Thought so.'

'Can I ask who gave you the tape, please?'

'Of course, you can.'

Joshi kept waiting for the next two minutes and then finally understood the real meaning of Kamran's answer.

Kamran and Joshi then talked about potential business associations and investments. They identified areas like cricket, real estate and Bollywood to be of particular interest. Kamran already had a footprint in these areas. Joshi just had to be his eyes and ears.

Kamran told Joshi that it was beneficial to be more involved with the cricket association in the state. That was going to be the future. The more they talked, the more Joshi got convinced that Kamran was not just a blackmailer but also that he was the future.

Joshi left for India a happy man the next day.

After a couple of days, true to his word, Aziz arranged all the documents and both the passports. He met Ibrahim bhai at the Gold Souk shop, cocky about having delivered at such short notice.

'Ibrahim bhai, no one—I repeat—no one can deliver at this speed. There is no . . .'

'Please see Rizwan on the way out.'

'Thank you, bhai.'

Aziz stepped out of the cabin and Rizwan gave him an envelope.

'All in there?'

'Plus a hundred. Ibrahim bhai likes you.'

'Thanks.'

As Aziz stepped out of the shop his cell phone rang. It was Yakub Mental from India.

'Salaam alaikum, bhai.'

'Wa'alaikum salaam, Aziz. Any news on the fucker?'

'No, bhai. I asked everyone everywhere but I am sure he has not landed in Dubai, bhai. I have put a prize out for him as well.'

'Okay. Let me know if you hear something.'

'Sure, bhai.'

The next day Mr Ibrahim Ali and his wife boarded an Emirates flight to Paris. A few hours later, Sonia looked at Kamran. She saw him sleeping peacefully for the first time since they had been on the run.

30

It was the start of the new century and Kamran and Sonia were surprised with the amount and nature of predictions regarding the impending Armageddon that were circulating. They were in a First World country and still there were people worried about the world coming to an end on the midnight of 31 December 1999.

There were more than two hundred prophecies about how the world would come to an end because of a date change.

They had been in La Chapelle, Paris, France, for the last few months and Jacques, their contact through Hussain bhai, had been most helpful. They were temporarily holed up in a one-bedroom apartment and Kamran was spending most of his time keeping a tab on what was going on and looking out for good opportunities.

Money was not an issue. At least for the time being. Kamran had liquidated all his assets through Hussain bhai and Hussain bhai had over time slowly routed all the money through hawala to Kamran.

Munna, Yakub and Farookh took over the city. All underworld activities in the city were distributed between the three and their factions. Kamran was completely out of the game. He was just busy collecting what he had left back home. The only person he kept in touch with was MLA Pramukh Joshi. They still talked regularly and Kamran kept suggesting and advising him on certain non-political agendas.

There were rumours that Kamran was dead. There were rumours that he was alive. There were also rumours that he was scared and in hiding. The last one being propounded generously by the notorious trio of Farookh, Yakub and Munna.

On the personal front Kamran was at peace. He was enjoying his anonymity. For the first time he looked forward to going home in the evenings. Kamran and Sonia started spending more and more time together. Kamran started learning French.

Sonia wanted to get married but never spoke about this with Kamran. He was well aware of her wish, but also chose never to speak about it.

Kamran had given Hussain bhai a list of things to do, the most important of which was to keep sending money to his mother in Qasimgarh. She was getting older and he wondered when he would get to see her. Police had landed up at his village when Kamran was on the run. Everyone had got to know what he was accused of but no one had believed it. Also, the fact that in the past he had donated generously towards the development of his village helped maintain his good reputation. Kamran remembered an observation from his past.

Money can buy happiness. It can buy smiles. Can make you forget pain. Those who say it can't can go fuck themselves. Money is not a bad thing in itself.

When Ruslaan's mother died, Hussain bhai arranged for everything on Kamran's behalf. Finally, that chapter had ended and Kamran was relieved on some level. Hussain bhai would also keep a tab over Hamid and his family. Miracles still took place in that house whenever crisis struck. Like when a miraculous loan enabled Hamid to buy his own taxi after he had lost his job. It was these small clues that reassured Hamid of Kamran's safety. Not only was Kamran well and fine but he was also biding his time. He knew the kid well. Kamran had never liked unfinished business.

Avinash Sharma kept chasing him. He knew that Kamran was not dead. The loss of his wife, Preeti, and his unborn child had spurred Avinash to the only mission in his life. Kamran had to be caught and the law had to punish him in a way that would be a lesson for all criminals. Avinash kept hunting for Kamran doggedly.

Kamran and Sonia travelled all over the world, especially Europe and the United States of America. Kamran had never known that the world was so big and that there was so much to see. Sonia taught him a lot about gadgets during the time. For a man who hadn't known anything about technology apart from cell phones, he now knew a lot about the big bad world of the World Wide Web.

Kamran couldn't believe it. He was surprised by the amount of information that was there on him on the Internet, including a red corner notice from Interpol. It was around this time that Kamran got the VHS tape digitized. Joshi's Santa adventure was now stored in two small pen drives. The VHS tapes were destroyed and the pen drives were securely stored in the locker of a Swiss bank.

Three quiet years passed. Kamran bought a couple of shops and a small restaurant in and around La Chapelle. There was a strong Asian presence here and after a slow start, his business started doing quite well. Back in Mumbai, the election results were announced. As expected, Joshi got the home ministry. Kamran had waited for his phone call. It came on the first day of his office itself. He had waited a long time for this day.

'Congrats, Joshi.'

'Thanks. Just wanted to let you know that I have not forgotten.'

'Appreciate that. It's about time.'

It was time that Kamran Ali Khan aka Ghalib Danger got back in the game.

There was another piece of good news that day. Sonia had finally found a place that she liked, a three-bedroom apartment on the top floor of a four-storeyed apartment on Rue de Cail in La Chapelle. Kamran saw the place the next day and fell in love with it too. It was going to be their home now.

One week after he assumed office, Home Minister Pramukh Joshi called a high-level meeting of the top brass of the Mumbai Police. In that meeting the respected home minister of the state gave them a clear-cut directive. Finish Farookh Khitkhit, Yakub Mental and this new chap Munna. The respected home minister also said that he wanted immediate results because the image of the state had been terribly compromised.

The eight men representing the top brass of the Mumbai Police walked out of the meeting acknowledging the fact that finally there was political will on display by such an honest politician. They, of course, didn't know that Santa Claus had a small role to play here.

For the next few months, encounters, arrests, raids became the order of the day and Farookh Khitkhit, Yakub Mental and Munna started feeling the wrath of the law. The law, when it chooses to, can be a real pain for those who think they are above it. The city started becoming safer. The swift crackdown on Yakub, Farookh and Munna started breeding hushed rumours.

Kamran Khan is alive.

The files compiled by Avinash Sharma on Farookh Khitkhit and Yakub Mental were reopened. After a period of time, Farookh and Yakub started getting toothless. Farookh decided to pass on his legacy to his son Majnu Miyan.

A few months later, in the winter of 2006, Majnu Miyan was shot dead in an encounter. Kamran had insisted on Joshi getting Majnu killed in broad daylight. It was Kamran's signature. The whispers became a little louder. Avinash smelled blood.

Farookh was distraught and decided to shut shop. He collected all his resources and put them in his line of defence. Soon he was an invalid don who could not leave the country because his passport had been seized and because he had more than twenty-odd cases pending in his name. He still lived in his stronghold, the Heera chawl area, and seldom ventured out.

Yakub's story was no different. Joshi's ultimatum to the Mumbai Police affected him the most. His dance bars had been completely shut down by the police. He kept getting summoned to court because of the various cases registered against him, as a result of which his other businesses got badly dented. After what had happened to Farookh, Yakub was forced to reconsider his situation and he sneaked out of the country in early 2007.

That left Munna completely powerless. Kamran detested Munna the most and had asked Joshi to take special care of him. Munna was repeatedly arrested and hurt during the next few months. The police were instructed to keep him on a very tight leash.

Kamran was just starting to get closer to his goal when Home Minister Joshi committed a blunder. A series of bomb blasts had rocked the central part of Mumbai and while speculation was on with no outfit claiming responsibility, Home Minister Joshi uttered the 'M' word and the 'I' word in a live press interview.

The opposition bayed for his blood and Joshi had to resign the next day.

Kamran was suddenly back to square one.

Pramukh Joshi remained his ally, however. He would help Kamran once again later in life. Actually, more than help. Joshi would be the one to ensure that Kamran was sent to Taloja and that he had the best of amenities there during the tenure of his stay.

But that would be after Kamran's arrest.

Avinash's efforts finally paid off. There was a number in La Chapelle, Paris, that used to call certain numbers in Mumbai on a regular basis. Amongst the numbers called in Mumbai was the number of the former home minister, Pramukh Joshi. Further investigations revealed that it was an Ibrahim Ali who had shifted to France about seven years back, just around the time Kamran Ali Khan had gone missing.

The law machinery started to move and Avinash with a team of officers from the CBI left for France after a month of intense red tape.

Avinash and his team of four CBI officers finally spotted them one day. Kamran and Sonia had stepped out of the VT Cash and Carry, Kamran holding a brown paper bag and Sonia with her hand wrapped around Kamran's. They didn't know that across the road and from inside the diner Avinash Sharma and his team were watching them intently.

'That's Kamran.'

'Are you sure?'

'You have a mother?'

'Yes.'

'Are you sure?'

The CBI officer had heard that Avinash was a jerk. Now he knew that absolutely, for sure.

They kept watching him for the next few days. Avinash, however, had something more painful in mind for Kamran.

Avinash went after Sonia.

A few nights later, when Kamran returned to his flat he found it unusually quiet. He went inside and kept his stuff and then heard Sonia's voice from the kitchen. She was talking animatedly to someone over the phone. Kamran sneaked upon her and then hugged her from behind. Sonia was rattled. She gave him a nervous smile and then returned to the phone.

'Listen. I have to go. You take care. Bye.'

Sonia disconnected the phone.

'That was Anjali.'

'How is she?'

'Good. She says her classmates are going for an excursion. She wanted to know if she could go.'

'You look jumpy.'

'No . . . Not at all. What will you have?'

'What did you say?'

'To?'

'Anjali.'

'About?'

'The excursion that she wants to go for?'

'Oh! I said I will let her know by tomorrow.'

'A glass of red wine.'

'What?'

'You asked me what would I have.'

'Oh!'

'You sure you are okay?'

'Sure.'

Kamran knew at precisely that moment that all was not okay. Kamran was really good at spotting lies.

Kamran woke up in the middle of the night to find Sonia missing. He walked into the drawing room. Sonia wasn't there either. Kamran saw that the light was on in the study and was seeping through the shut door. He could hear Sonia whispering on the phone.

He walked towards the study. The wooden floor betrayed him on the third step. Kamran sensed that Sonia had gone silent. He quickly retreated to the bedroom and lay down on the bed. A few moments later Sonia came stealthily and lay beside him. She lay there for half an hour and then went out of the bedroom again.

Kamran couldn't get more sleep that night.

Early next morning, Kamran got ready earlier than usual. He was looking at Sonia's phone that was lying on the kitchen table. Sonia must have left it there after the last call. Kamran wanted to see the list of incoming and outgoing calls but refrained.

A moment later, he let out a sigh, smiled and mumbled:

> *Kahoon kis se main ki kya hai*
> *Shab-e-gham buri bala hai*
> *Mujhe kya bura tha marna*
> *Agar ek baar hota!*

Kamran heard footsteps. Sonia entered the kitchen and looked at him. She hugged him tightly.

'Hi. You are up early?'

'Good morning.'

'Good morning. Coffee?'

Kamran raised his cup. Sonia smiled and headed towards the coffee machine. Kamran scanned her for a telltale sign. He was very good at this. He watched her as she went about the business of making herself a cup of coffee—but nothing.

No tell. That's the tell. This is bad. Really bad. I am fucked.

'I will see you in the evening.'

'Can you drop these before you leave for the office?'

Sonia peeled a sticky note from the fridge and walked towards him. Kamran took the note and looked at it.

'You will get these at Pierre's.'

Kamran looked at her. She caught his look and worked on it like a wringer. He blinked. She came closer.

'You okay?'

'Yes.'

'Sure?'

'Is it going to rain today, Sonia?'

'Do you want it to rain?'

'No.'

'So it won't.'

Kamran smiled at her and then kissed her. It lasted a touch longer from his end than the regular everyday goodbye kiss.

Still no tell. This is going to be really, really bad.

When he got down on the street, Sonia was at the window waving at him. He waved back and continued walking. Paul, the florist, called out to him.

'Bonjour!'

'Bonjour!'

'Is it going to raining today, Kamran?'

'Of course, Paul. You can place your bet and give me my twenty.'

'But you never take it when I give it to you.'

'If I take your money then you will stop winning. That's how it works. You keep my share for now.'

Paul was an honest man and so he never quite understood what Kamran meant.

Pierre's was just around the corner. Kamran entered the store. He knew the layout inside out. There were five rows of branded consumerables lined up neatly one after another. And then, of course, there were the dairy and meat products kept in freezers lined in the inverted U. Kamran picked a basket and started on the list.

He was on the fourth item on the list when he realized that the pregnant woman in front of him in the second row was not just another customer. This was the third time Kamran had caught her looking at him. She had got her bump right but her walk wrong.

He scanned the store. These were faces that he had never seen there. It had never happened in his three years in La Chapelle. The cashier, Julia, was a little too engrossed in her magazine today. There was a man looking at a cookie pack diligently. Actually, a little too diligently. The couple in the next aisle looked at him in sync.

Kamran didn't waste another moment. He walked towards

the pregnant woman with a smile.

It's in her handbag.

'Bonjour!'

The woman was surprised.

'Bonjour!'

'Puis-je vous aider?'

'Merci.'

Kamran signalled at her bump and asked, 'Quand vous êtes dus?'

As the woman fumbled for an answer Kamran caught her by her neck and drew the gun out of her handbag. The woman screamed. The other 'customers' in the store could barely react before Kamran had his hostage fully secured. Everyone sprang into action.

It was Kamran's SP 2022 trained at the woman's temple against nine other SP 2022s trained straight at him. Amid all the screaming and threatening, Kamran started to slowly inch towards the exit using the woman as his shield. He had barely reached it when he heard the sirens closing in on him.

Eleven National Police cars of various makes converged at the scene as Kamran froze at the glass door. The cops alighted and took position. A flash blinded Kamran. He retreated for a moment and then glanced at the terrace of the building across the street. A couple of snipers had already taken their positions. He looked around and spotted a few more. He looked ahead and saw the cops training their guns at the exit. He looked behind him. The cops in the store had also taken their positions.

He looked at his hostage. She was crying and pleading.

Kamran tightened his grip around her and kicked at the door. A hinge came undone and the door spilled on to the street. The cops took a step back. He walked with his hostage right on to the middle of the street and looked around. A helicopter flew right over his head.

His hostage was still crying and pleading. Kamran smiled.

You should have had the stomach for it.

Kamran reached for the stuffing under her jacket.

She didn't have any. Kamran lost a step. She was actually pregnant.

His grip loosened. The woman was surprised. She looked at Kamran. The gun dropped from Kamran's hand. The woman took a step and then another and then started running towards the cops lined on the other side of the street.

Kamran could only register a cacophony of overlapped screams. Cops on the street as well as cops from inside the store were all training their guns at him and were asking him to kneel on the ground.

And through that pandemonium he filtered out someone shouting his name. He didn't respond. It came through again. He turned. Sonia was standing behind a police cordon and screaming his name.

Wow!

Sonia was crying and screaming for him and standing next to her was SI Avinash Sharma of the Mumbai Police.

Really!?! Am I fucked or what?

He didn't know exactly when he was floored and pinned down but, while they were handcuffing him, Kamran Khan started counting, out of a very old habit.

CBI
Interpol
Maharashtra Police, India
National Police, France
Eleven police cars
About thirty-five cops
Six snipers

He then saw a couple of police choppers arrive at the scene and assume position overhead. Kamran smiled.

Not bad! Not bad at all.

31

Present Day

'. . . ELIGIBLE FOR BAIL!'

Kamran caught on to the last three words. There was a collective sigh in the courtroom. Kamran kept looking at the judge and heard the conditions set for his bail. It didn't matter greatly to him because he would be out of the country by the evening but still he listened with singular intent.

There were a lot of conditions. Once the judge was through and gone, Kamran turned to Vidya and smiled.

'Thank you, Vidyaji.'

'God knows what's going to happen to this country. Go and wait in the waiting room. I will join you shortly.'

Kamran walked out of the courtroom, led by Vidya's assistant and accompanied by a couple of cops. As Kamran stepped into the corridor, the media screamed for attention. Kamran walked near a window and waved to the crowd downstairs. He also flashed the victory sign. Kamran then turned in a 180-degree panorama making sure that no camera missed him.

Kamran wanted everyone to register him. There was a particular reason why he was doing this.

Farookh Khitkhit was watching the news when it flashed:

KAMRAN KHAN'S BAIL APPROVED

They kept running these four words. On the second run Farookh's swing stopped and on the third run, his heart.

Farookh Khitkhit died without a Khitkhit. Just a flutter in his heart and a small gasp.

In Dubai, Yakub Mental smashed the remote on the table and broke both the glass top and the remote. Sultan, his right hand, got worried.

'Yakub bhai, now don't burst a vessel.'

'Fuck! They fucking released the motherfucker.'

'Relax, bhai.'

'Fuck man. Unbelievable.'

'Bhai, it's getting late for the meeting. It's a half an hour drive. Forget about this. Let's go.'

'Fuck!'

Yakub and Sultan left for their meeting.

Kamran walked into the waiting room and slumped into the chair.

Finally.

He looked at Vidya's assistant. The assistant passed him a cell phone and left. Kamran dialled a number. Hussain bhai was at the other end.

'Hi. It's me.'

'Yes. All okay?'

'Yes.'

'Shukar.'

'Where are you?'

'Very close.'

'Is he ready?'

'Yes.'

'Bring him in.'

'Sure. We will be there in five minutes.'

Kamran disconnected the phone and then sent a text on another number.

'Are you ready? ARE YOU READY?'

Kamran waited. His phone beeped after a moment.

'YES, BHAI.'

Dubai was more than scorching hot that day. Yakub and Sultan were in the rear seat of the Hummer going for their meeting. The Hummer was doing a nice ninety on Sheikh Rashid road. Yakub Mental still couldn't believe that Kamran was out on bail.

'That fucking country I swear has gone to the dogs. Now the fucker will run. I am telling you the fucker will run, Sultan. That motherfucker . . .'

Sultan's phone rang. He looked at the display and took the call.

'Yes, bhai. One sec . . . Yakub bhai, your call.'

Sultan stretched the phone to Yakub Mental. A curious Yakub took the call.

'Hello.'

'Yakub Mental. This is Ghalib Danger this side.'

Yakub knew that it was the voice of death. He looked at Sultan. Sultan had taken out his gun and was pointing at Yakub.

'I . . . am . . . sorry, Danger bhai.'

'No, you are not but you will be when the first car runs over you.'

'What car?'

Sultan was waiting for these two words. He opened Yakub's side of the door in a flash and kicked Yakub with huge force. Yakub was thrown out of the moving car and by the time he stopped spiralling a Mercedes couldn't help running over him.

Kamran heard a few sounds and then disconnected. A few moments later he got another text. It was from Sultan's second phone and it read—*Gone*.

Kamran took a deep breath. His promise to Murli Highway had been honoured and how. Yakub was kicked to his death.

Kamran just had a few hours in hand and there was stuff to do.

Chintu's cell rang. He looked at the display. It was Avinash.

'He is a free man.'

Avinash disconnected the phone. Chintu was standing in the crowd outside the court. He quickly moved towards the exit and strategically positioned himself.

Hussain bhai reached with a group of people. They stood at the door and only Hussain bhai entered the room carrying a packet. Kamran got up and they both hugged each other. Hussain bhai had stayed in touch with Kamran even through the Taloja days but they were meeting after a very long time.

'Farookh Khitkhit is gone.'

Kamran was surprised.

'Was it me?

'In a way. He died watching the breaking news of your bail approval.'

Kamran shook his head.

'Khitkhit always had a weak heart, Hussain bhai.'

'That he had.'

'Is my bag ready?'

'It's waiting. We will check it out on the way to the airport.'

'Where is the guy?'

Hussain Bhai motioned at the crowd that had accompanied

him. A man who would easily pass off as a double for Kamran came forward and joined them.

'He will do?'

'He will do.'

'Do we have someone in the crowd outside, Hussain bhai?'

'About twenty of them.'

'Let's do it.'

Hussain bhai motioned for the boys to cover the door. Kamran started taking off his clothes. Hussain bhai gave him a packet that contained his new clothes. The 'double' quickly started wearing what Kamran took off. A minute later, Kamran was wearing a black T-shirt and light brown denims with white sneakers. The other man had already changed to whatever Kamran had been wearing earlier.

Someone from the crowd passed a pair of shades and a cap to the double. As soon as he put them on Kamran saw Hussain bhai's point.

Of course he would do.

Hussain bhai asked one of the boys to collect the clothes that were lying on the floor.

'Kamran, we will move now. You will finish here and then join me at the back of this building.'

'Ji.'

Hussain bhai hugged him again and the crowd moved out of the room. The double was in the centre and the small crowd was walking alongside. They were about to reach the exit when someone from the crowd drew the attention of the entire press towards the group screaming Kamran's name. Nineteen more people screamed and did the same.

These twenty people were planted by Hussain bhai according to Kamran's plan. A huge commotion ensued and Chintu, who was about to take out his gun and shoot, was nearly trampled by the overenthusiastic media. They just wanted a sound bite and a photo of the free Kamran.

The double was escorted to a parked van, which sped off in a matter of seconds.

A flabbergasted Chintu ran towards his bike, which was standing in the parking lot. He started it and hurried in pursuit of the van.

Vidya entered the room and was surprised.

'You changed?'

'Yes. New look. What do you say?'

'Sign these.'

Her attendant laid down a bunch of papers and Kamran went on a signing spree.

'Read it before you sign.'

'I am in a hurry.'

Kamran finished signing and then looked Vidya in the eye.

'Thanks so much, Vidyaji. If there is anything ever where I can be of any use to you then kindly let me know.'

'I hope that day doesn't come, Kamran.'

'I hope so too, Vidyaji, but life, as I have learnt, is a funny little business.'

'That it is. There is someone who wants to meet you.'

'Who?'

It was Vidya's turn to tease.

'Tell me once you know it.'

Kamran look surprised.

'Wait here.'

Vidya went away. A few moments later, a figure came and stood at the door. Kamran didn't have to look up. He knew who it was. Kamran started to smile and finally looked at Sonia.

Sonia was standing there in a blue salwar-kurta and Kamran immediately wished he had a gun on him. Sonia walked up to him and hugged him slowly. Her breathing got heavier and

Kamran tried to be as unaffected as possible, which was asking for too much considering the circumstances.

Kamran counted. It was six years on one hand. But, on the other, just like yesterday.

Kamran took her face in his hands. Sonia had tears in her eyes. Kamran's voice broke too.

'Why?'

Sonia started crying. Kamran held her tightly and whispered, 'Why?'

Sonia calmed herself and then started.

'A day before your arrest I had an appointment with my doctor . . .'

'Isabelle.'

'Yes. Dr Isabelle. I went to her and she confirmed to me that I was pregnant. I was overjoyed. I didn't have any clue as to how you would react but I was really excited. I wanted to tell you personally and I rushed out of the hospital when I heard my name called out.'

Six Years Earlier, La Chapelle, Paris, France

'Sonia!'

Sonia stopped and turned to find an Indian man facing her. He came up and introduced himself.

'Avinash Sharma. Mumbai Police.'

Sonia felt the ground give way. Avinash held her by the elbow.

'We need to sit and chat. Let's go to a cafe.'

They went and sat in the nearest available one. Avinash got a coffee for himself and a hot chocolate for Sonia.

'I don't want a coffee.'

'I know. You are pregnant and you would prefer a hot chocolate, right?'

'Right.'

'Here it is.'

'What do you want?'

Avinash sipped on his coffee.

'My wife was pregnant too. She was hoping for a boy, that idiot. I wanted a girl. It was a day like this, Sonia. Check-up day. The difference was that I was with Preeti on that day while you are alone. Kamran's boys came out of nowhere and shot at us. Preeti died. My baby died. Everything died that day, Sonia.'

Avinash said all this in a very matter-of-fact tone.

'I wanted to kill Kamran but my faith stops me.'

'Listen to it because mine says that Kamran couldn't have done it.'

'I know he did and that's the reason I am here. That you are pregnant now gives this entire story a touch of poetic justice.'

'What do you mean?'

'The CBI, the Interpol, Mumbai Police, the National Police, etc., etc. are all doing a round-the-clock surveillance on both of you, your house, your shops and your restaurant.'

'Please spare the scare and tell me what you want?'

Avinash smiled.

'Deliver Kamran to us. Testify against him in these courts here. Disclose his modus operandi and I will spare you and your child.'

'Or else?'

'I promise you that Kamran, you and your to-be-born child will all know what hell means in your lifetime. Sonia, the thing is that day those bastards did not just shoot my pregnant wife down, they killed something inside me as well.'

Sonia blinked.

'What the law has to do with Kamran that the law will figure but the complete punishment for Kamran is going to be pronounced by me. You will deliver Kamran to us. Kamran is not going to see you or your kid's face again. He should understand pain and loss.'

'What do you know about pain and loss?'

'Enough to know that everyone's is greater than the other person's.'

Avinash closed the discussion.

'If you try to be smart then let me warn you that encounter killings don't just happen in Mumbai; they can happen anywhere. If I don't get my way on this then no one will, Sonia. That, my dear, is a promise.'

Sonia knew that tone. It was not threatening. It was an announcement. Kamran used that tone and meant it all the time.

'I will call you in a couple of hours to hear your yes on this.'

Avinash left Sonia in the cafe and walked away.

He did call a few hours later but that conversation could not be completed because Kamran walked in right in the middle of it. Avinash called again around midnight. Sonia pleaded but he didn't relent. This happened through the night.

Finally, Sonia supplied Avinash with Kamran the next morning.

Present Day, Sewri Sessions Court, Mumbai

'I was scared and had no option.'

Kamran was overwhelmed by this new turn of events.

'If only . . .'

'What, Kamran, if only what?'

Kamran knew there was no point.

'I have a . . . ?'

'Son.'

Kamran took a deep breath.

'Is he . . . ?'

'Next room.'

Kamran shook his head. He caught Sonia's hand and came out of the room. They walked into the next room and saw a six-year-old boy sitting on a bench playing on a cell phone. Kamran noticed the curls and something tugged at his heart. He looked at Sonia.

'He's gone after you. He talks like you and smiles like you too.'

Kamran left her hand and walked up to him. He sat next to the boy and cleared his throat. The boy looked up. Kamran smiled. The boy smiled.

'What's your name, son?'

'Kamran.'

Senior Kamran sniffed. His cell rang. It was Hussain bhai calling. Kamran was getting late.

'Give me two minutes.'

Kamran disconnected and held junior Kamran's face and kissed him on the forehead.

'Why are you crying?'

'Because I got late, son.'

'How come?'

'It's a long story. I will tell you the next time we meet.'

Kamran kissed him again and hugged him tightly. Kamran didn't want to let go of that small soft bundle of himself. Kamran Junior was surprised but didn't mind. Finally, Kamran let go him and rushed to Sonia.

'I don't have time, Sonia.'

'I know.'

'I am leaving the country today. I will organize everything for you and him and get you guys over as quickly as possible.'

'I know.'

'Hell! There are so many questions . . .'

'In time. Right now you should go. This is my number.'

Sonia handed him a chit of paper. Kamran put it in his pocket and kissed Sonia. It lasted till the time Hussain bhai called again.

'I love you.'

'I see that.'

Kamran hugged her again and then left the room. Kamran sat in the car and Hussain bhai could make out that something was not right.

'What's the matter?'

'Nothing. Let's go to the bag.'

Chintu couldn't believe it. The van that he had been following stopped right outside Leopold in south Mumbai. The occupants got out and started walking in merrily. Kamran's double was now without the shades and cap.

Chintu was about to take out his gun when he realized the switch. He had been played and the moment the truth hit him was also the moment his phone rang. It was Avinash again.

'Hello.'

'They did a switch, sir.'

Chintu then explained to Avinash how he and the entire press had been conned. Avinash placed himself in Kamran's shoes and thought of the next few steps. It was a fairly simple deduction.

'I want you to go to the international airport right now and wait. He will turn up soon.'

'But, sir . . . it's a big airport.'

'Fucker, you are telling me. Just reach there and give me a call.'

It had started raining when Kamran reached the far end of the Mazgaon docks. The place had changed and altered a bit but not significantly. The car stopped at the other end of dock and Kamran stepped out of the car.

The bag that these guys were referring to was a gunny bag that was kept in the middle of the road. The bag was tied at the top and kept moving every once in a while.

There were a couple of people standing near the gunny bag and Kamran looked at one. The guy opened the knot and out popped Munna. Munna first fell on the ground and then looked around. He adjusted to the light and the rain and then finally saw the face of death—Kamran.

He started crying and dragged himself to Kamran. Kamran kept looking at him. The betrayal of Munna came back to Kamran.

Munna stopped himself and mumbled, 'Please make it fast. Kamran, please hurry before you have a change of heart.'

'Who said I had a heart? I don't.'

'You are all heart. I know it. Please make it fast.'

Kamran felt sorry for Munna. He stretched out. Somebody placed a gun in his hand. Kamran waved his gun and asked Munna to stand.

Munna stood up slowly. Kamran was glad that his tears were getting mixed in the rain.

Kamran emptied the gun.

Kamran had thought of a more painful death for Munna but he changed his mind when he saw Munna wanting to embrace death rather than plead for life.

Munna fell on the ground and yes, it was fast.

Chintu reached the international airport and called up Avinash.

'Now, sir?'

'Terminal 2C. It will either be an Emirates flight or an Air France one. My guess is another hour or so.'

'Okay, sir.'

Hussain bhai took Kamran to his place in Santacruz. A new

get-up was in the works along with new documents and papers.
Kamran had a quick shave. In about half an hour Kamran alias
Mr Vikas Malhotra was good to go and board his flight.
Kamran was completely unrecognizable.

They started for the airport. On the way Kamran was both
excited and anxious at the same time. He couldn't help taking
Hussain bhai into confidence.

'Hussain bhai, I have a son.'

'What?'

'Yes! Sonia and I have a son. Mashallah, he is just like me.'

'I don't understand.'

'Neither did I. I met them today. Hussain bhai, I will speak
to you in detail tomorrow. I need them with me as soon as
possible.'

'Sure.'

The car sped towards the international airport where Chintu
was wondering how he was ever going to find Kamran in this
sea of passengers and their families who had come to see them
off.

Kamran got off from the car and hugged Hussain bhai.

'Shukriya, Hussain bhai, for all that you have done.'

'It's okay. You have always been a favourite. Khuda hafiz.'

'Khuda hafiz.'

Kamran took his luggage and walked towards Terminal 2C.
Avinash, of course, had guessed right.

It was busier than usual. The airport was teeming with
people as Kamran manoeuvred his way to the entry when he
bumped into a guy who was busy looking all around. It was
Chintu.

'Sorry.'

'Sorry.'

They looked at each other and apologized. Kamran then
went and stood in the queue. Chintu was still looking around.

It was then that it struck Kamran. He turned and looked at Chintu again. Of course, it was Chintu. That innocent face had not changed at all.

'Chintu?'

Chintu turned around and looked at him. He couldn't make out who it was.

'Chintu, it's me. How are you doing, beta?'

Chintu then realized that the man was Kamran Khan. He trembled with fear. Kamran opened his arms.

'Come here.'

Chintu smiled and walked towards Kamran. He went and hugged Kamran.

'How have you been?'

'Fine, bhai.'

'What are you doing?'

'This, bhai.'

Chintu had already taken out his gun. He pumped in five silent bullets into Kamran and then let go of Kamran's body. Kamran fell in a heap and Chintu disappeared in a moment.

A crowd gathered around Kamran's body but nobody wanted to touch him.

Kamran smiled.

A worn-out sequence ran through his head.

EPILOGUE

The sequence that flashed in Kamran's mind in the last moments of his life was from years ago when he had gone to offer his thanks at the Haji Ali Dargah after receiving his brand-new taxi.

It was all from memory except for one small tailored change. Now with his last few breaths Kamran recalled the sequence.

Kamran closed his eyes and thanked Sayyed Pir Haji Ali Shah Bukhari at the mazaar. As he stepped out he bumped into Chintu.

'You are shining, Kamran bhai.'

'Pray for me, Chintu. It's a big day.'

'Nothing wrong can ever happen to you, Kamran bhai.'

Kamran ruffled his hair and gave him a fiver. He then sprinted down the causeway towards his parked taxi. He quickly started the taxi. As he put it into gear, he found Mirza waving ahead at him. Kamran leaned out to tell him that he was not running fares but Mirza spoke first.

'Beta, can you take me to Mohammed Ali Road?'

What timing? My first fare? First to Mohammed Ali Road . . . drop this gentleman . . . then head to Salma's. Should still make it on time. But still . . .

'Chacha, there is someone waiting for me. I have to go and talk about my nikaah today.'

Mirza smiled and blessed him.

'Good luck, beta. I will take another one.'
'Thanks so much.'

Kamran Khan had always wondered what would have happened if it had played out like this.

Hazaaron khwahishen aisi ke har khwahish pe dam nikle
   Bahut nikle mere armaan, lekin phir bhi kam nikle

   Daray kyon mera qaatil? Kya rahega us ki gardan par?
Voh khoon, jo chashm-e-tar se umr bhar yoon dam-ba-dam nikle

   Hui is daur mein mansoob mujh se baada aashaami
Phir aaya voh zamaana, jo jahaan mein jaam-e-jaam nikle

   Hui jin se tavaqqa khastagi ki daad paane ki
   Voh ham se bhi zyaada khasta e tegh e sitam nikle

   Khuda ke waaste parda na kaabe se uthaa zaalim
   Kaheen aisa na ho yaan bhi wahi kaafir sanam nikle

Hazaaron khwahishen aisi ke har khwahish pe dam nikle
   Bahut nikle mere armaan, lekin phir bhi kam nikle . . .